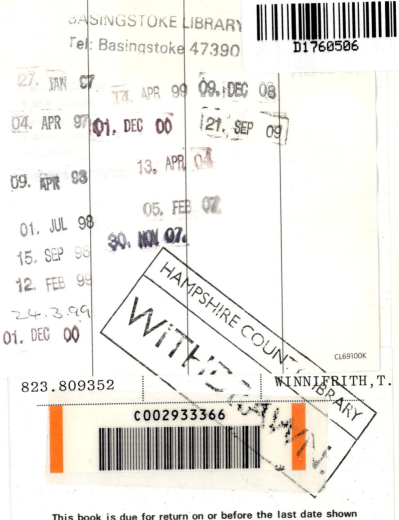

This book is due for return on or before the last date shown
above; it may, subject to the book not being reserved by
another reader, be renewed by personal application, post, or
telephone, quoting this date and details of the book. 100%
recycled paper.

HAMPSHIRE COUNTY COUNCIL
County Library

FALLEN WOMEN IN THE
NINETEENTH-CENTURY NOVEL

Fallen Women in the Nineteenth-Century Novel

Tom Winnifrith

St. Martin's Press

First published in Great Britain 1994 by
THE MACMILLAN PRESS LTD
Houndmills, Basingstoke, Hampshire RG21 2XS
and London
Companies and representatives
throughout the world

A catalogue record for this book is available
from the British Library.

ISBN 0–333–59191–7

Printed in Great Britain by
Ipswich Book Co Ltd
Ipswich, Suffolk

First published in the United States of America 1994 by
Scholarly and Reference Division,
ST. MARTIN'S PRESS, INC.,
175 Fifth Avenue,
New York, N.Y. 10010

ISBN 0–312–10173–2

Library of Congress Cataloging-in-Publication Data
Winnifrith, Tom.
Fallen women in the nineteenth-century novel / Tom Winnifrith.
p. cm.
Includes bibliographical references and index.
ISBN 0–312–10173–2
1. English fiction—19th century—History and criticism. 2. Women
and literature—Great Britain—History—19th century.
3. Prostitution—Great Britain—History—19th century. 4. Moral
conditions in literature. 5. Prostitutes in literature. 6. Sex
role in literature. I. Title.
PR468.W6W56   1994
823'.8093520692—dc20   93–15979
                                                                CIP

To Felicity who fell fortunately

Contents

Preface

I am grateful for help in preparing this book to Mrs Cheryl Cave, Mrs Debora Downing, Dr Gill Frith, Mrs Anne Rafique, and above all to Mr Kevin Ashby, whose tireless work with the word processor was combined with some acute critical observations.

References in the notes to texts by major authors are in all cases to standard editions. Thus for Austen I have used the Oxford edition edited by R. W. Chapman (Oxford, 1933). The individual novels were originally published as follows: *Sense and Sensibility*, 1811; *Pride and Prejudice*, 1813; *Mansfield Park*, 1814; *Emma*, 1815; *Northanger Abbey and Persuasion*, 1818. For Brontë I have used the Haworth edition, published by Smith, Elder (London, 1899–1900). The individual novels were originally published as follows: *Jane Eyre*, 1847; *Shirley*, 1849; *Villette*, 1853; *The Professor*, 1857. For Eliot I have used the Cabinet edition, published by Blackwood (London, 1878–80). The novels were originally published as follows: *Scenes of Clerical Life*, 1858; *Adam Bede*, 1859; *The Mill on the Floss*, 1860; *Silas Marner*, 1861; *Romola*, 1862–3; *Felix Holt*, 1866; *Middlemarch*, 1871–2; *Daniel Deronda*, 1876. For Thackeray I have used the Biographical edition, published by Smith, Elder (London, 1898). The novels were originally published as follows: *Catherine*, 1839–40; *A Shabby Genteel Story*, 1840; *Barry Lyndon*, 1844; *Vanity Fair*, 1847–8; *Pendennis*, 1848–50; *Henry Esmond*, 1852; *The Newcomes*, 1853–5; *The Virginians*, 1857–9; *Lovel the Widower*, 1860; *Philip*, 1861–2; *Denis Duval*, 1864. For Dickens I have used the Illustrated Library edition, published by Chapman and Hall (London, 1874). The novels were originally published as follows: *Sketches by Boz*, 1836; *Pickwick*, 1836–7; *Oliver Twist*, 1837–9; *Nicholas Nickleby*, 1838–9; *The Old Curiosity Shop*, 1840–1; *Barnaby Rudge*, 1841; *Martin Chuzzlewit*, 1843–4; *Dombey and Son*, 1846–7; *David Copperfield*, 1849–50; *Bleak House*, 1852–3; *Hard Times*, 1854; *Little Dorrit*, 1855–7; *A Tale of Two Cities*, 1859; *Great Expectations*, 1860–1; *Our Mutual Friend*, 1864–5; *The Mystery of Edwin Drood*, 1870. For Hardy I have used the New Wessex edition, published by Macmillan (London, 1975). The novels were originally published as follows: *Desperate Remedies*, 1871; *Under the Greenwood Tree*, 1872; *A Pair of Blue Eyes*, 1872–3; *Far from the Madding Crowd*, 1874; *The Hand of Ethelberta*, 1875–6; *The Return of the Native*, 1878; *The Trumpet-Major*, 1880; *A Laodicean*, 1880–1; *Two on a Tower*, 1882; *The Mayor of Casterbridge*, 1886; *The Woodlanders*, 1886–7; *Tess of the d'Urbervilles*, 1891; *The Well-Beloved*, 1892; *Jude the Obscure*, 1894–5.

1

Introduction

Who now reads the novels of Mrs Henry Wood? Dusty and un-
loved they lie on the back shelves of obscure libraries and remote
second-hand bookshops, but they must lie in considerable quan-
tities, since Wood wrote a great many novels, which went through
a great many editions. *East Lynne* sold at least half a million
copies, and deservedly it has been reprinted in the last ten years
as a monument to Victorian taste.[1] Promoters of cultural studies,
seen by some as an adjunct to, even a substitute for, the study of
literature, could do worse than take up the case of Wood. On the
one hand she is a tribute to the ephemerality of popular taste,
while on the other it might seem to make sense to study Victorian
culture through the medium of a popular Victorian text.

It is difficult, however, for students of literature to find much to
commend in Wood's novels. Their melodramatic plots and wooden
characters resemble those of a modern soap-opera to which they
have been compared.[2] She seems to have anticipated from television, though for less obvious reasons, the device of reviving a
supposedly dead character who returns to life, conveniently
disguised in green spectacles or a pink eye-shade.[3]. Her grammar
is deficient, her facts more so. Snobbishly she wrote about the
aristocracy, but clearly knew little about aristocrats. Jane Austen
would not have made the nephew of a newly created baronet
succeed him in the title.[4] Wood's husband and father were in
business, but she does not seem to know much about that either,
although money or the lack of it figure prominently in her works.
Unrealistically, if moralistically, the virtuous are usually rewarded
with wealth, while the wicked are usually ruined. The preaching
of this pious moral is rendered slightly less impressive by the
failure of the virtuous to be very generous with their money.[5]

It was the combination of the humdrum and the extraordinary
which made Wood so popular. Modern television serials rely on
a similar formula, and it may seem surprising that no enterprising
producer has adapted Wood for this medium. Such a producer

1

might have difficulties in reconciling to modern sensibilities Wood's firm conviction that for a married woman adultery is far worse that death.[6] In *East Lynne* the aristocratic but poor Lady Isabel Vane marries Archibald Carlyle and bears him three children. Suspecting her husband unjustly of an affair with Barbara Hare she elopes with the villainous Frank Levison whose name may carry some rather nasty anti-Semitic overtones.[7] Carlyle divorces her, and Levison deserts her. She is thought to have died in a railway accident, and Carlyle marries Barbara. But Lady Isabel is not dead. She has lost her looks and Levison's child in the accident, in which she is mistaken for another victim, but then recovers to return home to East Lynne as a governess suitably disguised in either green or blue spectacles. Here she undergoes agonies of jealousy at seeing Barbara and Carlyle together and is further made miserable by not being allowed to make herself known to her children, one of whom dies. Worn out, Lady Isabel dies too, having sought her husband's forgiveness on her deathbed.

This abrupt summary makes clear the terrible punishment Lady Isabel undergoes. So too does the long homily with which Wood sees fit to address her readers on the occasion of Lady Isabel's fall.

How fared it with Lady Isabel? Just as it must be expected to fare, and does fare, when a high-principled gentlewoman falls from her pedestal. Never had she experienced a moment's calm, or peace, or happiness, since the fatal night of quitting her home. She had taken a blind leap in a moment of wild passion; when, instead of the garden of roses it had been her persuader's pleasure to promise her (but which, in truth, she had hardly glanced at, for that had not been her moving motive), she had found herself plunged into an abyss of horror, from which there was never more any escape; never, never more. The very hour of her departure she awoke to what she had done; the guilt, whose aspect had been shunned in prospective, assumed at once its true, frightful colour, the blackness of darkness; and a lively remorse, a never-dying anguish, took possession of her soul for ever. O reader, believe me! Lady-wife-mother! Should you ever be tempted to abandon your home, so will you awaken! Whatever trials may be the lot of your married life, though they may magnify themselves to your crushed spirit as beyond the endurance of woman to bear, *resolve* to bear them; fall down upon your knees and pray to be enabled to bear them; pray for patience; pray for strength to resist the demon that would urge you so to escape; bear unto death, rather than forfeit your fair name and your good conscience; for be assured that the alternative, if you rush on to it, will be found far worse than death!

Poor thing! Poor Lady Isabel! She had sacrificed husband, children, reputation, home, all that makes life of value to woman; she had forfeited her duty to God, had deliberately broken His commandments, for the one poor miserable sake of flying with Francis Levison! But, the instant the step was irrevocable, the instant she had passed the barrier, repentance set in. Even in the first days of her departure, in the fleeting moments of abandonment, when it may be supposed she might momentarily forget conscience, it was sharply wounding her with its adder-like stings; and she knew that her whole future existence, whether spent with that man or without him, would be one dark course of gnawing, never-ending retribution.[8]

The repeated nevers and the exaggeration involved in the blackness of darkness may obscure the fact that even in this passage Wood is not uncompromisingly hostile to Lady Isabel. There are far from delicate hints that many erring wives may be more sinned against than sinning. Delicacy is not Wood's strong point, as can be seen by her tendency to prepare her readers for disaster in this work and others with ominous forebodings. It is probable that we have here in the reference to trials a discreet allusion to the change in the divorce laws in 1857, which had made divorce easier but still far from easy. Archibald Carlyle is of course no sinner and is indeed like other Wood heroes painfully honourable in both allowing a divorce and refusing to marry until he thinks Lady Isabel is dead. In fact all this nobility is to no avail, since Francis Levison refuses to marry Lady Isabel, the baby is killed in the train crash and Carlyle does unwittingly marry while his first wife is still alive. But at any rate Carlyle is pure, and that makes Lady Isabel's punishment and remorse even greater.

But both contemporary and modern critics have not been wholly satisfied with Lady Isabel's crime and punishment. Mrs Oliphant, who wrote more books and better books than Mrs Wood but with less financial reward, was almost as hostile to *East Lynne* as she was to another scandalous best-seller, *Lady Audley's Secret* – one of the many novels of the period with bigamy as its theme. What Mrs Oliphant objected to was the representation of vice as 'a purifying fiery ordeal, through which the penitent is to come elevated and sublimed'.[9] This seems a harsh judgement, and one almost suspects professional jealousy. Unlike M. E. Braddon, the author of *Lady Audley's Secret*, Wood was a woman of impeccable respectability. But modern critics have been eager to show ways in which Wood did sympathise with, even glorify, the sins she was condemning. Throughout the novel Lady Isabel is shown as kind and generous, even though she has no money, a dutiful daughter and a devoted mother, full of genuine religious feeling in spite of every kind of disaster. She does her best to escape Levison's clutches, and her attempts to do so are only foiled by the interference of her sister-in-law, her husband's preoccupation and her understandable if mistaken assumption that Carlyle's secret meetings with Barbara Hare are trysts in which they may indulge their adulterous passion, instead of attempts to help Barbara's brother.

The excuse of jealousy is almost sufficient to exculpate Lady Isabel from harbouring any immoral thoughts at all. Ladies were not supposed to have sexual feelings. Lady Isabel is a perfect lady, and so Barbara Hare must be brought in to make her even less guilty. It is different for the lower orders. Here the oddly, if appropriately, named Aphrodite Hallyjohn can encourage two admirers without any real hopes of marrying either, get her father shot as a result, and emerge to respectability as Mrs Joe Jiffin. Just to complete the class pattern we also have Barbara Hare who is allowed to have sexual feelings for Archibald Carlyle, and even through some unfortunate mistakes to declare them. This is not the conduct of a lady, and Barbara is later made to regret her outburst. All comes right in the end, and yet by having the slightly vulgar Barbara usurp her position Lady Isabel gains yet more sympathy. When her dying son asks after his real mamma we know whose side we are on.

It is probably not worth analysing *East Lynne* or setting up Lady Isabel and Barbara Hare as two sides of the same coin in the same way that feminist critics have sought to set up Jane Eyre and the first Mrs Rochester. Wood was a writer with strong views. Drunkenness and gambling, worldliness and flirtation are condemned in her novels as severely as adultery, even if they do not always lead to death, as they frequently do. In *Within the Maze* the greatest condemnation is reserved for the clergyman's daughter, Miss Blake, who spreads scandal and causes it by flirting with a clergyman given over to High Church practices. The statement of her prejudices, washed down with a powerful dose of religiosity, is so blatant that it is difficult to take Wood seriously as a novelist and it is now time to relegate her to her position as a Victorian wallflower and let others take the floor. And here we come to the difficulty that forms the subject of this book. The condemnation of fallen women shown by Wood appears at first sight to be shared by almost every nineteenth-century writer of any stature. Austen, except in *Mansfield Park*, is relatively kind to female sinners at the beginning of the century, and Hardy tried to be kind at the end, but like Gaskell and even Trollope he found it difficult. Tess and Gaskell's Ruth join Hetty Sorrel and Lady Isabel in expiating their sin with death. Here it is the fate of another female sinner, Lady Clara Pulleyn, who runs from her brutal and unfaithful husband, Sir Barnes Newcome, to elope with her childhood sweetheart Lord Highgate.

So Lady Clara flies from the custody of her tyrant, but to what a rescue? The very man who loves her and gives her asylum pities and deplores her. She scarce dares to look out of the windows of her new home upon the world, lest it should know and reproach her. All the sisterhood of friendship is cut off from her. If she dares go abroad she feels the sneer of the world as she goes through it; and knows that malice and scorn whisper behind her. People as criminal but undiscovered make room for her, as if her touch were pollution. She knows she has darkened the lot and made wretched the home of the man whom she loves best; that his friends who see her treat her with but a doubtful respect; and the domestics who attend her, with a suspicious obedience. In the country lanes or the streets of the country town, neighbours look aside as the carriage passes in which she sits splendid and lonely. Rough hunting companions of her husband's come to her table: he is driven perforce to the company of flatterers and men of inferior sort; his equals, at least in his own home, will not live with him. She would be kind, perhaps, and charitable to the cottagers round about her, but she fears to visit them lest they too should scorn her. The clergyman who distributes her charities, blushes and looks awkward on passing her in the village, if he should be walking with his wife or one of his children. Shall they go to the Continent and set up a grand house at Paris or at Florence? There they can get society, but of what a sort! Our acquaintances of Baden – Madame Schlangenbad and Madame de Cruchecassée and Madame d'Ivry, and Messrs Loder and Punter and Blackball and Deuceace will come and dance and flirt and quarrel and gamble and feast round about her; but what in common with such wild people has this poor, timid, shrinking soul? Even these scorn her. The leers and laughter on those painted faces are quite unlike her own sad countenance. She has no reply to their wit. Their infernal gaiety scares her more than the solitude at home. No wonder that her husband does not like home, except for a short while in the hunting season. No wonder that he is away all day; how can he like a home which she has made so wretched? In the midst of her sorrow and doubt and misery a child comes to her: how she clings to it! how her whole being and hope and passion centres itself on this feeble infant!. . . . but she no more belongs to our story: with the new name she has taken, the poor lady passes out of the history of the Newcomes.[10]

The *Newcomes* was written a few years before *East Lynne* and before the divorce laws had been changed. The two novels have certain similarities – Thackeray deftly steers, as Wood clumsily veers, between the middle-class world of the professions and the world of the aristocracy. Both works contain scenes in France and an election in which the righteous hero takes on the caddish villain. Lady Clara is of course a relatively minor figure and we cannot trace her punishment and remorse as we can follow Lady Isabel's. Even her new baby is swallowed up in limbo, not being conveniently carried away by death as is Hetty Sorrel's baby or Lady Isabel's or Tess's. Her punishment is not as bad as that of Lady Isabel, and it would be hard to be too cruel to one who has not left a pillar of rectitude for a cad, but left the odious Barnes for Lord Highgate who though rough has a warm heart and is conveniently quite rich.

What is uncomfortable for students of literature is that Thackeray seems slightly more unforgiving to Lady Clara than Wood is to

Lady Isabel. Admirably some of his bitterness is directed against the pharisaical critics of Lady Clara's conduct, but among these critics is Laura Pendennis, wife of the narrator, with whom Thackeray might be expected to be in sympathy, although his daughter reports that he did not like Laura.[11] There is something both comic and tragic about the way Laura lifts her long Victorian skirts out of the mire, refusing to visit Lady Clara until it is too late; and it might be possible to see the episode as a strangled satire against sexual squeamishness. This would not be how Thackeray's readers would have seen poor Lady Clara's story.

Thackeray by his own admission freely fornicated during his youth before his marriage. His wife went mad, and it seems unlikely that he remained chaste in the remaining years of his life when his wife was confined to a mental institution. An affair with a married woman, Mrs Brookfield, would appear to have been platonic, but one would have thought Thackeray should have been kind to sexual sinners or risk the charge of artistic insincerity. Eliot, in the eyes of the world, would seem almost as bad as Lady Clara, since she set up home with a married man after unsatisfactory love affairs in her youth. Charlotte Brontë by modern standards would hardly seem to have sinned in falling in love with her married Belgian teacher, but this sin was considered so grave that it could not be admitted for sixty years in spite of the fact that the heroes of her novels are married or Belgian or schoolteachers or a combination of these desirable attributes. The sexual life of both Dickens and Hardy is still shrouded in controversy, but the balance of evidence would suggest that they too were sinners and therefore should have been kinder to characters like Lady Dedlock and Eustacia Vye. Only Austen is totally free from the charge of sexual guilt, and she like Gaskell and Trollope and for that matter Mrs Henry Wood does seem quite kind to fallen women.

Thus to the charge of an incomprehensible attitude to sexual sin in nineteenth-century novelists we must add a further charge of artistic insincerity. It will be the task of this book to answer these charges by outlining ways in which novelists while accepting the conventional sexual code on the surface sought, if not to subvert it, at any rate to modify it by drawing different moral conclusions. These conclusions are of perennial interest and relevance and therefore of value even when the sexual code has changed as it has dramatically during the past thirty years. That is why we still read Eliot and Thackeray, Dickens and Brontë, Austen and Hardy in an age when adultery and illegitimacy, divorce and cohabitation have lost most if not all of the shame that once was attached to them.

Of course the subject is a complicated one. There is the problem of chronology. Historians of the twenty-second century will not find it easy to sum up twentieth-century British views on sexuality. They will probably content themselves with a facile comment to the effect that there was a major change in the 1960s, although anyone who lived as an adolescent in the 1960s would say that this comment was a gross generalisation.[12] In lumping together authors like Austen who was born in 1775 with Hardy who died in 1928 we clearly ignore similar shifts. These are hard to detect. Were the 1840s in which the Brontës wrote novels that were considered shocking an age of prudery or an age of prurience or both? In the 1860s there was a sudden rash of novels dealing with bigamy, apparently a way of including a heroine technically guilty but morally innocent. The novelists may have been seizing upon a temporary topical scandal or making some comment about the divorce laws.[13] Mrs Wood in *East Lynne* and *Verner's Pride* is so careful that by means of Lady Isabel's divorce she avoids bigamy in the first novel and by a case of mistaken identity avoids it in the second, but others were less squeamish. Queen Victoria reigned from 1837 to 1901, but though her own life was a model of marital propriety in contrast to those of her raffish uncles and son there is no reason to suppose that her subjects were equally proper. Her prime ministers certainly failed to set a very high standard if Gladstone is to be believed, and even he is under suspicion of sexual immorality because of his work among prostitutes.[14] The use of the word Victorian as a synonym for strait-laced with regard to sexual morality is therefore inaccurate unless it carries with it connotations of hypocrisy.

The six nineteenth-century authors I have selected all had comparatively short careers as novelists, but even in the case of Charlotte Brontë, whose four novels were all written within seven years, it is possible to detect a modification of her views toward sexual morality, and similar changes can be detected in all the authors considered. It is difficult to know whether these alterations reflect particular circumstances in the author's life or a general shift in attitudes. Rhoda Broughton said she began life as Zola and ended it as Miss Yonge.[15] But her career as a novelist started in 1864 and ended shortly before her death in 1920. There was a change in sexual attitudes and the depiction of sexual matters toward the end of the century. The naughty nineties and the swinging sixties are terms that reflect some kind of reality. In contrast Broughton's personal life does not seem to have been particularly interesting. In the writers we have chosen it seems to make more sense to pay attention to the particular context in which the author wrote, his or her own sexual life, and the reviews, kind and unkind, which greeted individual books. After all it was the savage attack on the immorality of *Jude the Obscure* that brought Hardy's career as a novelist to an abrupt conclusion.

This book is not a history of sexuality in nineteenth-century Britain, or even, to take a much narrower stance, a history of literary prudery. Both books should perhaps be written, but would be hard to write. It would be difficult to confine the subject to Britain. The two most famous adulteresses in nineteenth-century fiction are Emma Bovary and Anna Karenina. Both meet the conventional fate of erring females, but both receive more sympathy than British authors would have been allowed to display. The reception of Flaubert and Tolstoy in Britain similarly makes allowance for foreign laxity. America provides a different standpoint, but, even if we ignore Hawthorne and James, we are omitting some extremely interesting insights into adultery.

It is difficult to compare Anna Karenina and Emma Bovary, Hester Prynne and Merle Osmond. In Britain too there were wide differences in the sexual conduct of different classes. Aristocrats kept mistresses, slum dwellers sometimes did not bother to get married; but the middle classes for whom novelists wrote kept up a show of respectability. So much by the way of wild generalisation, but of course even the middle classes had outlets for sexual licence in prostitutes and pornography. If we concentrate on these outlets as some recent scholars have done we get a very distorted picture of British society, as distorted as that presented by the most decorous of Victorian novelists, Charlotte M. Yonge for instance, whose characters never seem to harbour any sexual thought.[16]

Even the narrower perspective of sexual prudery is one that is hard to keep clear. In charting the literary reception of the Brontës and recording the unkind reviews which accused them of coarseness I came to the conclusion that the years around 1848, the year of revolution, were ones in which authors and even authoresses had to be particularly careful in their depiction of sexuality or otherwise risk offending their public.[17] Professor Kathleen Tillotson in *Novels of the Eighteen Forties* took a contrary view to the effect that the decade in which Becky Sharp, Edith Dombey, Jane Eyre and Esther Barton sinned or nearly sinned was a decade relatively free from prudery as opposed to the next decade in which *Ruth* was so bitterly attacked, Lady Clara's downfall was so graphically condemned and even poor sad Lucy Snowe's dim love affairs came in for some criticism.[18] Jane Eyre does nothing wrong and it seems prudish to attack her, Esther Barton does everything wrong and it seems brave to mention her boldly as a prostitute. Becky Sharp and Edith Dombey are harder to pin down; since it is hard to know exactly how far they went on the road to ruin it is hard to decide what Thackeray and Dickens thought about this ruin. Ambivalence in attitude and ambiguity about the facts do seem to go hand in hand.

There is a much broader series of books to be written on Victorian attitudes to women.[19] Attitudes to women as sexual beings are clearly only a part of such a study, although an important part. By calling our book boldly *Fallen Women* we beg the important question why it is only through the falls of female protagonists that sexual and social changes are recorded. But attitudes to women as frail vessels did not change much through the century. Nor did women gain much in legal or political rights. The Married Women's Property Act, passed in 1867, was some small improvement, but the fight for female suffrage was largely a twentieth-century phenomenon. It is not until *Jude the Obscure*, the last novel to be studied in this book, that we meet in Sue Bridehead the first female character eager for genuine independence.

Many readers of this book now take female independence – financial, legal and sexual – for granted. There are still vestiges of nineteenth-century sexual attitudes. There is still a double standard. Parents of both sexes are more worried about their daughters' virtue, as it is sometimes quaintly called, than about their sons'. Except in very progressive circles it is still unusual for the woman to make the first sexual advances. But attitudes have changed dramatically in recent years and are clearly very different from those permitted to be expressed in the nineteenth-century novel. Modern readers may find *East Lynne* laughable; what would Mrs Henry Wood make of modern readers?

Modern readers do not find the great nineteenth-century texts laughable, although they do find the sexual contexts baffling. It is partly an attempt to explain these contexts that this book has been written. Inevitably this entails a good deal of biography. This may seem rather an old-fashioned form of criticism, although if we look at the spate of biographical studies in the last ten years, biography would seem to play its part in the study of the nineteenth century.[20] As has already been suggested, most male and female nineteenth-century authors will turn out to have had sexual lives as interesting as their twentieth-century counterparts, and this does give a piquant flavour to the insights into sexuality which appear in their novels.

2

Austen

Jane Austen's novels revolve around love affairs, successful and unsuccessful, decorous and indecorous, sublime and ridiculous. In contrast to this variety and in contrast to the thesis outlined at the end of the last chapter Austen's own life seems rather tame. Though the mysterious affair at Sidmouth was sad, and though the hastily accepted and as hastily rejected proposal of Harris Bigg Withers seems comic, we look in vain for the likes of Darcy or Wickham, Mr Knightley or Mr Elton in their creator's life. Literary scholarship, which has not been able to give a name to Austen's clergyman admirer on the Devonshire coast, has found a few potential suitors, but is unlikely to come up with many skeletons in this particular cupboard.[1] Even if there were any – and this seems improbable – the lapse of time and the protective care of the Austen family seem certain to have buried them for ever. Unlike eminent Victorians, ripe for biographical deconstruction in a more cynical age, Jane Austen found her biographers in that Victorian age. Her nephew's memoir presents a portrait of Christian piety and gentlewomanly serenity which it is hard to contradict, especially in the absence of any primary evidence in the shape of correspondence, which we expect to have been discreetly censored.[2]

Discretion and good manners are rather difficult but important keys to Austen's life and works. She belonged to a sector of society, still just recognisable in England today, which is inured to public service and has an interesting private life, but is reluctant to talk about political events or personal affairs. Affectionately caricatured as Mrs Miniver, members of this class, particularly female members, lower their stiff upper lip to gossip about the village fête while their loved ones are on dangerous missions and invasion is threatened. And so Austen, living in Kent or Southampton or Bath, near Britain's naval defences or near the place where invasion was threatened, with her two sailor brothers providing extra information and anxiety, hardly mentions the war against France in her novels or in her letters. Nor at first sight does she seem to be interested in the social, religious, intellectual and sexual revolution which accompanied the French Revolution and the Napoleonic wars.[3]

We are principally interested in the sexual revolution, but it is now generally agreed that Austen, though she mentions public events rarely in her letters and hardly at all in her novels, was keenly interested in the controversies of the day. The old idea that Austen, like Catherine Morland, would, if the conversation turned to politics, turn to silence, is now unfashionable. It is not doubted that Austen was involved in the war of ideas; what is in doubt is what side she took in this war. Her sex, her quiet country background, her Tory associations, even the Oxford education of her brothers all point to a different kind of involvement with politics from that we have come to connect with revolutionary Romantic poets. Wordsworth thought it very heaven to be young in the French Revolution and fathered an illegitimate child; Coleridge was mistaken for a French spy and became involved in rather difficult sexual entanglements; and Byron, whose amours were notorious, supported the revolution both at home and abroad. We would not expect similar political or sexual attitudes from Austen. But she was an intelligent woman from an intelligent family. Her letters do mention the war against France and her reading of the newspapers. Newspapers are mentioned in *Northanger Abbey*, politely by Henry Tilney, as dispellers of ignorance for the naive Catherine Morland in a neighbourhood of voluntary spies.[4] The idea that in her quiet rural backwater Jane was somehow protected from knowledge of politics and war is peculiar in that Charlotte Brontë in a much more remote backwater was known to be interested in public affairs and indeed retrospectively in the Napoleonic wars, memories of which lingered in the Dorset countryside in Hardy's day. Austen had much more personal involvement with the French Revolution and French wars than either Brontë or Hardy, whose interest in history and politics sometimes seem rather remote and pathetic like Branwell Brontë's and Jude the Obscure's interest in the Classics.

It is true that we have no direct evidence that Austen ever read or thought about the work of Mary Wollstonecraft, the author of *Vindication of the Rights of Women (1792)*, rightly seen through her life and her works as a pioneer of feminist thought. Wollstonecraft's irregular private life, her illegitimate child, her marriage to the revolutionary philosopher Godwin and even her tragic death in childbirth were not the kinds of subject that one would expect to be mentioned in Austen's letters. They were freely used by Wollstonecraft's anti-Jacobin opponents to discredit her feminist views which seemed so revolutionary at the time, though they seem quite reasonable to us. It is therefore difficult to be certain how Austen reacted to Wollstonecraft's ideas or her life. Her aloofness and a general lack of interest in abstract ideas is typical of a certain kind of conservatism with which Austen has been associated by conservative critics. Radical critics have seen a more intelligent Austen attacking established values in, for instance, presenting a whole host of parents, from the Bennets and the Bertrams to Mr Wodehouse and Sir Walter Elliot, as both selfish and stupid. People are anxious to have Jane Austen on their side; and feminist critics have brought her onto theirs by showing Austen's dislike of feminine sentimentality both in the swooning heroines of the juvenilia and the disapproval of such fantasy figures as Wickham and Willoughby.[5]

Disapproval of feminine fantasies would however qualify not only Austen as a feminist, but also one of Wollstonecraft's strongest opponents, Hannah More, whose *Coelebs in Search of a Wife* (1808) is part of the Evangelical revolution against Jacobinism. This later reaction is different from the original anti-Jacobin movement, not least because of the decorum of its language. We do know about Austen's views on More: they are not friendly. Austen says that the Miss Webbs approved of Hannah More; she did not like the Miss Webbs, who sound rather like the Miss Steeles in *Sense and Sensibility*. She later seemed to change her mind about Evangelicals, but on her first reading of *Coelebs* she said she did not like them. In originally referring to Coelebs as Caleb, Austen may just be making a mistake, but this might be an obscure joke involving the novel *Caleb Williams* (1794), written by Wollstonecraft's husband, Godwin, whose work she certainly knew.[6]

The case of Caleb versus Coelebs makes it clear that not only is it difficult to decide what side Austen took in various controversies, but also that the very nature of the sides is hard to determine. The Evangelical movement at the beginning of the nineteenth-century was a radical movement in religion, but conservative in its political and sexual attitudes. In talking of Hannah More in

1811 Austen expressed disapproval of the Evangelicals, but later in 1814 when considering her niece Fanny Knight's suitor, John Plumptre, suspected of being an Evangelical, she says she is by no means convinced that we ought not all to be Evangelicals. Confusingly she adds that she and her niece disagree not about the true nature of Christianity but about the meaning of the term Evangelical.[7] The years 1811 to 1814 cover the period in which *Mansfield Park* was composed. This is a novel in which religion plays a considerable part and for which affairs in the Knight household probably provided some inspiration.

In 1813 Austen spent a considerable period of time at her brother's house in Kent. In spite of her careful enquiries about hedgerows in Northamptonshire it is hard to avoid making comparisons between *Mansfield Park*, allegedly in Northamptonshire, and Godmersham House, certainly in Kent. Edward Knight, like Sir Thomas Bertram, had a large and fairly unruly family. His wife, being dead, could hardly be compared to the ineffective Lady Bertram, but both families missed the guiding influence of a strong mother. Fanny Knight, Austen's favourite niece, can be compared to Fanny Price, oddly favoured by her creator, even though the former, born to flower among the Kentish gentry, seems so unlike her namesake, born to wither as a poor relation. But the Knights did have poor relations with naval connections, like the Prices. Reading Jane Austen's letters of the period from 1807 when she was living in reduced circumstances at Southampton until her death we do find ourselves reminded of Fanny Price's resentment against her smart relatives.[8]

It is a mistake to think of characters in books as being the same as characters in real life, and mercifully students of Austen have not been subjected to the pressure to equate the lives and the works of a creative novelist as have students of the Brontës. If we said that Fanny Price was modelled on Fanny Knight and the serious Edmund Bertram modelled on John Plumptre, we would have to assume unusual prescience on the part of Austen, as no proposal had emerged until after *Mansfield Park* had been published. On the other hand the Plumptres were old friends of the Knights, well known to Austen in 1813 and perhaps before. Nor were they a family without intellectual distinction, the kind of family against which Austen would seem to have chafed in her later novels and letters. The *Dictionary of National Biography* is full of Plumptres; and two in particular would seem to be of direct relevance to some of the controversies in which *Mansfield Park* and its author would seem to have been engaged.

John Plumptre, the father of Fanny Knight's suitor, was the elder brother of Robert Plumptre, master of Queen's College, Cambridge. The latter had a large family, two of whom achieved distinction in very different directions. James Plumptre was a man who outbowdlerised Bowdler in producing versions of plays and poems designed to avoid bringing a blush to the cheek of a young person. His edition of *The English Drama Improved* appeared in 1812. His sister Anna was of a different temper. She translated Kotzebue, although it was not her version but that of Mrs Inchbald to which Austen refers in *Mansfield Park*, a book full of references to Shakespeare, an author whom James Plumptre suitably improved. Anna Plumptre on the other hand consistently adopted a Jacobin line and declared that Napoleon was welcome in England to put the aristocracy in their place.[9]

Like the Bertrams the Plumptres would seem to take different views on politics in general and sexual politics in particular. It still remains hard to find out what Austen thought about either debate. References to sexual matters in Austen's letters are few and far between. We do not know how much has been censored. Fanny Knight, who snobbishly described her aunt as common, may have been alluding to her unVictorian frankness, but we do not have much evidence of this frankness, although on birth and death Austen is refreshingly free from prudery and mawkishness. Odd remarks in the letters do seem to show a sensible and realistic attitude. Lord Craven's installation of a mistress at Ashdown Park is described in 1801 as a little flaw and unpleasing.[10] In the same year there is the episode of the adulteress whom Austen met in Bath. 'I am proud,' she declares, 'to say that I have a very good eye at an Adultress, for tho' repeatedly assured that another in the party was the *She*, I fixed upon the right one from the first.'

Modern biographers have not had such luck in identifying this mistress. She was Miss Mary Cassandra Twisleton, fairly remotely connected to the Austen family through a complex series of marriages between cousins. She had been divorced in 1797 by her husband, the future Lord St Vincent, for adultery. Halperin confuses her with her sister Julia, and Honan, following Chapman, assumes that she was committing adultery in 1801 with a Mr

Evelyn, mentioned in the same letter. The latter author goes on to make much of Austen's daring in going for rides in the phaeton of the dangerous Mr Evelyn. Even Le Faye, an extremely reliable recorder of Austen's life and that of her family, assumed that Miss Twisleton's adulterous partner in 1797 and presumably in 1801 was her future second husband, Richard Graves, whom she married in 1807. This seems improbable in view of Mr Graves's youth. In 1801 Mary Twisleton may not have been committing adultery with anybody, and certainly she is unlikely to have been involved with the elderly, married Mr Evelyn. She could have been called an adulteress because she had committed adultery. Thus Austen, though her tone is flippant, is quite stern and unforgiving about her cousin's shortcomings in the past, and of course must be relieved of the charge that she herself flirted with adultery in the shape of Mr Evelyn, who was clearly a harmless eccentric gathering groundsel for his birds.[11]

In 1808 Austen comments on the elopement of a Hamsphire neighbour, Mrs Powlett, with Lord Sackville. This story was mentioned in the newspaper with only the initials of the participants. There are obvious links with the elopement of Henry Crawford and Maria Rushworth, where again initials in the newspaper give the game away. Austen calls the original incident a sad story, observing that she would not have suspected Mrs Powlett who had staid the sacrament quite recently.[12] This religious reference has been taken as a sign of the greater moral seriousness that characterises *Mansfield Park*, although, as we have seen, Austen is fairly unforgiving to Mary Twisleton eight years earlier. Maria Rushworth in fiction is treated even more savagely, but she is more closely related to the characters in *Mansfield Park* than Miss Twisleton or Mrs Powlett were to Jane Austen; and therefore her sin is seen as more grievous.

In January 1809, some six months after the scandal, Jane wrote two letters to Cassandra about the conduct of the Rev. Dr Richard Mant, rector of All Saints Southampton, and her old friend Martha Lloyd.[13] Clearly remarks like 'Martha and Dr Mant are as bad as ever' and 'as Dr. M. is a clergyman, their attachment, however immoral, has a decorous air' are intended as a joke; and the suggestion that Mrs Mant had fled to the house of her married daughters was part of this joke. Dr Mant, sixteen when he matriculated in 1761, was an elderly and respected man, former headmaster and father of a future bishop.[14] Martha Lloyd was a very old friend of the family. Her marriage to Austen's brother twenty years later did cause a mild stir because of her age, but her life otherwise would seem to have been totally free from scandal. She remained Austen's close friend; and Dr Mant is mentioned respectfully both before and after these two letters. It is totally preposterous to suggest that the two could have been involved in an actual affair, and that is why Austen can make her sly allusions safe in the knowledge that nobody could take them seriously.

Unfortunately at least one modern critic has failed to see the joke. Roberts mars a pioneer attempt to set Austen in her historical context by describing Mant heavy-handedly as a clergyman who had broken his marital vows, confusing in the process Martha's responses with those of Mrs Mant and accusing Austen of cynical irony towards clergymen.[15] There is of course irony in these letters, for instance the delicate irony is placing decorous and immoral where they stand instead of in the reverse order, but this irony is lost on Roberts. His misinterpretation, like the earlier confusion about Jane's conduct with Mr Evelyn, is a sad reflection on how we are liable to judge other generations by the standards of our own. Austen treated the misbehaviour of her third cousin and of various aristocrats light-heartedly in her youth, although she disapproved of this behaviour. In middle age she seems to have grown more serious, but could still make a joke about what she would have regarded as a terrible blow, namely the involvement of a close friend in an adulterous affair with a married clergyman.

In 1813 Austen expresses some sympathy for the Princess of Wales in her dispute with the future George IV. Some have thought disgust at this royal misconduct discoloured *Mansfield Park*.[16] Earlier there is more sympathy with another royal personage, the Duke of Sussex, whose relationship with Lady Augusta Murray was irregular though domestic.[17] The aristocratic Pagets in the centre of conjugal infidelity and divorces are condemned in 1817.[18] All this disapproval makes Austen into a very moral person, although by some Victorian standards she might seem to have erred in mentioning the cause of this scandal or indeed in offering the brisk if sensible advice that separate bedrooms might prevent excessive breeding.[19] Fanny Knight would have disapproved of such a remark, although there were several scandals in the life of her family.[20] In contrast there is little evidence of any sexual misconduct in the lives of any immediate member of Austen's family, although Philadelphia Hancock, George Austen's half-sister, may have been the mistress of Warren Hastings, and a cousin, Frances Austen, is said to have made a disgraceful match.[21] Eliza de Feuillide was certainly flirtatious, although there is no evidence to assume that she was the model for Mary Crawford or Lady Susan or any other of Austen's attractive but wicked characters.[22] According to Mary Mitford Jane Austen was flirtatious in her youth,[23] and so too after a fashion are Emma Woodhouse and Elizabeth Bennet, her most autobiographical heroines. But there is a large gap between flirtation and fornication, and no evidence that Austen ever committed or contemplated the latter. In a book devoted to Victorian prudery, Jane Austen is no Victorian; but while all our other authors can be accused of some sort of sexual laxity, Jane Austen died a virgin.

All the novels revolve around courtship and marriage. In all cases the virtuous heroine in spite of difficulties wins the hand of the equally virtuous hero, while male sexual sinners like Willoughby and Wickham, Henry Crawford and William Elliot are both disapproved of and punished. The punishment involves both social stigma and a union with a woman very hard to love. Female sinners receive equally short shrift. It is very hard to prove adultery against Isabella Thorpe or Lucy Steele or Mary Crawford, although they can be accused of being heartless and mercenary. Lydia does elope with Wickham, and is punished for her sins with a description of the later years of her marriage which rivals those of Swift in both cruelty and brevity.[24] It is however the fate of Lydia which should pull us up short in dismissing Austen as a genteel spinster, Victorian before her time. For the attitude that her sin is a terrible disaster, bringing disgrace and infamy on her innocent family, even if it does not lead to death or Australia, is one held by the insufferable Mr Collins whose tactless relief that he is not a member of this family must make it clear that both Austen and her readers are out of sympathy with him. Likewise we must take comfort from the following grave sentence:

> Unhappy as the event must be for Lydia, we may draw from it this useful lesson; the loss of virtue in a female is irretrievable – that one false step involves her in endless ruin – that her repu-

tation is no less brittle than it is beautiful – and that she cannot be too much guarded in her behaviour towards the undeserving of the other sex.

These are sentiments of which a Victorian reviewer might be proud, although they also have the air of someone imitating Dr Johnson. They are of course uttered by Mary Bennet,[25] whose portentous aphorisms are gently mocked throughout the novel. Mr and Mrs Bennet are naturally deeply shocked by what has happened to their daughter, but once Lydia is properly married to Wickham all is well, and the young pair can do no wrong, in at any rate Mrs Bennet's eyes. Mr Bennet's irony and his guilt at his neglect of his younger daughter makes it hard to guess what he thinks. What does he mean by saying that Wickham is his favourite son-in-law? Sensible people like Elizabeth and Darcy and Mr Gardiner work hard to ensure that Wickham does the decent thing by marrying Lydia, taking the reasonable view that such a marriage, though not perfect, was better than the disgrace and the worry of Lydia unmarried, perhaps pregnant and abandoned. Such a view, while clearly not that of the high Victorian period when one slip would have doomed Lydia to eternal disgrace, is probably one that would have been common among most readers of Austen until twenty years ago. Now perhaps we are less willing to allow that women who compromised themselves with a worthless man would do better to marry him than try for a fresh start.

'Let other pens dwell on guilt and misery.'[26] So Austen begins the final chapter of *Mansfield Park*. Others might think that she had dwelt on the subject for too long. The elopement of Maria Rushworth and Henry Crawford occurs simultaneously with that of Maria's sister Julia and Mr Yates, a coincidence vaguely reminiscent of the unexpected whims of fate which Austen satirised in the early novel *Love and Freindship*. Maria is of course married to the stupid Tom Rushworth, and it is presumably the breaking of her marriage vows that enables her conduct to be differentiated from that of her sister, as wickedness and vice are distinguished from folly. Julia eventually marries Mr Yates, while Maria is unable to persuade Henry Crawford to marry her, or her father to receive her, and is punished for her criminal conduct – the strong words used by Austen – by having to live with Mrs Norris.

There are obvious parallels and differences between the treatment of the sexual scandals in *Pride and Prejudice* and their handling in *Mansfield Park*. Sir Thomas Bertram, like Mr Bennet, is aware that he has failed as a parent; Lady Bertram is more ineffective and more pathetic than Mrs Bennet. The happy marriage of Edmund Bertram and Fanny Price follows the disaster in the same way as the marriage of Elizabeth and Darcy follows the elopement, but whereas in *Pride and Prejudice* the hero and heroine seem sensible and uncensorious as opposed to the priggish Mr Collins and Mary Bennet, in *Mansfield Park* it is Fanny and Edmund who are the prigs, while Mary Crawford is blamed for seeing the behaviour of her brother in terms of folly rather than vice.

This change of attitude has been explained by a change of heart in Jane Austen as she grew older and more affected by prevailing Evangelical seriousness about moral conduct. Since the writing of both *Pride and Prejudice* and *Mansfield Park* took place over a number of years it is difficult to make much of the lapse of time between the two novels. Other late novels like *Emma* and *Persuasion* are not particularly hostile to sexual indiscretion. There is some feeling against William Elliot in *Persuasion*, and the first hint that he is not an upright man comes when we learn that he is lax about travelling on Sundays, but it is possible to exaggerate the extent of Austen's conversion to the Evangelical movement. We have seen how two passages in her letters point in opposite directions. A third passage that has been used to show that *Mansfield Park* was a novel about ordination turns out to be wrongly punctuated.[27] In her last fragment *Sanditon* the conceited seducer Sir Edward Denham appears to be treated as more foolish than wicked.

There is a difference, as Austen sees, between the conduct of Maria on the one hand and Julia on the other. The breaking of marriage vows and the disruption of a third party's happiness, even if this third party is the fairly worthless Thomas Rushworth, are not crimes committed by the eloping lovers, who may still be brought into the fold by the marriage ceremony. Rather sadly, if tolerantly, Henry Crawford does not seem to be punished for causing so much misery and guilt, although Austen protests against this. Unlike Wickham and Lydia who end up unhappily married; unlike Julia and Yates who end up married; unlike Maria who ends her days with Mrs Norris, an even more unhappy pairing than Wickham and Lydia, Henry Crawford would only seem to suffer the loss of Fanny; and in spite of her virtue we sometimes feel this is no great loss.

In condemning adultery as worse than fornication, and in seeing a woman's lapse as something worse than a man's, Austen is hardly revolutionary, and it is difficult to see her as a pioneer of feminist thought. In novels other than *Mansfield Park* and *Pride and Prejudice* where an elopement does not furnish the main crisis there is less emphasis on sexual misconduct, but the same attitude is shown towards this misconduct. In *Northanger Abbey* Isabella Thorpe is condemned, not because she and Frederick Tilney become lovers, but because she flirts with Tilney for mercenary motives although engaged to James Morland. Such conduct may seem less reprehensible than the breaking of the marriage vow, but it does involve the breaking of a promise in the same way as Catherine was forced, on this occasion through no fault of her own, to abandon her undertaking to go for a walk with the Tilneys because John Thorpe carries her off to Blaize Castle. Punctilious behaviour in small matters often accompanies carelessness over large moral issues, but rarely so in the novels of Jane Austen.

In *Sense and Sensibility* Willoughby behaves very badly towards Marianne Dashwood again for mercenary reasons, but he does not actually seduce her. He has seduced Miss Williams, and this shows us what an unreliable and disreputable man he is; but since we see and hear much more of Marianne than we do of Miss Williams it would seem that it is unfaithfulness and unreliability in general rather than sexual misconduct in particular that is to be blamed. Darcy makes much the same point about Wickham's behaviour to his sister. Colonel Brandon is thought by Mrs Jennings to be the natural father of Miss Williams. The information is delivered as a shocking piece of scandal, but, as Mrs Jennings is rather a vulgar woman, it is difficult to know how Austen thought the information should have been delivered. Presumably not at all, since the accusation is false, although like most pieces of scandal it contains the germs of truth, since Brandon had contemplated eloping with Miss Williams's mother, romantically to Scotland, where he would presumably have married her at Gretna Green. Brandon does not seem to be particularly blamed for this piece of rashness, and we sometimes feel that this escapade in his past has been inserted to add a touch of Byronic glamour to his flannel waistcoat. His contemplated indiscretion is made all the worse by the fact that the lady in question is subsequently unhappily married to his own brother. Indeed so confused is Brandon's narration that on a careless reading it looks as if he contemplated the journey to Scotland after this unhappy marriage. In fact after the marriage Brandon is out of the country, and the unfortunate lady runs away not with him, but with someone described boldly as her first seducer, who is the father of Miss Williams. Her subsequent fate as a woman who had lost her reputation is described with more clarity and more charity than that of many Victorian ladies, but she meets the inevitable early death, bequeathing her daughter to Colonel Brandon.

Following in her mother's footsteps Miss Williams falls early a prey to Willoughby's seductive charms. Brandon is very hard on her seducer: 'He had already done that which no man who can feel for another would do. He had left the girl whose youth and innocence he had seduced, in a situation of the utmost distress, with no creditable home, no help, no friends, ignorant of his address'.[28] Presumably Brandon had intended to do better for the girl's mother. We must make some allowances for the fact that *Sense and Sensibility* began its life as an epistolary novel, and authorial support for Brandon's outbursts seems limited. Eleanor's forgiveness of Willoughby seems, like Elizabeth Bennet's reconciliation with Wickham, to err on the side of kindness. Unlike Wickham, Willoughby does not seem to suffer for his sins. 'He lived to exert, and frequently to enjoy himself. His wife was not always out of humour, nor his house always uncomfortable; and in his breed of horses and dogs and in sporting of every kind he found no inconsiderable degree of domestic felicity.'[29] It is a fate not altogether unlike that of the villain of *Locksley Hall*, who 'will hold thee, when his passion shall have spent its novel force/ Something better than his dog, a little dearer than his horse'.[30] Willoughby's transformation into the typical Victorian squire seems undeserved. Even less deserved is Edward Ferrars's reward of a comfortable living and Eleanor as wife, after he would seem to have acted not with Byronic wickedness but Shelleyan weakness in becoming virtually affianced to two ladies at the same time. For all Lucy Steele's scheming and vulgarity, for all Eleanor's understanding forgiveness, and for all Ferrars's desperate attempts to do the right thing, it is hard to avoid this conclusion and with it the conclusion that Austen is a little soft on her male sinners.

There is of course no question of Ferrars and Lucy having slept together, although Lucy might have wanted to entrap him in this way, but in the different social standards of the day it is difficult to see all that much difference between the way Willoughby behaves and the way Ferrars behaves.

In *Emma* there is much flirtation, but little sexual scandal. Almost every young female character seems at one stage to be likely to marry almost every eligible male character, but there is little except gossip and intrigue behind these courtships. Early on in the novel Mr Elton finds himself entangled with two or possibly three different women, but unlike Edward Ferrars he is not really to blame for this entanglement. Harriet Smith's illegitimacy is clearly a source neither of embarrassment nor disgrace, and Emma at any rate thinks she is a good deal more suitable for Mr Elton than the upstart Miss Hawkins. Emma imagines an affair between Jane Fairfax and the future husband of her friend Miss Campbell. Since this affair exists only in Emma's imagination we cannot tell how far it proceeded; it is clearly delightfully shocking in Emma's eyes, whereas the real engagement of Jane Fairfax and Frank Churchill comes as something of an unpleasant surprise.[31] Although there would seem to be nothing improper in their conduct, the secrecy, even slyness, involved would seem to carry some element of disapproval with it – the kind of disapproval that would necessarily follow a clandestine affair within or before marriage. In contrast, when Emma discovers her love for Knightley she is quite open about it.

By the time of her later novels Austen was discovering the predicament of many Victorian heroines, full of sexual energy but thwarted by convention from stating their love. It was the Brontës' flouting of this convention that brought upon them the wrath of the reviewers. In *Persuasion* Austen had to rewrite chapter 18 to solve Anne Elliot's predicament, and some readers may feel she does not solve it very satisfactorily, although we are clearly meant to contrast Anne's demure behaviour with that of Louisa Musgrove who literally throws herself at Wentworth and as literally, but fortunately not metaphorically, becomes together with her sister Henrietta in the famous scene at the Cobb a fallen woman. The subsequent mutual transfer of affection that occurs both with Louisa and Captain Benwick is a rather ironic comment on the shallowness of sexual attraction, and is perhaps an important comment, in view of the annotations from Byron, on the silliness of the Romantic movement.[32]

Anne herself feels more deeply, but it is clear that she is sexually attractive since not only Wentworth but Charles Musgrove and the wicked William Elliot fall in love with her. Sexual wickedness in *Persuasion* is confined to the persons of William Elliot and Mrs Clay, and the very terse passage at the end of the novel which announces that Mrs Clay has left her somewhat dubious position in Sir Walter Elliot's household to take up the definitely disgraceful situation of a place in London under William Elliot's protection.[33] The word protection is an interesting Orwellian euphemism, used sarcastically by William Wilberforce in the House of Commons in 1812, suggesting William Elliot is some kind of Sir Galahad when he is clearly nothing of the kind, marrying first for money, then swindling Mr Smith, then running off with the not very attractive Mrs Clay presumably to ensure that she could never marry his uncle and thus by bearing heirs deprive him of the title. Mrs Clay presumably hoped to become Lady Elliot by fair means or foul, but we feel that her hopes are doomed to be disappointed. As in *Mansfield Park*, although this time Austen does not say so, it would seem that the man came off better than the woman as a result of this scandal. All William Elliot loses is the chance of marrying Anne Elliot, although he had less chance than Crawford had with Fanny Price since Wentworth's presence was more vigorous than Edmund Bertram's. The fact that William Elliot is attracted to Anne Elliot, although no particular element of self-interest is attached to a marriage with her, is a further indication of the sexual power of Austen's last heroine.

We do not know how Austen would have developed her sexual themes in *Sanditon*. Would Sir Edward Denham, so frankly described as a seducer, have been a major or a minor character; and would they have been treated in comic or tragic fashion? The recent attempt by another lady to conclude *Sanditon*, suggesting that Sir Edward is a minor comic unsuccessful suitor, is as good a guess as any.[34] Sir Edward's title is a reminder of a certain hostility to the aristocracy displayed in Austen's life and her mature novels. A real life model for Sir Edward, attested by Fanny Burney, is not impossible.[35] The peerage, in the shape of Lord Orville, appears in *The Watsons*, although it seems unlikely that the most humble of Austen's heroines should aspire so high. In *Lady Susan* we have a smart aristocratic adulteress, who is much more attractive than her dim daughter and dull sister-in-law; and we can well understand why Mr Mainwaring is prepared to sacrifice his rather shrewish wife in favour of her. Nevertheless the novel ends with all Lady Susan's plans foiled, her daughter married to the man she hoped to seduce, the Mainwarings united and herself fobbed off with the booby she had hoped to foist on her daughter.

With Lady Susan we come back to the world of *Mansfield Park*, where the attractive, seductive urban world of the Crawfords is eventually defeated by the stodgy but right values of Edmund Bertram and Fanny Price. The presence in *Mansfield Park* of Kotzebue's play *Lover's Vows* is a reminder of the division and of which side Austen takes. Fanny and Edmund disapprove of the play, and when Sir Thomas returns their disapproval seems justified. It is hard for modern readers to grasp the point *Mansfield Park* is trying to make, since most modern parents would be only too pleased to find their children acting in a play instead of in front of the television, and if their children were as old as the Bertram children they would long ago have relinquished their authority. It was not so in Austen's time, and if we are looking for a modern analogy for the production of *Lover's Vows* in *Mansfield Park* we have to think of a teenage drinks party that has got out of hand. Both kinds of youthful escapade involve the moving of the furniture. In addition Kotzebue was both a sexual and a social revolutionary. The baron is shown to be a fool; Agatha's disregard for the marriage vow is not frowned upon; and Amelia boldly declares her love for Anhalt without bashfully waiting like Fanny Price and Anne Elliot for some encouragement.[36]

Sir Thomas Bertram disapproves of *Lover's Vows*, and so we should think did Jane Austen, though we know that the Austen family acted plays in their youth and that Jane Austen visited the theatre at Bath and in London. Yet play-acting was not wholly respectable and it grew less respectable as Austen grew older. Another relative of hers, sister-in-law of the adulteress, was herself both an adulteress and an actress. This was Charlotte Twisleton, who had five children by her husband, the Rev Thomas Twisleton. He then, in a life that seems to be more like a novel by Mrs Henry Wood than by Jane Austen, married again and became Archdeacon of Colombo, and although he began life as the second son of a man who was not even recognised as Lord Saye and Sele it is from this second marriage of the second son that the present Lord Saye and Sele descends. Austen speaks once not very kindly of the Rev Thomas, but her views on his wife would probably have been harsher. She would have appreciated the way in which the title has descended.

In her views on sexual morality Austen hardly seems a revolutionary. She seems to accept without question the patriarchal idea that women's role was to marry and that women should enter marriage as virgins. We have shown her as apparently accepting the double standard whereby men are allowed a little indiscretion without doing much damage to themselves, although here she does allow herself some questions when she says of Henry Crawford's adultery, 'that punishment, the public punishment of disgrace, should attend in a just measure *his* share of the offence is, we know, not one of the barriers, which society gives to virtue'.[37] There was of course a debate on this question set in motion by the publication of Richardson's *Sir Charles Grandison*, a book much read and admired by Austen, as to whether men could be expected to be paragons of virtue. Austen seems to take the sensible view that most men were neither Lovelaces nor Grandisons, although she does not allow herself many opportunities of exploring male consciousness. Brontë knew fewer men, but was less cautious. In treating of female virtue Austen wisely saw sexual morality as part of human morality, although not the only part as some Victorians would have it; or completely separated from moral considerations as some modern thinkers would assert. Her upbringing led her to uphold the institution of marriage as something worth preserving, even in the case of bad marriages like that of Rushworths or the Wickhams, unequal marriages like that of the Bennets, or dull marriages like that of Mr and Mrs Collins.

There is probably not quite enough evidence in Austen's life to show how she reacted to contemporary attacks on the institution of marriage. Her novels would suggest she dealt with marital problems in a way that was politically unengaged but morally alert. Adultery is seen as a practical disaster since it usually leads to material ruin; but also a moral disaster because it involves a lack of sensitivity to the claims and susceptibilities of others. It is not seen as a moral disaster just because women must not know about sex outside marriage. Austen came from a close-knit family. When disaster hit this family, as it did with Aunt Perrot's arrest for shop-lifting, Henry Austen's bankruptcy and even Jane's fatal illness, they loyally closed ranks.[38] Adultery makes it impossible, as *Mansfield Park* shows, for the ranks to be closed, for it disregards the most intimate ties of the social fabric.

A woman's adultery is worse in Austen's eyes than a man's because people assume it is, and therefore it involves a more fundamental breach with the family unit. But for a man to commit adultery is still a contemptible breach of social virtues and a degradation of the moral character. Unlike Lady Isabel Carlyle, whose fall turns her into a bad woman although actually she is still full of sensitivity and compassion and still devoted to her family, Austen's fallen women display selfishness and insensitivity before and after their technical fall which is just part of their badness. And her fallen men display the same faults.

This is a perfectly reasonable moral standpoint. It runs counter to the views of Mrs Henry Wood, which we may term Victorian. Wood assumed with her readers that sexual activity outside marriage was a terrible sin, especially for the women concerned. It also runs counter to some contemporary attitudes to sexuality, where sexual activity before marriage is almost regarded as normal, where women are judged in the same terms as men, and where the only real sexual crimes are hypocrisy, violence and repression. Austen clearly fits into neither camp. We have seen the danger of judging events in her life by contemporary standards. There is an equal danger if we regard her as a Victorian. Our next five novelists did all write their novels in Victoria's reign, and all were writing under the kind of pressure that led to the absurdities of *East Lynne*, although Brontë was fairly ignorant of Victorian values and Hardy fairly contemptuous of them.[39]

3

Brontë

Charlotte Brontë's views on Jane Austen are well known. G. H. Lewes sent her *Pride and Prejudice* to read after the publication of *Jane Eyre*, thus neatly linking the first three authors under examination. She was not impressed, comparing the work of her predecessor to a neat, well-ordered garden and complaining of the lack of poetry and by implication of passion in it. The verdict is an unfair one, although it is sometimes echoed by modern readers. To do her justice, Brontë did add, in a passage which editions of her letters unaccountably omit, praise of Austen for her lack of windy wordiness and her clear common sense. But in general she dismisses her as too prim and proper, a Victorian writing before her time. The verdict she gave on Austen to Lewes was repeated in a letter to W. S. Williams.[1]

This correspondence is more revealing for what it reveals about Brontë herself. If she attacks Austen for her spinster-like prudery – and this seems to be the gist of her complaints – then Brontë herself appears to be someone writing outside her prudish times; and this was indeed the verdict of many of her reviewers. Not all the reviews were hostile, and not all the hostile reviews were particularly critical of Brontë's discussion of sexual morality. There was confusion between the three Brontë sisters, with Anne Brontë's *Tenant of Wildfell Hall* coming in for a special measure of abuse, although oddly her earlier *Agnes Grey* had been compared to the work of Austen. One suspects that the distinctly shocking *Wuthering Heights* dragged the other novels into the mire. By the time we come to reviews of *Shirley* and *Villette* reviewers seemed to expect the Brontës or Bells to be shocking and found cause for disgust in reading about Shirley whistling or using slang.[2]

Such contemporary verdicts on Brontë seem as misplaced as Brontë's own verdict on Austen, but they have emboldened modern readers into seeing her as a standard bearer of revolt against Victorian values. Thus the portrait of Bertha Mason as the Mad Woman in the Attic has become the symbol of Victorian women imprisoned by convention from behaving as sexual beings. Bertha is seen as the other side of Jane herself, both women with sexual desire not harnessed demurely to the family; both equally bullied by oppressive males. In the other novels, Frances Henri, Caroline Helstone, Shirley Keeldar and Lucy Snowe similarly assert themselves. Meanwhile conventional women like Blanche Ingram and Ginevra do not seem troubled by erotic thoughts, but play the conventional enticing game of courtship and marriage. They are clearly objects of disapproval.

It has to be said that this interpretation of the Brontë novels, though interesting and at times providing fresh insights, can be exaggerated. In the first place Brontë was no revolutionary. In politics a Tory, a keen admirer of the Duke of Wellington and a supporter of the Church of England with all its faults, she did not rebel against Victorian values because she did not know what these values were. Her poverty and isolation prevented her from keeping up with literary fashions. Only after the publication of *Jane Eyre* did she start reading contemporary fiction which her publishers sent to her, and significantly her last two novels after this crash course of reading gave less cause for complaint to the reviewers. In her youth she had read widely and unusually books from abroad and from a previous generation with less strict rules about sexual expression and sexual attitudes.[3] This reading made her seem more of a sexual revolutionary than was really the case, for Brontë's life was not conducive to sexual revolt. She remained throughout her life like Jane Austen a pious and practising member of the Church of England. It is true that she herself and the country in general moved away from the pure Evangelical morality of Mr Brontë to which Austen seemed to be moving, a morality that placed special emphasis on sexual continence; but she was a member of a church that valued monogamy highly, which had an all male priesthood, and did not have much time for female independence. Brontë must have felt the claims of this church even if at times her instincts pulled her in the opposite direction.[4]

In her early twenties Brontë received proposals of marriage from two curates. Unlike Charlotte Lucas she did not accept them, and the refusal does her credit. The curates in question seem rather preposterous characters, but so was Mr Collins, and Brontë's prospects after her father's death would have been a great deal worse than those of her fictional namesake. The love affair with

M. Heger was quite a different matter and caused Brontë confusion and guilt. Branwell Brontë's affair with his employer's wife, real or imagined, showed adultery in a sordid light. Later possible romances with James Taylor and George Smith were so decorously conducted that it is almost impossible to discover what happened in them. Mr Nicholls's proposal was tepidly received, and like a dutiful daughter Brontë initially seemed to pay undue heed to her father's opposition, although this opposition and a desire for companionship in a lonely old age may have combined to win Mr Nicholls's case for him.

This is hardly the life of a sexual revolutionary. It is true that under the demure façade hidden fire was burning. From her early teens well into her twenties Brontë was pouring forth an incredible farrago of verse and prose, full of characters passionate and unrestrained, whose lives are indecorous in the extreme.[5] Her principal hero Arthur Wellesley, Marquess of Douro, Duke of Zamorna, Emperor of Angria, has more mistresses than he has titles, and his courtiers are not models of marital fidelity. The fact that the Angrian stories were written at different times about different periods in Zamorna's life makes it difficult to keep track of exactly who is married to whom, and the way people die and come to life again is an additional source of confusion. Sometimes, especially in one notable tale where Zamorna has a double,[6] it looks as if Brontë wanted to have her cake and eat it by making her hero both a Byronic rake and a dutiful husband. At other times she appears to have been worried by the influence the world below had on her and to have made more than one effort to free herself from her Angrian fantasies.[7]

It was M. Heger who curbed Brontë's imagination though more in his capacity as teacher than as lover. Already, before going to Belgium, she had written stories like *Ashworth*, which is far more realistic than most Angrian tales, although it still contains Angrian characters. *The Professor*, written after M. Heger's literary education, has a deliberately sober introduction. Guilt over M. Heger and shame over Branwell may have helped keep fantasies about Zamorna in check in the later novels. In arguing that they still emerge in a symbolic way in *Jane Eyre* feminist and deconstructionist critics seem to ignore just how tawdry these fantasies are. Selfish and masterful, with a train of women eager to fall into his arms, Zamorna is a cardboard character, not one we should admire. Many other male characters, notably his chief rival, Alexander Percy, Duke of Ellrington, fall into the same category. The absurd setting, involving country houses with Regency architecture placed in the middle of Africa, adds to the unhealthy impression of unreality. Worse still, the women in Angria, with the possible exception of the spirited Mary Percy, Ellrington's daughter and Zamorna's wife, tend to fall into the two Victorian stereotypes of angel or harlot. Two of Brontë's later and better stories, *Mina Laury* and *Caroline Vernon*, exemplify this dichotomy, although the long-suffering and virtuous Mina does break all the rules by being technically Zamorna's mistress. On the whole, however, Brontë's juvenilia with their swooning heroines in unreal situations seem to be set in the same escapist world that Austen satirised in her juvenilia; and after reading Brontë's condenscending remarks about *Pride and Prejudice* one hates to think of the asperity with which Austen would have dismissed Brontë's early stories in which characters do either run mad or faint.[8]

She would have been less harsh to the mature novels, although *The Professor*, in spite of its sobriety, has a very odd hero. A single man without any fortune, he seems obsessed by thoughts of a future wife. Any woman he meets is regarded in sexual terms. His Seacombe cousins and his sister-in-law Mrs Edward Crimsworth are appraised and found wanting. He stares eagerly at the unavailable girls at the Crimsworth dance; pines to see into the garden of the girl's school; thinks that Madame Reuter is going to make love to him; thinks that Mademoiselle Reuter is in love with him even when she is engaged to Monsieur Pelet; and appraises his female pupils by their physical attributes. He looks at himself in the mirror and finds himself not very handsome, but is so confident of his charms that he thinks that he and Madame Pelet are likely to start an affair, even though he has by that time met and fallen in love with Frances Henri. He discusses his love affairs freely and frankly with Hunsden and Pelet, although distressed by the former's Yorkshire bluntness and the latter's Gallic sensuality.

Austen does not include scenes where male characters talk to each other on their own because she had not heard them and in entering a domain of which she knew nothing Brontë was playing a dangerous game. Branwell, not a very reliable or very normal recounter of masculine conversations, may be one source for Crimsworth's sensual thoughts and talk; at other times we feel that Brontë has transferred the schoolgirl chatter of friends like Ellen Nussey to Crimsworth and his friends. For Crimsworth and his sexual longings, though strong, are essentially innocent. *The Professor* attracted no hostile comment for coarseness, but this may be because people were unwilling to attack Brontë posthumously. It may also be because the manuscript was frequently revised after the publication of *Jane Eyre* and its shocked reception, although these revisions, a few of them from the bowdlerising hand of Mr Nicholls, do not seem to have added or subtracted much.

In spite of his feminine characteristics Crimsworth retains some of the old Angrian features. His aristocratic education at Eton has given him a haughty mien and he seems to think women are impressed by despotic gestures. Mademoiselle Reuter is impressed to such an extent that she contemplates leaving Pelet for his subordinate because of his air of lofty disdain. Frances Henri on the contrary is impressed by her teacher's kindness, even though he is unnecessarily patronising about her faults in English. She also shows her independence at the end of the novel in first insisting on keeping her job, then setting up her own school. While extremely respectful to Crimsworth, whom she insists on calling Monsieur, she is prepared to state her own point of view and can keep up an argument both with him and Hunsden. We are meant to contrast her modesty, virtue, intelligence and spirit with the duplicity and subservience of Madame Pelet, and the contrast does work and is in keeping with modern feminist thought, awkward though Crimsworth's masterful characteristics are.

The Professor was written almost immediately after Branwell's disastrous liaison with Mrs Robinson had been revealed and fairly soon after the débâcle with M. Heger in Belgium. Revulsion at the former affair and perhaps guilt at what might have happened in the latter show themselves in two long tirades against self-indulgence and possible adultery.[9] The repetition, length and savagery of such phrases as 'hideous and polluting recollections of vice' and 'a body depraved by the infectious influence of the vice-polluted soul' are perhaps blemishes in a short, fairly quiet novel, but show how far Brontë had moved away from Angria, and how removed she is from any sympathy with sensuality in spite of Crimsworth's broodings on women. Most of the female characters in the novel are despised by Crimsworth for defects of intelligence or morality. When Frances Henri's virtue and intellect become apparent, her beauty shows through and he derives pleasure from 'contemplating the clearness of her brown eyes, the fairness of her fine skin, the purity of her well-set teeth, the proportion of her delicate form; and that pleasure I could ill have dispensed with'.[10] In contrast his other pupils, because of their stupidity, do not attract him, since sullen tempers, disfiguring frowns, coarse gestures and muttered expressions detract from their beauty.

Some girls like Sylvie, destined for the convent, are irredeemably plain, though virtuous. Leonie Ledru, though less virtuous, has a parchment-like skin; and would have fared better if she had been a boy, in which case she would have been the model of an unprincipled attorney. Eulalie, Hortense and Caroline are the beauties of the class, stupid, unprincipled and unchaste. Eulalie and Hortense are large girls, Caroline though small has coarse hair and lips as full as those of a hot-blooded Maroon. Both remind us of the first Mrs Rochester, while the slight, apparently timid but really quite spirited Frances Henri prefigures Jane Eyre. Almost all Charlotte Brontë's villainesses are large women, their full figure apparently being a sign of sexual wantonness. We are not surprised that the deceitful Mademoiselle Reuter, who in a sense deceives both her husband and Crimsworth, marrying the former for convenience and falling for the latter's old Etonian charm, ends up by weighing twelve stone.

The Professor then contains the contrast between its virtuous heroine, capable of love and full of spirit but channelling her sexuality correctly, and a series of rather reprehensible women who use their sexuality to entrap men and have no morality or intelligence as a counterbalance. We also have the rather pathetic Sylvie as the dried-up future nun to show the dangers of having no sexual feelings at all. It is difficult to see anyone from Jane Austen to Victorian reviewer to modern feminist critic quarrelling with the preference for Frances Henri, or the theme of the novel stated in this somewhat crudely schematic way, although we can cavil at Brontë's statement of her thesis; and of course with Crimsworth as narrator and *homme moyen sensuel*.

Jane Eyre, clearly a much more impressive novel, poses more problems of evaluation and elucidation. Austen would naturally have disapproved of its melodramatic coincidences and deplorable hero as Mrs Humphry Ward did a hundred years later. Victorian critics were divided into those who attacked the novel's moral coarseness and those who praised its stern moral purpose, while modern interpretations insist in finding new surprising and sexually revolutionary statements in a novel with a theme at least as old as *Pamela*, of the girl from a humble background who preserves her virtue and wins her reward.

Jane Eyre opens with the heroine involved with a trio of minor characters who seem to come straight out of the pages of *The Professor*. John Reed is the bullying male, fawned upon by his mother and sisters; we are not displeased that he comes to a sticky end. Georgiana is the brainless beauty who uses her sexuality to marry for position, not love; we are not surprised that she achieves her aims by marrying a worn-out man of fashion. Eliza Reed is the shrivelled spinster, less admirable because more calculating than Sylvie; we are not disappointed that she ends up in a convent. Jane Eyre starts without any of the advantages of the Reed children, but like Frances Henri wins her way to wealth and marriage and happiness, although there are many difficulties on the way, as there are for Crimsworth and Frances Henri.

The first difficulty Jane meets is the inflexible regime of Lowood under the charge of Mr Brocklehurst, rightly seen as a symbol of Victorian repression although not necessarily as a symbol of patriarchal authority. The famous comparison of Brocklehurst to a pillar, to which St John Rivers is also likened, shows links between the two men. In hinting at phallic symbols[11] critics have rightly shown not only Brocklehurst's maleness but also his power as the director of an all female school and the rigidity with which he exercises this power. St John Rivers exercises similar control over his household, refusing his sisters' friendly overtures and trying to bend Jane to his will. Mr Brocklehurst, it is true, has power over Jane and her fellow schoolgirls, Miss Temple and her fellow mistresses not just because he is a man, but because he is rich. Mrs Squeers holds a similar position of power over Nicholas Nickleby and Smike, although of course the Squeers family are less prosperous. But there is a kind of sexual mastery about Mr Brocklehurst, as shown by the fact that he is almost the only person married, as well as being the only man, in the Lowood establishment. Miss Temple has to leave the school to marry a clergyman. In insisting on straight hair and modest dress while imposing a Spartan regime on the girls and mistresses at his school Brocklehurst is curbing the sexuality which he hypocritically flaunts when he brings in his well-dressed family. Rochester assumes that, as all the nuns in a convent are in love with their director, so all the girls love Mr Brocklehurst. Jane naturally denies this, but Rochester's casual remark, as well as showing the way Brontë equates the extreme low-church atmosphere of Lowood with the High Church and Catholicism, also reveals Brocklehurst as a symbol of male sexuality.

This of course links Brocklehurst with Rochester. It is now fashionable to see Rochester as a symbol of unjust male power, unfairly imprisoning his wife and Jane; dominating by his masculine authority a house full of female dependents and a house-party full of fashionable guests. Against this authority Jane revolts, as the first Mrs Rochester tries to revolt, by running away, only returning to him when he is tamed and broken, if not actually rendered harmless by being castrated. Interestingly Brocklehurst is not punished in the same way, merely suffering a slight diminution of his authority after the outbreak of the fever which carries off Helen Burns. Rochester loses his sight and one arm, a punishment which is likely to owe more to the biblical injunction about plucking out eyes than to any Freudian symbolism.

Rochester needs to be punished, because on any account he has sinned. Only a series of coincidences and the timely intervention of Jane's uncle saves him from the crime of bigamy. He deceives Jane Eyre and almost entraps her into a bogus marriage which would have left her a fallen woman in the eyes of the world and rendered her children illegitimate. Adèle Varens and Jane's dreams about children are subtle reminders of the latter possibility. By the rather stern standards of Austen it could be argued that Rochester deceives Blanche Ingram into thinking he was going to marry her, although it could be argued that Blanche deserves such deception. When his first marriage is discovered he adds insult to injury by asking Jane to run away with him to the South of France as his mistress. He has had good practice with mistresses in France as the episode of Cécile Varens makes clear. His free recounting of his adventures with Cécile to the innocent governess was another way of raising Victorian hackles. Mrs Humphry Ward, herself no stranger to public controversy with the publication of *Robert Elsmere* (1888), and not entirely hostile to a little sexual licence, as shown in the *History of David Grieve* (1892), still found Rochester shocking at the end of the nineteenth-century.[12]

But of course, as Rochester noted when he talked about a conventional impediment, and Eliot complained when she said that she could not see what all the fuss was about in *Jane Eyre*, the central moral issue which makes Rochester wicked and Jane heroic turns out in many people's eyes to be a broken-backed dragon.[13] Rochester could have divorced Bertha Mason had she not been mad, and had he not presumably condoned her mad drunken adultery. His explanation of his four years of marriage, not narrated under ideal circumstances, makes it clear that he was more sinned against than sinning. Thackeray and Eliot knew the difficulties of divorcing a mad or bad wife, and the terrible heartfelt attempts to try and make up to such a wife, which rebounded on the innocent partner. Modern readers are less appreciative of such difficulties. Divorce is no longer a disgrace, certainly not a disgrace if one is the innocent partner. Divorce can easily be obtained, however guilty either party is, and however hard either partner has tried to preserve or destroy the marriage. Madness is no defence against, as it should be no cause for, divorce. We are of course very tolerant of divorced couples, and even if all else fails tolerant of couples living together unable or unwilling to obtain a divorce. This makes it very difficult for modern students to understand *Jane Eyre*; and both they and the literary critics they read are in difficulties when trying to explain why Jane has to flee.

Jane has to flee, but not to the South of France, where Rochester having won her forgiveness invites her after revealing another string of mistresses: Giacinta in Italy; Clara in Germany. He also virtually tries to rape her though he later denies such an attempt. Again as in *The Professor* Brontë seems to imagine men as the victims of inescapable sexual urges and rather surprisingly forgives such men.[14] There is perhaps less reason for surprise when we realise that there are many similarities between the predicament of Charlotte Brontë and that of Edward Fairfax Rochester. Both had fallen in love with another person, from whom the marriage tie would seem to separate them forever. Both wrote poems expressing this unfortunate state of affairs. These poems are different at several vital points, but not at the most vital point. The narrator of Brontë's poem is female; begins in a subordinate position; acknowledges respect turning into love even if this love is unlawful; and then finds all turn into dust and ashes as a successful rival takes the prize away. In *Jane Eyre* Rochester's poem of course has a male narrator and there is no note of subservience; nor does the poem end with disaster, being delivered well before the discovery of the first Mrs Rochester. Brontë's poem fits none of her fictional characters, but does exactly correspond to her position with M. Heger.[15]

Modern critics are unable to explain why Jane left Rochester or indeed why she did not accept his offer to be his mistress in the South of France. They ignore repeated pleas that such conduct would be offensive in the eyes of God and man, because such pleas carry no conviction in modern times. Instead they try and find explanations as to why any union with Rochester half-way through the novel would be offensive to modern sentiment. It is argued that Rochester does not appreciate Jane as a woman, treating her at one level as a kind of doll to be dressed in pretty ornaments, at another as an elf or fairy, a mere figment of the imagination. There is justice in both charges, although to use the former to attack male dominance as opposed to the dominance of wealth is to ignore Brontë's persistent hostility on behalf of the downtrodden governess against her rich employers, male and female. Rochester's frequent references to Jane as an unreal being are a trifle tiresome to the reader, but to condemn them is to ignore that element of teasing which any happy pair of lovers will recognise, and which Brontë seems, though not so fortunate, to recognise when she makes Jane tease Rochester at the end of the book. Rochester is not all that easy to slot into the patriarchal pattern.

It is claimed that he, like John Reed, Mr Brocklehurst and St John Rivers is the only male dominant in a house of females, but this is not actually true. The house-party is full of other men, Colonel Dent, Lord Ingram, Sir George Lynne, who might seem superior to Rochester with their titles, but whom he dominates with his personality, as he clearly dominates Richard Mason. In the past, first his father and brother, then Cécile Varens's other lover had got the better of him; and this may have strengthened his resolve to be masterful. Jane refuses to accede to his masterful ways and thus earns his respect.

In his conduct toward Bertha Mason Rochester does his best. We must not write *Jane Eyre* from the pages of Jean Rhys's *Wide Sargasso Sea*.[16] Bertha is both intemperate and unchaste. With the example of Branwell in front of her Brontë could not be sympathetic towards drunkenness and immorality. In seeing parallels between Bertha and Jane, and in turning Jane into the mirror image of Bertha critics ignore obvious differences between the small poor sober chaste Jane and her large loose-living rich predecessor. Some students of *Jane Eyre* can see nothing wrong in running off with a middle-aged man, as a succession of university novels seems to suggest that this is the norm rather than the exception. Such students in a desperate attempt to explain Jane's conduct quote a film version of *Jane Eyre*, which has the heroine say that she could not come to Mr Rochester's bed knowing that the first Mrs Rochester was in the same house, but these are not lines in the original novel.[17]

Where Rochester behaves badly is in deceiving Jane. When he meets her again at Ferndean he claims that once his first wife had been discovered and Jane had refused his offer to come to the South of France he never intended to take Jane by force or persuade her to abandon her resolve. We do not know whether to believe him. His other, earlier, claim that once Jane was his wife he intended to undeceive her is less confident and certain. He says, 'I wanted to have you safe before instilling confidences',[18] but we do not know how far these confidences would have gone. Rochester's action, which he initially calls cowardly, shows a lack of knowledge of Jane's moral strength. Later, when he acknowledges his sin and proclaims rather dramatically that he 'would have sullied my innocent flower – breathed guilt on its purity',[19] we see Rochester overcome by Jane's views, which are so inflexible that we need the clumsy supernatural voice of Rochester before she can revisit Thornfield with a clear conscience and without risking temptation.

Jane Eyre's pilgrimage from Thornfield to Moor Head makes painful reading. We are not surprised that when she meets Rochester again she gives an expurgated account of her sufferings. When she eats the mess of potage fit for pigs there is an obvious parallel with the prodigal son who had left loose living and harlots to go back to his father; and this is presumably a reflection on the life of bodily ease and moral degradation that Jane would have led as Rochester's mistress. The shadow of prostitution as well as destitution hangs over Jane's desperate attempts to support herself by exchanging her handkerchief and gloves for food. Charlotte Brontë may or may not have read *Sketches by Boz*. In one of these sketches, entitled 'The Pawnbroker's Shop', Dickens describes a genteel young lady selling her trinkets; an obvious prostitute decked out in rouge and gaudy clothes; and a broken woman reduced to utter degradation by her terrible life, and imagines how in time each character may sink to a lower state. There is of course no suggestion that Jane would sink so low as to sell herself. On the contrary this is the fate she has escaped, and we are reminded of this fate, known in the old cliché as a fate worse than death, by Jane's sufferings; just as she reminds us of the temptation to become the successor of Céline, Giacinta and Clara, and how little Rochester would think of her if she did.[20]

On the other hand, as has been brilliantly shown by Mary Poovey, governesses were linked with prostitutes as well as with lunatics.[21] By taking children away from their mothers they were seen as foes to the domestic ideal in the same way as prostitutes who took away men from their wives. Sometimes, as happened in two cases in the family of Austen's niece, it was the sons of the family who became entangled with the governesses.[22] Lady Eastlake's famous hostile review of *Jane Eyre* plays on these fears, and *Shirley* is an answer to them, as indeed is *Jane Eyre*, because, as even Lady Eastlake had to admit, Jane's own morality is unimpeachable.[23]

After this period of suffering we have the strange courtship of St John Rivers. Like Mr Brocklehurst, St John is the only man in a household of women, a stern Evangelical clergyman, harsh to Jane and unpopular with modern and contemporary readers alike. Unlike Mr Brocklehurst, St John mortifies his own flesh as well as others', and inspires affection in people like his sisters and respect in Jane, who ends the novel with a warning of his impending martyrdom. There is no blatant example of his hypocrisy as there is with Brocklehurst; and yet we feel that St John is not being quite straightforward in his dealings either with Rosamund Oliver or Jane herself. He is clearly attracted to the former and admits as much, but thinks she will make an unsuitable wife for a missionary. This may indeed be true, although in a way St John seems deliberately hostile to the whole area of sexual attraction. Jane, without any ties in England, hard-working and humble, even offering her services as a translator of Hindustani, may seem more suitable than Rosamund as an unpaid curate. St John proposes marriage on the grounds that it would be impractical for Jane and him to travel unchaperoned without attracting censure, and it is unconventional of Jane not to see the force of his arguments. But St John is sexually attracted to Jane; his jealousy of Rochester makes that clear, although it takes a different form from Rochester's much more open and attractive jealousy of his sexual rival. Brontë manages to convey all this very well in spite of the demands of Victorian decorum which Jane can break, although she attracted censure for doing so, but which St John, a clergyman, cannot be allowed to break.

Unfortunately Jane does not love St John with his regular good looks, but prefers Rochester whom she calls ugly to his face. In making Rochester less handsome than St John in the same way that Edgar Linton is said by Emily Brontë to be better looking than Heathcliff, *Jane Eyre* is a powerful statement of the power of sex and the right of women to make their own sexual choice, and in this sense is a book which straight-laced reviewers were right to find shocking and modern feminist thinkers are right to find refreshing. For making the hero conventionally handsome is a way of anaesthetising sex and in addition appears to deny sexual rights to the large section of the population not blessed with good looks.[24]

Between writing *Jane Eyre* and completing *Shirley* Brontë, as well as losing her brother and two sisters in a series of blows which would have curtailed anyone's exuberance, had read a number of reviews which found her novel and those of her sisters very shocking. We know that she resented such reviews and even tried to incorporate an answer to one of them in *Shirley*; but she may also have tried to restrain her own boldness. Certainly there is plenty of interest for feminists in the story of Shirley's independence and Caroline's resentment against her uncle's neglect of her aspirations, and even in the account of the narrow lives of the spinsters, Miss Ainley and Miss Mann, or the satirical account of the arrogant airs of the young curates with which the novel opens. But on sexual matters Brontë is reticent.

Of the novel's two heroines Shirley, the unconventional heiress with her masculine name and behaviour, might seem to be the obvious channel for unorthodox sexual views. In fact in rather a tame fashion Shirley says she longs to find and marry a man who is her superior and in even more tame fashion sees this ideal in the colourless Louis Moore. Shirley resents her inability to join in the world of masculine politics, but can do little about this except for organising the subordinate task of providing relief for the families of the workers. Only in her rather mystical speeches such as in the chapter including Eva's dream does Shirley live up to her role of challenger of the accepted code, and the invocation of nature as a great female force is too vague to be a real statement of a new sexual role for women.[25]

In spite of this vagueness and her tame submission to her tutor Shirley is an attractive character and she does have some fine lines, as when she declares that man considers a good woman to be a 'queer thing, half doll, half angel', whereas a bad woman is almost always a fiend. There is some exploration of the nature of this bad woman in the strange description of an imagined voyage to the seas north of Scotland full of dangerous bull-whales and a siren-like mermaid described as 'temptress terror! monstrous likeness of ourselves'.[26] There may be some reference to Thackeray's observations on Becky Sharp here.[27] Shirley seems frightened of sexuality, and in her rejection of her uncle's matrimonial plans for her she is equally hostile to Sam Wynne's vulgar profligacy, and arranged marriages in general which lead to love outside marriage. Her other unsuccessful suitor, Sir Phillip Nunnely, has a name which suggests he is not potent enough. But Louis Moore is hardly dynamic. It is awkward that Shirley, who refuses Robert Moore's proposal, should not say something to relieve Caroline's fears. What has happened to feminine friendship and sexual frankness?

Caroline Helstone, like Anne Elliot, is prevented by convention from declaring her love for Robert Moore and falls into a decline as a result. A political quarrel between Moore and Caroline's uncle causes a rift between the two families. Deprived of the sight of Moore Caroline cannot eat or sleep. She wants to earn her living and has sad thoughts on the sterile life of old maids. Her friendship with Shirley revives her a little, although it is a new cause of anxiety that Moore, whose financial position is poor, transfers his attentions to her from Caroline. It is additionally awkward that Moore, after just turning from being Captain Wentworth into being William Elliot, should emerge as one of the heroes of the novel, as unsatisfactory a character as his brother. Eventually, after he is wounded and after the contrived intervention of Martin Yorke, Robert and Caroline are brought together, although the double wedding at the end of the novel does not seem very romantic.

The difficult circumstances under which *Shirley* was written, the need to avoid charges of coarseness and the inclusion of political themes in the novel all conceal the fact that Brontë is stating a feminist thesis to the effect that women do have social and sexual needs and that society as constituted has no very good way of satisfying those needs. The materialistic Robert and the nebulous Louis reinforce this message, which is however weakened by Caroline's conventional prettiness and Shirley's forceful personality and wealth. In *Villette* the inconspicuous and not particularly attractive Lucy Snowe is a bold new departure. The sexual symbols swirl around in a baffling way. Shirley's masculine ways and name are obviously meant to tell us something about the role of the sexes. So too are Lucy Snowe's appearance as a man in woman's clothing in the play and the way in which Lucy gets a cigar-case and Graham Bretton a woman's turban at the concert. It is difficult, however, to see exactly where these symbols are pointing; and *Villette*, though clearly a powerful statement about a woman's right to be as independent as a man, is also a very difficult book to interpret in a definite way. Perhaps this is one of its strengths.

There is obviously a clear statement of hostility towards flirtatious women who use their sexuality to entrap men and then make them unhappy. We see such a portrait in the brief account of Mr Hume's wife early in the novel, and she lives again in the portrait of her niece, Ginevra Fanshawe, whose cruelty to John Graham and outrageous flirtation with Alfred de Hamal meet with the narrator's scorn, although they are not punished. Ginevra's elopement and Mr Hume's separation from his wife seem to suggest, though they do not exactly entail, sexual misconduct; but as in Jane Austen's novels it is bad behaviour in general rather than sexual immorality in particular that is condemned.

Zelie St Pierre and Madame Beck also try and entrap Paul Emanuel by their sexual snares, although these are of a different order from those in Miss Fanshawe's armoury. It is perhaps not surprising that Paul Emanuel makes unreasonable accusations against Lucy for her scarlet robe and coquettish ways. Lucy's pink dress cannot make her into a scarlet woman, but Paul Emanuel is of course partly right in that Lucy is in love with John Graham and wishes to attract his attention. Victorian convention prevents her from doing this openly and even from admitting her love to the reader except in a contorted and reluctant fashion.

Paul Emanuel partly subscribes to this convention, to which he adds a foreign Catholic flavour. His prudish censorship of his pupils' reading and his disgust that Lucy should be looking at the undraped Cleopatra contrasts with the British common sense of John Graham who is unmoved by the Cleopatra and even unmoved by the acting of Vashti, described as both wonderful and immoral, in words that seem to sum up Charlotte Brontë's divided attitude to female sexuality.[28] Both heroes seem to have mixed feelings. In spite of his bowdlerising activities Paul Emanuel says he abhors prudery; and although Lucy Snowe thinks of him as wedded to virginity, his interest in her and jealousy of John Graham makes it clear that he is not. In contrast, John Graham for all his coolness, and the extraordinary statement that his mother is a better woman than Cleopatra, falls an easy victim to the sexual charms of Ginevra and Paulina.

We of course form a different impression of both heroes at different stages of the book. John Graham turns out to have faults undreamt of when Lucy Snowe first recognises him, and never really explained, while Paul Emanuel undergoes a curious change from a dreadful little man, 'a mere sprite of caprice and ubiquity', into a constant knight in shining armour, failing Lucy only through his absence.[29] John Graham's faults would appear to spring from masculine vanity and lack of imagination. He enjoys creating a flutter in the heart of Lucy Snowe, with little thought of any unhappiness he may cause. At the beginning of the novel he is equally careless about the young Polly. When he meets Lucy on her arrival in *Villette* after she has lost her trunk his English good manners demand that he give her help and direct her part of the way towards safety. Significantly he does not see her all the way across the park to the inn he had recommended. To do so might have embarrassed both parties and ensured that Lucy's reputation was in some sense compromised. Nevertheless the abandonment of Lucy in the streets of Brussels leads to trouble, though eventually to the fortunate discovery of Madame Beck's establishment, just as the withdrawal of Dr John's friendship after the visit to the theatre leads to loneliness, although eventually to the discovery of Paul Emanuel's love.

It is of course not for some time that Lucy Snowe announces that the stranger who helped on her arrival is Dr John, and it is even later that she acknowledges that he is her godmother's son, although she has recognised him. She is also tardy in announcing that the donor of some violets was Paul Emanuel. This concealment on the part of the narrator has aroused some complaints against a novel which has in any case a most peculiar narrative method, but it does fit in with a novel that deals with the hidden nature of female sexuality. Hostile criticism of *Jane Eyre* and her own conventional church upbringing would seem to have led Brontë to feel that a woman's sexual needs could not and should not be openly expressed. Yet she acknowledged the presence of these needs and despised the conventions in which they were masked, while recognising the need for a moral framework to control them. This framework was not supplied by man-made convention, still less by rigid High Church or Low Church rules and regulations, but is something that men and women have to work out for themselves. This makes Brontë a very modern thinker, and it is small wonder that her stature has risen in the last thirty years, which have seen a sexual revolution, or that she has become a patron saint of feminist critics. It is true that in her portraits of male sexuality she sometimes blunders, displaying an ignorance which neither Austen nor Eliot shows; but once we have seen through the surface respectability which made Brontë a favourite author among Victorians after a few initial shocks, we can see that she is probably the least 'Victorian' author in this study.

4

Eliot

Compare and contrast the lives of Charlotte Brontë and George Eliot. So one might set an undergraduate essay and receive some obvious answers. Both women in their lives and in their books laid stress on the need to love and be loved. Both reflected but in a way rejected the Evangelical teaching of their youth, although Eliot carried her revolt further. Both put a great deal of themselves into their heroines and drew upon their acquaintances to provide models for their other characters, although the game of finding real-life models for the people in Eliot's novels has never been carried so far as it has been in the cases of *The Professor, Jane Eyre, Shirley* and *Villette*. The central episode in the lives of both novelists, apart from their success as authors, was falling in love with a married man, but Eliot, whose love unlike Brontë's was returned, took the unusual step of going off to live with her lover, G. H. Lewes. Finally both women married unexpectedly, late in their lives, although in each case the marriage lasted a tragically short time and had little influence on literature.

George Eliot could not marry Lewes because he had condoned his wife's affair with Thornton Hunt. She thought the divorce laws absurd and throughout her association with Lewes considered herself a married woman. Society did not. The story of George Eliot's career as an author involved a difficult rise to something like respectability as the earnest morality of her novels overcame objections to the irregularity of her marital status. Initially some very coarse remarks were made about her, and even when she was a famous author women were still reluctant to acknowledge her.

The savage letter of Thomas Woolner to William Bell Scott on 4 October 1854 refers to Eliot as a '– – – – – ', an interesting if hardly colourful variant on the euphemism 'fallen woman'. The letter, quite apart from fairly striking allusions to hideous satyrs and stinkpots of humanity, contains a rather unkind picture of the relations of Lewes with his wife and Thornton Hunt, suggesting that Lewes was quite happy sharing Agnes with his lodger. Such accusations are hard to prove, although Woolner's hysterical outburst does suggest that morals were lax in Lewes's literary circle.[1]

This was a circle to which Eliot gained access through her friendship with John Chapman, another improbably modern character. At one stage he appeared to be carrying on an affair with the young Eliot in the house in which both his wife and his mistress were living. Even today there are areas of society in which eyebrows would be raised at the sexual conduct of both Lewes and Chapman, as there would have been at the behaviour of another early friend of Eliot's, Charles Bray. The story of Eliot's friendship with Dr Brabant and Herbert Spencer has a slightly comic note, as so often sexual relationships have when one party's expectations are so different from those of the other. Eliot's role was rather different in the two cases, but neither Victorians nor moderns could accuse her of anything except a certain naivety on either occasion. Eliot's female friendships, in spite of her embarrassingly addressing Sara Hennell and having her foot kissed by Edith Simcox, seem to have been disregarded by her contemporaries and probably should be by us.[2]

We should be less willing to ignore the probable affair with Chapman and the certain affair with Lewes. Haight, though cautiously circumspect, assumes that in 1851 Eliot was involved in something more than holding hands when staying in Chapman's house.[3] He bases this assumption on Chapman's diary which in spite of excisions and erasures, themselves a sign of irregularity, still gives sufficient evidence of jealousy on the part of Chapman's wife and mistress to make it clear that something unusual was going on. The affair, if it was an affair, was short-lived; but subsequent remarks attributed to Eliot and Chapman do not contradict its existence. In a recent article Holbrook assumes that Eliot slept with Chapman very early on during her stay in his house, basing his remark upon the single initial 'M', twice repeated and suitably excised.[4] Certainly it is impossible to know exactly what went on, as it is in the case of another equally magnetic uncertainly married man and a younger impressionable woman, Charles Dickens and Ellen Ternan, but there is more than late twentieth-century moral laxity to suggest that both affairs did take place. In a way, the very absence of evidence suggests concealment, and concealment suggests guilt. Guilt would also explain, though it would not excuse,

Chapman's and Eliot's great squeamishness when it came to regulating standards of sexual propriety in the literature that was submitted to them for inclusion in the *Westminster Review*.[5]

An earlier affair with Chapman might make the decision to live with Lewes as his wife more explicable. It is impossible to exaggerate the boldness of this decision. Modern critics who, for instance, condemn Eliot's brother for breaking off relations with her, regard the conduct of Lewes and Eliot as quite unexceptional as indeed it might be thought in the 1980s.[6] The 1850s thought differently. Even the enlightened circle in which Lewes and Eliot moved was shocked. Combe wondered whether there was insanity in her family; Bray, though loyal, called Eliot's actions imprudent, and Chapman, perhaps jealously and certainly hypocritically, blamed Lewes for leading Eliot astray. Most importantly of all, Eliot herself, though stoutly defending her decision to live with Lewes as entirely moral, was not exactly open about proclaiming this decision to the world – not announcing it to her family until three years after she had left for Germany.[7]

In spite of these dubious associations Eliot was able to produce novels which seem quintessentially Victorian both in their high moral seriousness and fairly uncompromising attitude to sexual sin. Other fallen women die or are sent to Australia. Poor Hetty Sorrel suffers both fates. Maggie Tulliver is scarcely more fortunate or more favoured, even though it is made clear that she is technically innocent and dies a virgin. Other older sinners like Mrs Transome and Lydia Glasher are hardly treated with sympathy. It is true that male sinners receive equally short shrift. Tito Melema and Harleigh Grandcourt die prematurely and horribly, and Arthur Donnithorne suffers almost as much as Hetty. At least Eliot cannot be accused of subscribing to the double standard, although her work has been less subject to feminist rereadings than that of other female nineteenth-century novelists.

We have seen that she and Chapman were very cautious in their policy with the *Westminster Review*, in for instance urging that books by Eliza Lynn Linton, a very odd barometer of moral taste, should be toned down. Eliot's anonymity was carefully preserved by Lewes in her early years as a novelist. In both cases commercial rather than moral factors were at work. Eliot herself refers, rather sadly, to 'grave reasons for not speaking on certain public topics' and to 'the peculiarities of my own lot'. It would have been difficult for her to have been outspoken; and not surprisingly she is remarkably careful in charting sexual misdemeanours.[8] Thus Hetty's pregnancy, although advanced, comes as something of a surprise. The discovery that Harold Transome is Jermyn's son occurs after some increasingly heavy hints about Mrs Transome's behaviour in her youth, but all these hints are discreet. Some readers may feel that Eliot is too discreet about the sexual lives of Dorothea and Lydgate. In *Daniel Deronda* she says 'it has long been understood that the proprieties of literature are not those of practical life.'[9] Tessa in *Romola* is introduced as a mother before we know she is Melema's mistress, although the mock marriage which renders her innocent should have given us the clue. There is curiously little about sex in *Romola*, although writing about a foreign country in a different age might have provided a pretext, as it did for Thackeray, for being a little more free in the treatment of sexual matters. There are glancing allusions to the vices of the Medici, but even Savonarola's fulminations against wickedness are curiously general.

Tito's behaviour with Tessa is of course deplorable and deplored, as he is deceiving both her and Romola, but his particular deception is not nearly as important in the novel as his neglect of Baldasarre, or the selling of Bardi's library, or the political chicanery which leads to the death of Bernardo. By the time Romola finds out about Tessa she is already disillusioned by her husband, and even hopes that the mock marriage might be a real one and thus dissolve the tie between her and Tito. We do not see any parallel to Arthur Donnithorne's gradual yielding to sexual temptation with Hetty, although the insidious nature of sin is well explored in the account of Tito's failure to do anything about Baldasarre.

Perhaps *Romola* can provide an insight into Eliot's sexual teaching. She did not regard her conduct with Lewes as immoral and in her letters speaks of French moral laxity and the importance of the marriage tie as seriously as any Victorian. To one who does not believe in the sacraments, sexual relations outside marriage are not bad in themselves, but are to be condemned because they involve falsity, selfishness and cruelty to others. Tito is not really condemned for his conduct to Tessa. This comes about not through self-indulgence but from a wish to escape from the pressures of his other sins. He does of course like to be liked, and Tessa's touching if cloying devotion supplies this want. It is his wish to be popular that leads to his downfall, and much the same can be said of many Eliot's other sinners, notably Arthur Donnithorne.

In *Scenes from Clerical Life* there are a number of characters who offend against Victorian respectability but are sympathetically treated. The Rev Amos Barton is·supposed by local gossip to be having an affair with the Countess Czerlaski who is also supposed to be having an affair with a man who is in fact her brother. Neither accusation is true, but the Countess is guilty of selfishness and Amos of foolishness, faults which eventually bring the saintly Milly Barton to her death. Her ill health is increased by her frequent pregnancies; and there is a discreet note of disapproval for this aspect of Amos's selfishness. Nevertheless neither Amos nor the Countess behave as badly as Milby gossip would have liked them to have behaved, or possibly as their originals did behave.[10]

In *Mr Gilfil's Love Story* Eliot is at pains to show her hero in his unromantic old age as if to point out the importance of love in such apparently unpromising vehicles. Mr Gilfil's love affair with the beautiful Caterina Sarti in his youth is a romantic one, complicated by Tina's passion for Captain Antony Wybrow, the heir to Sir Christopher Cheverel. Wybrow is the prototype for such aristocratic seducers as Arthur Donnithorne, but he does not actually seduce Caterina, merely trifling with her affections. Caterina shows her love in a very unladylike fashion and when this love is thwarted plans to murder Wybrow. Her Italian blood might be seen as an excuse for these aberrations from sexual good conduct, but the aberrations are not condemned, even though after marrying Gilfil Caterina meets with the conventional early death reserved for the erring Victorian female. The murder planned but not executed is an idea to which Eliot returns with the story of Laure in *Middlemarch* and Gwendolen Harleth in *Daniel Deronda*. It reinforces the contention that in sexual morality George Eliot was more interested in corrupt states of mind than in corrupt actions.

In *Janet's Repentance* Janet Dempster is repenting not of immorality but of drunkenness to which she is driven by her husband's cruelty, although no unfaithfulness is involved. She is helped in her struggle by Mr Tryan, an Evangelical clergyman, with whom she is clearly in love, but she is only allowed to give him a chaste kiss, on his deathbed. Mr Tryan has had an affair in his past, for which he is duly repentant; and first impressions of

Eliot as an austere denouncer of sexual immorality must be altered by this portrait, since clearly he is the best of the clergymen in *Scenes from Clerical Life*, practising a form of Christianity in action which comes very close to Eliot's own creed. Research into real-life models of Eliot's characters suggests that she subtly altered the sexual element in these early stories.[11]

Both *Scenes from Clerical Life* and *Adam Bede* were hailed as masterpieces of realism with virtually no protests against looseness of morality, as might have been made against the description of Hetty Sorrel's seduction by Arthur Donnithorne.[12] Similar seductions were probably quite common in Victorian times, often leading to pregnancy, but fortunately rarely to infanticide. Sometimes a husband was found who with or without connivance or financial reward was persuaded to marry the girl and give the child his name. Such a possibility is hardly raised in *Adam Bede*, whose hero's assault on Arthur Donnithorne makes it clear that he would not have submitted to such a solution. The timing of Hetty's pregnancy is described with clinical accuracy. One suspects the hand of Lewes here. George Eliot had no first-hand experience of being pregnant, but Lewes as well as having some scientific training must have observed his wife's pregnancies with unusual interest.

Arthur Donnithorne and Hetty Sorrel presumably make love for the first time two days after the dance on the young squire's twenty-first birthday which is celebrated on 30 July. Two and a half weeks later on 18 August Adam discovers Arthur kissing Hetty, strikes him and warns him that the affair must cease, although he is not aware that it has gone to the lengths it has. The warning is given in the Old Hermitage, which is clearly the illicit love-nest, as is shown in Arthur's concealment of Hetty's handkerchief. Arthur writes to Hetty, who then in a lukewarm way begins to respond to Adam's courtship. On 2 November she becomes engaged to Adam, but discovers she is pregnant some weeks later. She does nothing about this, hoping vaguely for the best, until the middle of February when she leaves home in the hope of finding Arthur. The baby is born on 27 February; Hetty kills it and is tried for murder. Her execution is fixed for 15 March, the very day when she and Adam were to be married. Arthur Donnithorne brings the reprieve just in time, but Hetty is still transported to Australia, where she dies shortly before she is due to return home.

'There's a sort of wrong that can never be made up for.'[13] These are Adam's final words in the novel, and he is equally harsh to Arthur Donnithorne, both on the night of 18 August when he thinks there has been a flirtation and in March when he hears of Hetty's arrest. 'He taught her to deceive – he deceived me first.'[14] And of course Arthur is guilty, the stages of his temptation being described with the same mixture of sympathy and ruthlessness as were applied later to the downfall of Tito Melema, whose wickedness, however, is not confined to sexual indiscretions. Like Tito, Arthur is anxious that the world should think well of him, and this prevents him from making a full confession to Mr Irwine, whose gentlemanly tact is a further obstacle to frankness. He does admit in his interview in June that he has temptations, but has done nothing wrong at this stage except meet Hetty rather too often and arouse her interest. The confession is abandoned because he is reluctant to admit that the mild flirtation could become serious.

Two months later matters are different, and Eliot condemns Arthur again. 'Our deeds determine us as much as we determine our deeds. . . . There is a terrible coercion in our deeds which may first turn the honest man into a deceiver, and then reconcile him to the change – that the second wrong represents itself to him in the guise of the only practicable right.'[15] Many a modern second marriage has been forced along these lines by older and wiser people than Arthur, who is very young and does feel uncomfortable during the short period when he is sleeping with Hetty. Not confessing the truth to Adam, though it led to terrible trouble, may have seemed at the time the best answer for all concerned. There is a fair amount of evidence to show that Eliot condemns Arthur not for sexual misbehaviour but for dishonesty to Mr Irwine, with whom he was economical with the truth; to Adam, whom he deceived; to Hetty, whom he never intended to marry; and to himself, whose better nature he ignores.

This broadening of Eliot's purpose to include an investigation of all morality and not merely sexual morality is of course helped by Eliot's Victorian reticence in dealing delicately with sexual matters. We can only guess at the outcome of the dance by Mr Poyser's ironic words that Hetty would remember the day when she was an old woman. The time and place of Hetty's seduction are only shown by Arthur's hurried mention at the dance of a meeting in the wood and by his furtive hiding of Hetty's handkerchief, a fairly innocent garment. Hetty's pregnancy is only announced by a reference to a great dread. This great dread comes on her 'some weeks', but not, we think, many weeks, after 2 November, and she is therefore guiltless of accepting Adam while knowing she is carrying another man's child. One could accuse her of thoughtlessness in not considering the possibility that she might be pregnant, and indeed since she must have conceived before 18 August she ought to have been worried by 2 November, although a combination of Victorian innocence and unhappiness over Arthur's desertion might be considered some sort of excuse. It is difficult to know how ignorant Victorian women were about menstruation because the subject was too delicate to mention. Modern teenagers are less delicate, but they tend only to be convinced they are pregnant after the second period is missed.

On discovering her pregnancy Hetty should have told Adam, but he was not an easy man to tell. It would also have been hard for Hetty, even if she had been so inclined, to seduce Adam into thinking that the child was his. Such a calculated response would in any case have been difficult in view of the time involved, especially as the birth of the child, premature but alive in late February, would indicate that it was conceived in early August. It is necessary if slightly awkward for the plot that the child should be born prematurely since otherwise Hetty could hardly travel uncomfortably around England without her condition being more obviously noticed. Nevertheless the premature birth does raise interesting possibilities.

The date of the conception of Hetty's baby, whose sex is never revealed, may seen as unimportant as the number of Lady Macbeth's children. George Eliot could have dated the initial seduction earlier, Adam's discovery of Arthur and Hetty later and the engagement of Adam and Hetty at a point where the child could have been passed off as Adam's. But she did not. Mr Irwine's look of relief when Adam tells him that somebody else is involved with Hetty makes it clear that he suspects Adam of making Hetty pregnant. This relief turns to redoubled pain when he learns that Arthur is the culprit. Some Victorian readers might have found it odd that Mr Irwine could have suspected the virtuous Adam, and most modern readers find it odd that he could have thought Hetty capable of infanticide on discovering that she was pregnant by her future husband. The Poysers are of course a proud family and in the circle of that family a premature pregnancy would have caused distress if not disgrace. Maggie Tulliver causes distress to her family, and she is not pregnant, nor likely to be.

It looks as if Eliot has carefully constructed the story of Hetty's seduction to rule out the possibility that she could have hoped to pass off one man's child as another's. This is one sin of which she is not guilty. Her affair with Arthur lasts less than three weeks; she is only seventeen, he, four years older, is more to blame than she is, and we do not feel disposed to condemn her very savagely either for becoming pregnant or for taking desperate measures when she is pregnant. Eliot seems more severe, but it is clear from her narrative that Hetty is not being castigated for her seduction but for the silliness and selfishness that leads up to this seduction. As is the case with Arthur Donnithorne, we hear a great deal of her feelings before she has actually fallen. Arthur's gifts lead her to fantasies about being married to him and becoming a grand lady. Her social snobbery is part of the general shallowness that leads Eliot to compare her to a rootless plant. Like Arthur she has the chance of confession in the chapter entitled 'The Two Bed Chambers', but Dinah's honest appeal is no more successful than Irwine's tactful reticence. Both Arthur and Hetty suffer because, being imprisoned in their own selfishness, they can find nobody with whom they can discuss their hopes and fears, not even each other.

All this goes to show that, whereas *Adam Bede* at first sight seems a classic tale of vengeance on a fallen woman, it eventually becomes clear that Eliot is attacking very much more than the sexual behaviour of two very young people. In *The Mill on the Floss* there is in fact no sexual misbehaviour, and yet Eliot is almost as severe to Maggie Tulliver, with whom she has much in common, as she is to Hetty Sorrel, whose brainless prettiness she plainly dislikes. There are a number of features in the novel which seem to correspond to incidents in Eliot's own upbringing at Griff House, and relations between Maggie Tulliver and Tom do seem fairly close to those between Eliot and her brother Isaac, whose disapproval of her liaison with Lewes lasted until the latter's death. Maggie is forgiven earlier. Her generous and romantic impulses lead her into difficulties, first with the gypsies and then with Philip Wakem. Although Wakem's father has illegitimate

children, Philip, being both crippled and pathetic, hardly represents much moral danger, whereas Stephen Guest is dashing and
conventionally handsome. Eliot is not particularly good at describing such men and Stephen like Ladislaw seems rather a
hollow character. But she is good at revealing the attraction Maggie
feels for Stephen; the fatal indecision she shows in rowing down
the river with him; her feelings of remorse at the damage she has
done; her refusal to add to this damage by doing what society
expects and marrying Stephen; and finally the bitter reproaches
she meets on her return.

Tom Tulliver's attitude is typical of Victorian masculine nar-
rowness. His earlier harshness to a similar mistake in Maggie's
childhood when she neglected to feed his rabbits should have
prepared us for his inability to distinguish the finer shades of
morality. Sexual morality is seen in black and white terms, and
Maggie's unmarried state is worse than death after she has compromised herself. The ending of the book renders this judgement
ironic as well as wrong, but does in some way redeem Tom as
well as Maggie. St Oggs would have tolerated Maggie 'if she had
returned Mrs Stephen Guest after a few months of well chosen
travel with a post-marital trousseau'. There might have been a
few misgivings, but 'public opinion which is always of the feminine gender would have eventually found the marriage wonderful and romantic, and condemned people who refused to visit the
happy pair'.[16] But without a wedding ring and a trousseau Maggie
is degraded and an outcast, a moral taint to the neighbourhood.
Dr Kenn, the widowed clergyman of the parish, sees that it is
difficult for Maggie to marry Stephen and difficult for them to
remain unmarried in the neighbourhood, but his efforts on
Maggie's behalf merely result in more tittle-tattle, to the effect that
in her shameless way she is now setting her cap at him. Stephen
Guest, who is more to blame than Maggie, gets off very lightly in
all this gossip.

Maggie's failings fade into insignificance when compared with
those of the society that condemns her. She is technically innocent, but feels herself guilty and tries to make amends for her
guilt. Eliot was technically guilty, but felt herself innocent and
devoted her life to writing novels showing the difficulty of making moral decisions and passing moral judgements. Her final
statements of this difficulty comes toward the close of *The Mill on
the Floss*.

The great problem of the shifting relation between passion and duty is clear to no man who is capable of apprehending it: the question, whether the moment has come in which a man has fallen below the possibility of a renunciation that will carry any efficacy, and must accept the sway of passion against which he had struggled as a trespass, is one for which we have no master-key that will fit all cases. The casuists have become a byword of reproach; but their perverted spirit of minute discrimination was the shadow of a truth to which eyes and hearts are too often fatally sealed – the truth that moral judgements must remain false and hollow, unless they are checked and enlightened by a perpetual reference to the special circumstances that mark the individual lot.

All people of broad, strong sense have an instinctive repugnance to the men of maxims; because such people early discern that the mysterious complexity of our life is not to be embraced by maxims, and that to lace ourselves up in formulas of that sort is to repress all the divine promptings and inspirations that spring from growing insight and sympathy. And the man of maxims is the popular representative of the minds that are guided in their moral judgement solely by general rules, thinking that these will lead them to justice by a ready-made patent method, without the trouble of exerting patience, discrimination, impartiality – without any care to assure themselves whether they have the insight that comes from a hardly-earned estimate of temptation, or from a life vivid and intense enough to have created a wide fellow-feeling with all that is human.[17]

The *Mill on the Floss* brought Eliot some notoriety, and, with her identity generally known, there was some criticism of the moral tone of the novel.[18] These two facts may be connected, but it would be unjust to say that criticism definitely induced caution in the next phase of Eliot's career as a writer, though this is possible. Certainly there is little specifically sexual in *Silas Marner*, where Godfrey Cass has made an imprudent marriage which he wishes to conceal in the same way as young men and women wish to conceal equally disreputable but more irregular sexual encounters. It is indeed hard to remember that Eppie is Godfrey's legitimate offspring; clearly he does not deserve her, and his efforts to win her away from Silas Marner at the end of the novel meet with well-merited failure. One could say that Godfrey's guilt and appropriate punishment are further illustrations of Eliot's contention that it is not the use or abuse of the marriage tie which is the decisive factor in passing moral judgements on sexual matters. Rather it is the way we behave, whether married or not. Godfrey is as rash and selfish as Arthur Donnithorne, as cruel and deceptive as Tito Melema, and is lucky to escape worse punishment than he receives when his guilty secret is exposed. The fact that this guilty secret is not seduction or bigamy, but a disreputable marriage, does not alter the pitiless judgement, although as always Eliot reserves some pity for Godfrey's predicament.

Silas Marner was published in 1861. It was later published in the Cabinet Edition of the Works of George Eliot with two shorter stories. Sex is hardly present in 'Brother Jacob', originally published in 1864, and strangely absent in 'The Lifted Veil', written in 1859, though the latter story hinges around the hero Latimer's marriage to the evil and sensual Bertha Grant, hailed somewhat improbably as the equivalent of Bertha Mason by feminist critics.[19] In *Romola*, as we have shown, there are no evil women, and Tito's wickedness in the sexual sphere is merely part of his pliable corruptibility. Romola's attraction to Tito is delicately handled. Our final vision of her helping to bring up the family of Tito and Tessa seems odd, although it is perhaps worth remembering the mutual devotion of Eliot and Lewes's sons.

Romola was the first of the four long novels which engaged Eliot in a great deal of historical research. Some contemporary critics bemoaned the absence of the pastoral realism which characterises the early novels, but few could doubt the novelist's moral seriousness; and with the writing of *Romola* Eliot began to be generally accepted in society. In *Felix Holt* she risked disapproval by a fairly frank discussion of the temptations facing Esther Lyon and Mrs Transome, although attention is diverted from them by the topical political issues and the complicated and improbable plot which ensures that Esther is heiress to the Transome estates. Esther is not the daughter of the saintly Rufus Lyon, whose chivalrous courtship of her mother is the object of some spiteful gossip, but is brought up by him. Somewhat surprisingly we find her reading Byron, dismissed angrily by the virtuous Felix Holt as a 'misanthropic debauchee' writing about 'the most paltry ever puppets that were pulled by the strings of lust and pride.'[20] In spite of his reputation for radicalism, of which Felix ought to have approved, and subversion which he would not have liked, Byron continued to be widely read during the nineteenth-century, being for instance recommended, with reservations, by Charlotte Brontë to Ellen Nussey.[21] But it is not really Byron that Eliot is condemning; it is the false romanticism which could easily have led Esther astray. Later we find her reading *René* on a Sunday, dismissed as mawkish trash by Felix, who sometimes sounds like a more savage version of the Eliot who wrote the article entitled 'Silly Novels by Silly Women Novelists'. The example of her adopted father and of Felix eventually prevail, making the Byronic heroes look tawdry and giving Esther a new sense of morality and reality, and in spite of strong erotic feelings, fairly frankly described, she is saved from the fate of marrying the attractive but egotistical Harold Transome by the discovery that his wife had been a slave from Smyrna. The connection with Byron is made clear.[22]

Less obvious are the connections between Mrs Transome and Esther. But the older woman, whose tragedy is the best part of the novel, has also had a defective education with too many French novelists including Chateaubriand, the author of *René* – and an interest in stories of illicit passion.[23] Indeed her education is worse because it is not deep or consistent. Mr Lyon sees that Esther is reading Byron; Mrs Transome picks out for her private reading the lighter parts of dangerous French authors. This education and a spoilt and selfish nature encourage Mrs Transome, married to a feeble and unattractive husband, to start an affair with the handsome and odious lawyer Matthew Jermyn. Passion and vanity start the affair; self-interest and a desire to preserve reputations prevent it from being openly acknowledged. But Harold is Mr Jermyn's son.

This revelation does not come until the end of the novel, although we have many pointed references to scandal and gossip in the past, Mr Jermyn's surprising hold over Mrs Transome and the absence of any resemblance between Harold and Mr Transome. There is even the frank statement that the Transomes sleep in different bedrooms. We also have Mrs Transome's guilt and fear, described on numerous occasions as dread, the same word used to describe Hetty Sorrel's realisation that she is pregnant. This link between Eliot's two major fallen women draws attention to the same mixture of compassion and ruthlessness with which both the younger and older sinner are treated. Mrs Transome may have been thoughtless and vain, but does she really deserve the long years of fear and the final relevation, made worse by the fact that Harold has quarrelled with Mr Jermyn? Eliot is insistent that we have to live with the consequences of our deeds, but Mrs Transome is doubly punished both by Jermyn and Harold, men who are 'selfish and cruel' and who care only for 'their own pleasure and their own pride'.[24] Pleasure and pride are what has destroyed Mrs Transome, but Esther abandons her inheritance and any idea of marrying Harold, and turns back to her father and Felix after an education in real life.

Education is also mentioned in *Middlemarch*, although not to such an extent. Dorothea has a narrow Puritan bookish upbringing and is shocked by the Classical statues and Renaissance paintings which her uncle has brought back from his travels. When she is married her uncle encourages her to read authors like Smollett: a little broad, but permissible in view of her married state. It is clear from these two references that Dorothea is sexually innocent before her marriage, and enters her marriage to Casaubon, which is probably not consummated, in ignorance, giving an added irony to Mr Brooke's second observation.

Rosamund Vincy has also had a limited education. 'At that time,' Eliot says 'young ladies in the country, even when educated at Mrs Lemon's, read little French literature later than Racine, and public prints had not cast their magnificent illuminations over the scandals of life.'[25] She therefore has to wait until after her marriage to make the discovery that women, even after marriage, might make conquests and enslave men. It may seem odd that too much French literature destroys Mrs Transome and too little destroys Rosamund Vincy, although Rosamund is more shallow and more vain. Technically she remains innocent, although she might not have done so if Ladislaw had not been in love with Dorothea. Morally of course she is almost as much the murderess of her husband as the actress Laure is.

The introduction of Laure as an episode in Lydgate's youth is presumably meant to serve as a warning which he does not take. There are spots of coarseness in his nature and his education in the indecent parts of the Classics is a sign that he is too much inclined to be governed by his sexual appetites, unlike Felix Holt who says improbably that he will quell them by a diet of vegetables, and unlike Dorothea who pays too little attention to sexual matters when considering Casaubon as a husband. In marrying Casaubon Dorothea displays her ignorance almost as a defect, but this innocence is necessary for an understanding of Ladislaw's courtship of Dorothea and her reception of it.

In *Middlemarch*, Eliot's longest and greatest novel, there are no real fallen women. The nearest we get to this dangerous subject is the presence of Joshua Rigg, the natural son of Peter Featherstone. The illegitimacy in *Middlemarch* is boldly stated, though clearly a disreputable fact. Rigg has an undistinguished frog-like face, but oddly is the vital agent in changing the destinies of all the main characters in the novel, apart from Dorothea and Casaubon, since he reveals Ladislaw's parentage and Bulstrode's villainy; robs Mary Garth and Fred Vincy of their inheritance but enables Fred to gain self-respect; while poor Lydgate nearly has his life ruined because he is implicated with Bulstrode in the death of Raffles, Rigg's stepfather. Curiously the only other reference to illegitimate sex is the apparently casual mention of idle gossip about the possibility that Lydgate owes his preferment to the fact that he is Bulstrode's natural son.[26] This gossip is clearly wide of the mark since Bulstrode's sexual morality is as unimpeachable as Lydgate's aristocratic birth, but it is of course ironic in view of the later connection between Lydgate and Bulstrode. A natural son is not to blame for his own birth any more than Lydgate is to blame for the death of Raffles, and yet Bulstrode is clearly guilty of something, as is dimly appreciated by the servants who look after Raffles and think of him as one of the unfortunate 'cousins' with whom rich folk are connected.[27]

It may be that Eliot, by drawing our attention in these two references to natural sons, wishes to point out the contrast between sexual morality seen in black and white terms and the much more subtle web of moral decisions which affect the main characters. Most of the troubles of Bulstrode, Lydgate and Fred Vincy are connected with money rather than love, although financial difficulties do lead to marital troubles. In the case of Dorothea the reverse is true. We hear a great deal about financial difficulties, something about matrimonial incompatibility and virtually nothing about sexual matters. How different *Middlemarch* is from modern life.

And yet not all that different. Eliot cannot describe impotence; and yet it is generally recognised that Casaubon is impotent.[28]

Images of sterility, useless keys and shallow rills carry the point subtly, perhaps too subtly for modern students accustomed to more blatant sexual honesty. Casaubon's disappointment before the marriage and Dorothea's bitter tears after it reinforce the point. A reference, albeit an obscure one, to disappointment about an heir would seem to indicate that Casaubon is sterile if not impotent. It is true that remarks by Sir James Chetham and Will Ladislaw about Casaubon as no better than a mummy and a white-blooded coxcomb could be put down to masculine jealousy. It is also true that alleged models for Casaubon like Mark Pattison and Dr Brabant would seem embarrassingly virile. On the other hand surprisingly little use has been made of Mrs Cadwaller's description of Casaubon as a 'great bladder for dried peas to rattle in' or the name of Casaubon's parish which is Lowick.[29]

Dorothea's second husband, Ladislaw, won little acclaim among contemporary critics, and modern critics have hardly been kinder. His marriage with Dorothea, disapproved of by the conventionally Victorian Sir James Chetham, has won equal disapproval from less conventional and less Victorian writers. Once we have understood Casaubon's impotence we can understand and approve of Dorothea's eagerness to marry Ladislaw, even though like a Jane Austen heroine she finds it difficult to show this eagerness, and it needs Rosamund Lydgate of all people to break down the barriers of reserve. Sir James Chetham disapproves of any second marriage and particularly that of Dorothea with a handsome foreign adventurer. In such a world it is difficult for Eliot to make a plea for the right of women to choose their own sexual destiny, but this plea, though obscurely phrased, is present in *Middlemarch* and is one of the achievements of the novel.

By the time she came to write *Daniel Deronda*, published in 1876, Eliot had painfully won her way to respectability as England's leading moral novelist. In her last novel, in spite of the long Jewish sections, there is a great deal of room for the discussion of women, fallen, virtuous, and betwixt and between. Lydia Glasher, the wife of an Irish officer, had misbehaved with young Henleigh Grandcourt ten years before the story opens. She bears him four children, but is compelled to live in the gloomy isolation of Gadsmere where there are no gentry in carriages to be met, and the curate's wife and the curate himself were either ignorant of anything to her disadvantage or ignored it. Grandcourt had toyed with the idea of marrying her even though she would not have been received in society. She is anxious for this in order to secure provision for her children, but Grandcourt is too lazy and selfish to make amends. He fights a duel with Colonel Glasher, in which neither party is hurt, and is at one stage willing to work for a divorce, to which the colonel objects. But when Lydia's husband dies Grandcourt's ardour has diminished, although he is unable to disentangle himself from the connection.

The arrival of Gwendolen Harleth changes matters. Inspired by her beauty and an untamed quality about her, Grandcourt decides to marry her. His confidant Lush tells Lydia, who meets Gwendolen at the Whispering Stones. Her revelations drive Gwendolen away to the continent where we have met her, spoilt and discontented, at the opening of the novel. It is difficult to know whether Gwendolen would have accepted Grandcourt's proposals if it had not been for Lydia; certainly she is attracted by his insolent languor. When her family loses her fortune she has an added motive for marriage, which her mother and uncle clearly desire; but she does have scruples about Lydia. She stills these scruples, but a terrible letter from Lydia on the night of her wedding returns to haunt her.

The marriage is an unhappy one. Grandcourt's egotism and hollowness are soon revealed. He treats his wife with superficial politeness, but at all times wishes to assert his mastery over her. Her friendship with Deronda is the object of some coarse innuendo. This friendship is in fact innocent, although after Grandcourt's death it is clear that she is in love with him. Unfortunately Deronda is in love with Mirah, the Jewish singer whom he has rescued from suicide. Mirah's youth on the stage has been an unhappy one, and her father exposed her to all kinds of moral danger. When Deronda rescues her he is worried by the thought of possible scandal and has to house her with the Meyricks. Grandcourt assumes that Mirah is Deronda's mistress with the contemptuous words, 'men can see what is his relation to her'.[30] He is equally contemptuous and wrong about the relationship between Daniel and his wife.

Of the three main female characters clearly the most interesting is Gwendolen. Lydia's role as a fallen woman and as a single parent is treated without condemnation, but without much sympathy. Her bitterness is understandable but also inexcusable. She ruins any chance Gwendolen could have had of happiness with Grandcourt. It might be argued that such happiness would have been impossible as Grandcourt has a withered heart. But Gwendolen herself is shallow and selfish, and one must remember the strong element of sexual attraction that Grandcourt has. His continual cigar smoking might be seized upon as a phallic symbol, but the passage describing Gwendolen's feelings as she drives towards Ryelands on her wedding night is surely more significant.

> Gwendolen had been at her liveliest during the journey, chatting incessantly, ignoring any change in their mutual position since yesterday; and Grandcourt had been rather ecstatically quiescent, while she turned his gentle seizure of her hand into a grasp of his hands by both of hers, with an increased vivacity as of a kitten that will not sit quiet to be petted. She was really becoming somewhat febrile in her excitement; and now in this drive through the park her usual susceptibility to changes of light and scenery helped to make her heart palpitate newly. Was it at the novelty simply, or the almost incredible fulfilment about to be given to her girlish dreams of being somebody – walking through her own furlongs of corridors and under her own ceilings of an out-of-sight loftiness, where her own painted Spring was shedding painted flowers, and her own foreshortened Zephyrs were blowing their trumpets over her; while her own servants, lackeys in clothing but men in bulk and shape, were as nought in her presence, and revered the propriety of her insolence to them: – being in short the heroine of an admired play without the pains of art? Was it alone the closeness of this fulfilment which made her heart flutter? Or was it some dim forecast, the insistent penetration of suppressed experience, mixing the expectation of a triumph with the dread of a crisis? Hers was one of the natures in which exultation inevitably carries an infusion of dread ready to curdle and declare itself.[31]

A Victorian virgin on her wedding night might be thinking of penetration and the foreshortened trumpets of angels as vague symbols of the sexual act, dimly imagined with works of art as the only guide. Some Victorian virgins lay back and thought of England, gazing up at the ceiling which may well have been suitably embellished with angels. Was Gwendolen in either or both of these categories? One would have thought so, were it not for the intrusion of the sinister word 'dread'. This is a word which we have seen previously attached to Hetty Sorrel's fears for the future in her pregnancy and Mrs Transome's fears of the exposure of her past. In both cases dread involves sexual guilt. How is the word applicable to the newly-wed Gwendolen Grandcourt?

One can imagine that Gwendolen was a girl with a past who perhaps feared an exposure as a non-virgin on her wedding night. Her cousin Rex is shown to be a sexual failure through his incompetence as a horse-rider, so different from the skill of Grandcourt, and this preference for sexually mature men might suggest premature sexual knowledge on Gwendolen's part. Again Gwendolen's first appearance in the novel is at the gaming tables, and this role with Becky Sharp as an example hardly suggests virginal innocence. The novel would gain an added bite if we were meant to be contrasting the supposedly virginal and aristocratic Gwendolen with the allegedly promiscuous and proletarian Mirah, only to discover the roles were reversed. Even if not technically a fallen woman Gwendolen seems dangerously fast, and in drawing her portrait Eliot may be giving her views on the contemporary debate about the 'girl of the period'.[32]

But it is very hard to be definite about Gwendolen's loss of innocence – even harder, in the absence of evidence, than to discover the truth about Eliot's relationship with Chapman. The way that Gwendolen's dread is brought home to her is through the discovery of Lydia Glasher's letter which accompanies the diamonds. This letter makes it clear that Gwendolen, even if she were sexually innocent, is morally guilty in stealing Grandcourt from one who is his wife in all but name. This episode does have autobiographical reverberations. Eliot was accused of stealing Lewes from his wife. Almost certainly this is false. Some think she was a source of discord in the relationship between Chapman and his wife and his mistress. Almost certainly this is true. In her life Eliot offended through sexual behaviour that appeared to flout moral conventions. In her works she showed that moral conduct does not depend upon sexual conventions, and Gwendolen joins an impressive list of sinners, male and female, whose misbehaviour is unconnected to their marital misdemeanours.[33]

Victorian convention made it impossible to describe sexual

activity in detail. We do not know for certain whether Maggie Tulliver or George Eliot was guilty of more than foolishness; how far Casaubon was guilty in not recognising his impotence, or Lydgate his sexuality; whether Hetty Sorrel was more guilty in murdering her newborn child, or Rosamund Vincy in causing the death of her unborn child; just how far Mrs Transome had some excuse for her dread or Gwendolen cause for hers. But all of them are in some sense sinners just as Tito Melema is a sinner, even though in his case his sin in going through a form of marriage with Tessa whom he makes very happy is so much less severe than marrying Romola of whom he is totally unworthy.

Gwendolen is punished less severely than Tito for her misbehaviour, but is still punished. Sexual attraction without spiritual affinity is no recipe for a successful marriage. Deronda and Mirah do have spiritual affinity, as Deronda's painfully established Jewish origins make clear. So too are Miss Arrowpoint and Herr Klesmer united by a common love of music, although the marriage between them is condemned as a *mésalliance*. It is also said that he married her for her money, as Grandcourt might have been tempted to do, although Miss Arrowpoint is not favoured with beauty. We do not hear enough about this marriage, which is eventually accepted by the society that sees nothing wrong in the marriage of Gwendolen and Grandcourt in spite of the ugly gossip about his past. Gwendolen's uncle, one of Eliot's best if unkindest portraits of the worldly clergyman, chooses to ignore gossip about the almost certain baronet, the probable peer. Mr Gascoigne comforts himself with the thought that, 'if Grandcourt had really made any deeper or more unfortunate experiments in folly than were common in young men of high prospects, he was of an age to have finished them'.[34] When Grandcourt dies, Mr Gascoigne is indignant that Lydia Glasher rather than Gwendolen should be made heir to the bulk of his fortune; he ignores his previous knowledge of Grandcourt's dissipations which he had hoped 'would be swept into private rubbish heaps, and never present itself as an array of live caterpillars, disastrous to the green meat of respectable people'. This remarkable image is not very kind to respectable people. Nor is Mr Gascoigne's second observation: 'The effect is painful in more ways than one. Female morality is likely to suffer from this marked advantage being given to illegitimate offspring'.[35]

Such an observation is tactless, being addressed to Sir Hugo Mallinger, popularly if wrongly thought of as the natural father of Deronda. Sir Hugo in his comfortable way is less angry with Grandcourt for making Lydia Glasher's son his heir than is Mr Gascoigne. He is a man of generous spirit, part of his generosity consisting in allowing everyone to think that Deronda is his son. Such generosity does not cost him dear, and one could hardly have a better illustration of the way in which Victorian society adopted double standards. George Eliot had first-hand knowledge of this double standard and she disapproved of it. Her novels are full of male sexual sinners who are punished for their sin. Grandcourt is the last in a long line of self-indulgent men whose misdeeds find them out in unexpected ways. It is true that Hetty Sorrel and Maggie Tulliver, Mrs Transome and Gwendolen Harleth also meet terrible unhappiness which in their different ways they deserve, but it should be clear that it is not sexual immorality for which they are punished. Indeed Maggie Tulliver and Gwendolen probably do not commit any form of sexual immorality any more than do Dorothea or Rosamund, both of whom suffer for marrying for the wrong reasons.

Eliot was a keen student of Dante.[36] In both the *Inferno* and the *Purgatorio* lust is the least serious of the seven deadly sins, though Francesca's attractiveness in the fifth canto is the symbol of the insidious nature of all temptation, of which sexual temptation is only a part. In the *Inferno* the fruits of sin are punished, while in the *Purgatorio* the roots of sin are purged, and Eliot is really more interested in corrupt states of mind than in corrupt acts. It is one of the features of Eliot's moral teaching that sexual morality is always subordinate to all morality. It is a bad feature of many of her Victorian contemporaries and modern successors that sexual morality is regarded as the most important part of morality and that sexual acts are seen as more interesting than the frame of mind from which these acts emerge.

5
Thackeray

As a man and as a male author Thackeray faced different problems from those faced by Eliot, Brontë and Austen. We have shown how the standards of sexual behaviour expected of women during the nineteenth-century differed from those expected of men. Henry Crawford can sin and get away with it, Mr Rochester can have a string of mistresses, attempt bigamy and still be forgiven. In contrast, Maria Rushworth after an unfortunate marriage pays a horrible price for her attempt to escape from this marriage, although not as horrible as that paid by Hetty Sorrel in her attempt to make a fortunate marriage. Eyebrows are raised at the conduct of Maggie Tulliver and even of Jane Eyre, although they are guilty of nothing more than indiscretion. Brontë and Eliot were reluctant to admit their female identity as authors. Men could visit the Lewes ménage, but women could not. Men could and did profit from the infamous double standard, not suffering the risk or the disgrace of pregnancy and thus being less likely to suffer the shame or the scandal of sexual exposure. Male authors are perhaps less inclined than female to challenge the standard, although they had less to lose if they made such a challenge.

Dickens is said by Emerson to have declared that he would not expect his son to be chaste.[1] This remark may not be wholly serious, but we would not expect anyone to make such a joke about his daughters. Thackeray had two daughters, and it was perhaps anxiety for their reputation that kept him from being too sexually outspoken. They repaid him in turn by trying to keep his reputation unspoiled. Unlike other authors in this study, Thackeray's descendants became part of the literary establishment and were able to exercise a powerful control over this reputation.[2] Thus a biography of Thackeray, expressly forbidden by the author himself, becomes both harder and easier to write. We can contrast the fate of Austen, Eliot, Brontë, Dickens and Hardy, all of them subjects of official biographies or memoirs, written shortly after the author's death, or in Hardy's case, shortly before it, and all subject to more candid and less adulatory scrutiny thereafter.

With Thackeray for life and for letters we are dependent on the admirable Ray who somehow has to combine the roles of, and sometimes inevitably falls between the stools of, the nineteenth-century hagiographer and the twentieth-century literary detective.[3] This is particularly relevant in sexual matters. Writing before the sexual revolution of the 1960s and heavily dependent on Anne Thackeray and her family for source material Ray is understandably reticent about Thackeray's amours. A new, more candid biography is badly needed: it is sometimes difficult to know whether the lack of such a biography is caused by, or is the cause of, a recent fading in enthusiasm for Thackeray's novels.

Ray is however perfectly adequate in showing up Thackeray's ambivalence. He made strangled protests against Mrs Grundy, but himself exercised stringent censorship as editor of the *Cornhill*.[4] He repeatedly refers with disapproval to coarse masculine banter as likely to offend ladies, although he himself indulged in this kind of boring jovial clubman's talk, albeit of the relatively innocent banality of "tis true 'tis titty, 'tis titty 'tis true'.[5] He himself was aware that Victorian standards of propriety were not immutable; in *Vanity Fair* Miss Crawley has to moderate the racy language of her youth, and the novels about the eighteenth-century are full of references to the loose conversation of both men and women.

Thackeray's father had like many Anglo-Indians of the period a half-caste mistress and an illegitimate family, and there is something vaguely disreputable about the life of his maternal grandmother. However, the influence of a mother as strongly virtuous as Mrs Pendennis is likely to have outweighed these factors, as Thackeray's father died when he was very young and he knew Mrs Becher when she was fairly old.[6] This does not mean that Thackeray was as virtuous as Pendennis. Thackeray tells us as much.[7] Like Pendennis, Thackeray attended Charterhouse and Cambridge, and as a young man was not unduly troubled by financial considerations. Or by moral considerations. Neither educational establishment was famous in the early nineteenth-century for stern sexual morality, although later reformers like Dr Arnold made public schools and universities less deplorable. Thackeray's portraits of Charterhouse and Cambridge became increasingly blurred by sentimental nostalgia, although in the early *A Shabby Genteel Story* he is fairly savage about what passed for a gentleman's education.[8] He himself left Charterhouse two years before Arnold became headmaster of Rugby, and had left Cambridge seven years before Queen Victoria began her long reign, during which the two universities were gradually reformed.

We know about Thackeray's youthful indiscretions.[9] The collapse of his family's finances in 1833 may have curbed his appetites. In 1836 he married Isabella Shawe who fell insane in 1840 shortly after the birth of their third child. Valiantly, in spite of financial difficulties and the hostility of his mother-in-law, Thackeray struggled with this problem, which eventually became insoluble. Like Mr Rochester and G. H. Lewes he was tied to a wife whom he could not divorce. Unlike other authors in this study he was denied any outlet for sexual passions in which he had already indulged. More honest than most Victorians he complained about the absence of this outlet, writing surprisingly to his mother on the subject. The desperately platonic affair with Mrs Brookfield is well recorded by Ray. It was at its height between 1847 and 1851, but casts a shadow over all the novels. Avuncular friendships with people like Sally Baxter whom he met in America could have been some small compensation. His two daughters and his mother may have helped to keep him outwardly respectable. A stricture of the urethra, probably the result of some venereal disease consequent upon the indiscretions of youth, should have acted as an ugly reminder against sexual licence. Jokes about visits to the incontinent, like Dickens's visits to the Continent with Wilkie Collins probably involved more wishful thinking than actual sinning.[10]

Thackeray wrote a great deal. In spite of his comparatively short life his poverty as a young man and his position as a public figure in middle age led to constant demands upon his pen. His correspondence like that of Jane Austen has fallen victim to family censorship. His early writings for periodicals are full of originality and wit, and in disregarding these we are ignoring the recent interest in these shorter works as part of Thackeray's progress as a writer toward the peak of *Vanity Fair* before an abrupt descent to the dreary plains of the other major novels.[11] Oddly the early Thackeray works like *The Book of Snobs* and *The Yellowplush Papers*, though extremely instructive on many aspects of Victorian society and rightly praised for their brilliant touches of colour, do not have a great deal to say about sexual matters. Nor can they be said to display Regency licentiousness as opposed to Victorian decorum. It could of course be argued that harping on sex in a short story was more likely to be offensive than a mention of sex in a long novel.[12]

It is true that *Catherine* (1839–40) is by mid-Victorian standards deplorably slack in not condemning more openly the immorality of the heroine, although the account of her death, censored in almost any modern edition, makes the conventional fate of the erring Victorian ladies almost palatable. *Barry Lyndon* (1844) describes the story of a male sinner, largely based upon an actual character in the eighteenth-century, to which Thackeray twice returned as a possible outlet for describing sexual activity more freely. And yet Barry Lyndon, though a rogue, is not nearly as wicked in sexual matters as Mr Rochester: indeed he is more sinned against than sinning, and most of the sexual sin in *Barry Lyndon* occurs in the digression, again based on a true story, entitled 'The Tragical History of the Princess of X', in which Thackeray with typical ambivalence combined sympathy with the sinner and condemnation of the sin.[13]

There is some indication of changing Victorian standards in Thackeray's other early attempt at a novel, *A Shabby Genteel Story* (1840). He was fond of the story and eventually returned to it in *Philip* twenty years later. In both narratives an important issue is the fact that Dr Firmin, alias George Brandon, is involved in an irregular union with Caroline Gann or The Little Sister, as she is known in *Philip*. The latter coy title is an indication of an increasing sympathy with this particular fallen woman, marked by an increasing reluctance to spell out the exact details of her fallen state, although great emphasis is placed in the latter novel on a marriage ceremony, conducted with some degree of legality by the disreputable Reverend Hunt. The bogus wedding was a stock device of Victorian writers to enable their heroines to have the cake of rectitude and eat the fruit of sin. Hardy resorted to it in the magazine version of *Tess of the d'Urbervilles*. In *A Shabby Genteel Story* Thackeray makes no bones about Brandon's wickedness, but seems to regard it as perfectly natural that young men should set out to 'ruin' young women of Caroline's class. He is prepared to do the same to her sisters. The subject is declared to be a delicate one, but is not handled particularly delicately. At one stage it is clear that Brandon makes improper advances before any marriage to Caroline. These she indignantly rejects. Brandon condemns her for her prudery. The marriage which is no marriage ends the story. It is fairly brave of Thackeray to mention the mock marriage, accepted by Caroline, after the rejected improper advances.

In *Philip* there seems some doubt as to whether the marriage is legal, but Caroline for the sake of Philip is unwilling to make any claims, since to do so would render him illegitimate. Dr Firmin's villainy is more than once mentioned in terms of exaggerated disapproval, but we almost feel that he has been punished sufficiently, and rather strangely his ruin is due, not to the exposure of his relationship with Caroline, or even to the blackmail of Hunt, but to financial speculation. Thackeray's last completed novel, by all accounts a feeble affair, has little to say on sexual matters. Philip's adolescence, unlike that of Pendennis or Harry Warrington or most young men in Thackeray's novels, does not seem to involve any sexual escapades or any vice beyond cigar smoking. It is hinted that he is a desperate fellow and no doubt some critics could turn the cigars into phallic symbols, but it looks as if by the end of his life Thackeray has finally succumbed to Mrs Grundy. Opportunities to explore sexual sin could have been seized at the end of *A Shabby Genteel Story*; most of them are missed in *Philip*.

In studying Thackeray's six full-length novels we find more than one reference to Mrs Grundy who in fact dates to the end of the eighteenth-century, a time when young men could be described as behaving as young men did behave. The famous comment in the preface to *Pendennis* that, 'since the author of "Tom Jones" was buried no writer of fiction has been permitted to depict to his utmost power a MAN',[14] expressed Thackeray's dissatisfaction with the restraints of the nineteenth-century. Some critics attacked him for overstepping the mark, others for steering too close to it. Modern writers are more likely to accuse Thackeray of cowardice and dishonesty, as he is reluctant to tell us exactly what happened, and we are left to explore his far from subtle innuendoes, like 'boys will be boys', a phrase used to explore Philip's cigar smoking and the more deplorable vices of his predecessors.

In depicting women Thackeray seems even more crude. There

are virtuous angels, like Mrs Pendennis and the cloying Laura who returns like Mrs Grundy to haunt the reader in the later novels with her pharisaical comments on her erring fellow females. Then there are the wicked women of whom Becky Sharp is clearly the first and the best. Since their wickedness cannot be exactly described, and since the major heroes cannot be painted as men, wicked women tend to become minor characters. Thus in the short and feeble novel *Lovel the Widower* Elizabeth Prior has the makings of a Becky Sharp in that she rises from humble if not disreputable beginnings to marry her master, but she retains her virtue in the process, and the spice of wickedness had to be provided in small doses in the shape of her companion, Miss Mantonville, whose fall from a rainbow in the theatre is not her only lapse. The governess, as has been shown, was regarded as particularly dangerous in Victorian times. Sadly Thackeray himself suffered from scurrilous gossip through *Jane Eyre* being tactlessly dedicated to him. He needed governesses to educate his girls, had to make sure they were painfully plain, and is reported to have taken refuge against the rumours by declaring that he had six children by Currer Bell and slew them all with his own hand.[15]

This anecdote, if true, shows that Thackeray cannot be dismissed as a typical Victorian prude. In standard Victorian novels like *East Lynne* the fallen woman is clearly guilty of sexual immorality, and with varying degrees of condescending broadmindedness the author pities but never pardons her fall. Thackeray is more subtle. We do not know for certain if Becky Sharp is guilty, of what she is guilty, and how far Thackeray disapproves of her guilt. Examination of Thackeray's manuscripts increases the uncertainty about both male and female guilt.[16] Male sinners can get away with sexual misdemeanours in their youth; George Osborne and Rawdon Crawley both make several conquests, Mr Osborne leering hideously over George's exploits with what he calls the pink bonnets and uttering the standard sexist excuse that boys will be boys. George Osborne makes an assignation with Becky Sharp when both parties are married to someone else, and this is clearly wicked, although George's death at Waterloo prevents the matter from going any further. How far did matters go with Lord Steyne, or how far would they have gone if Rawdon Crawley had not been released from gaol?

'Was she guilty or not? She said not: but who could tell what was truth which came from those lips: or if that corrupt heart was in this case pure?'[17] The servants' hall, Rawdon Crawley and Lady Jane Crawley unite in finding against Becky. Mr Wenham says to Rawdon that he and Mrs Wenham were invited to dinner on the fatal night, but Wenham is an unreliable source, later responsible for spreading calumny against Mrs Crawley in the years of her decline. Lady Jane may be moved by jealousy, since her husband is not altogether unmoved by Becky's charms, or she may be spurred on by Becky's neglect of her son, but in general Lady Jane is an attractive if insipid character, a great improvement on Laura Pendennis, though less interesting than Amelia who is foolishly on Becky's side, while the virtuous Dobbin is against her. Rawdon refuses to forgive his wife, and the episode of the thousand pound note which she keeps makes it hard for him to be forgiving, although this note at any rate raises the possibility that Becky is technically guiltless of adultery, but guilty of a treacherous mercenary flirtation. Thackeray was wise enough to see that there are forms of sexual sin outside the sexual act, and clearly we are on Rawdon's side in disliking these.[18]

After the collapse of the marriage we enter upon a period of Becky's life which, as Thackeray says, 'he must pass over with that lightness and delicacy which the world demands – the moral world, that has, perhaps, no particular objection to vice, but an insuperable repugnance to hearing vice called by its proper name'.[19] There are later rather obvious sexual references to the siren's hideous tail, although it is still not exactly clear what form of immorality Becky produced in this disreputable period. We hear of gambling, not paying bills, the brandy bottle and the rouge pot, disapproval from the strait–laced and acquaintance with disreputable male characters of the likes of Major Loder and Captain Rook, but only the latter would seem to indicate the likelihood of sexual indiscretion, and even this is not certain. A descent into semi-prostitution seems unlikely as Rawdon gives Becky a respectable allowance, and she tries to maintain respectability, but seems very poor. Major Dobbin is extremely shocked when Becky moves in with Amelia, and this would seem to hint at some moral taint. The idea that sexual immorality was somehow infectious seems a strange one, but we shall find it again in the conduct of Laura Pendennis.

On the other hand it is in connection with Dobbin and Amelia that Becky shows surprising generosity when she reveals that George had offered to elope with her before Waterloo. It is odd that she should have preserved his note through so many vicissitudes of fortune, and in fact the note is not necessary as Amelia has already sent for Dobbin who has realised she is not worthy of him. Thus Becky's action seems principally to show her in a good light, and we end reading *Vanity Fair* as we began, by questioning Thackeray's attitude to fallen women, just as Amelia, praised for her piety and devotion to her first husband and son, is shown to have a selfish and stupid shallowness about her that makes us question the virtuous wife.

Pendennis and *Henry Esmond* were written during and just after the long drawn out Brookfield affair, in which Thackeray behaved with a Dobbin like rectitude, although he probably wished he was George Osborne, while Mrs Brookfield found herself in the position of Amelia probably without any strong inclination to play the part of Becky Sharp. Cross currents from this affair swirl across both later novels. Both heroes are painfully virtuous, although exposed to numerous temptations. Pendennis falls in love with Miss Costigan, Blanche Amory and Fanny Bolton before Laura finally claims him. His affair with Fanny causes deep, indeed fatal, pain to Helen Pendennis and the virtuous Laura, but it is in fiction entirely innocent, although in real life, as Thackeray clearly, if cynically, saw it would probably not have been. Laura and Helen are unduly censorious, especially as in her youth Pendennis's mother had been involved in an even more innocent love affair with Laura's father. It is difficult to disentangle Thackeray's hostility to their pharisaical attitude from his praise of their virtue. Miss Costigan and Fanny remain chaste almost by accident and are rewarded with suitable spouses in the shape of an elderly aristocrat and virile young surgeon, neither of course quite as suitable as the virile and gentlemanly Pendennis. Blanche is flirtatious and ends her life in the novel more dubiously as a Parisian literary lady, whose husband fights duels. As a predecessor to Beatrix she is probably the most interesting heroine in *Pendennis* and in spite of her dubious ancestry it is difficult to see why both Pendennis and Foker spurn her.

With Pendennis unable to behave like Tom Jones it is only minor male characters who are able to indulge in sexual misbehaviour. Sir Francis Clavering marries for money, but has establishments in St Johns Wood which he can ill afford. Foker pursues actresses, whom he can afford, rather more successfully than he pursues Blanche Amory. Thackeray is very indulgent to this young man, heir to a vast fortune, destined to marry an aristocratic cousin, one of nature's boys who will be boys. More interestingly we have the case of stunning Warrington, a good brain and a good oar, a good friend and a good man, who is able to attract even the coldly chaste Laura, but is unable to marry her as he is unfortunately married, like Mr Rochester, to a woman inferior to himself in class, intelligence and honour. She seems a sad warning to men that it is not always better to marry than burn, and the fate of Warrington acts as a kind of counterblast to the accusations of Helen Pendennis to the effect that the affair with Fanny nearly involved a sin and a crime. Pendennis does not actually commit this crime, but we are left asking the question whether it is more sinful for young men to sow their wild oats with the likes of Fanny, or marry unwisely and live unhappily ever after. The question is raised early on when the virtuous but worldly Dr Portman comes to remonstrate with Pendennis about his affair with Miss Fotheringay. He is appalled to learn that Pendennis contemplates marrying the girl, cynically assuming the affair had no honourable conclusion. Pendennis indignantly rejects the worthy clergyman's insinuation that marriage is an impossibility – 'What else, Dr Portman . . . do you imagine would be my desire?'[20] Dr Portman is knocked down by this sudden assault, and indeed the party of virtue finds it difficult to think of any counter-attack when offered the choice of a dishonourable marriage and a disreputable affair. It is the even more worldly Major Pendennis who disentangles his nephew from the Costigans; he would of course have been more tolerant of any liaison with Fanny Bolton.

It might be argued that heroes should neither wish to marry girls of low origin nor indulge in extra-marital liaisons with them; and in Henry Esmond Thackeray produces such a hero, stately, virtuous and honourable just like Sir Charles Grandison, to whom he is compared. Henry is the fruit of what appears to be an illicit union between Thomas, third Viscount Castlewood, and a humble Flemish lady, and his bastardy is mentioned frankly at the opening of a novel which is not conspicuous for sexual frankness. It later of course turns out that Henry is not illegitimate after all, Thomas and Gertrude having been secretly married before his birth, but after his conception, and this enables our hero to show conspicuous nobility in not claiming a title which is really his. The title had passed to Francis, fourth Viscount Castlewood, who is no model of marital fidelity, deserting his admirable wife for other ladies whose status is not exactly made clear, one of them being described as a Princess of Drury Lane. Francis is killed in a duel by the wicked Lord Mohun who has made advances to Lady Castlewood, which in a curious way do not dishonour her, and the title passes to young Frank Castlewood, a charming scapegrace who is entrapped into marriage by a Catholic lady on the continent. Thackeray does not make much of this mismatch, but in Frank's comically misspelt confession of his marriage there is confusion as well as misspelling. Castlewood says he had married Clothilda of Wertheim because he was anxious to sow his 'wild otes'.[21] One usually assumes that sowing wild oats involves indulgence in youthful indiscretions, frequently sexual, before settling down in a respectable fashion. Castlewood seems to wish to combine both processes. Perhaps this confused combination is a sly reference to Dr Portman's dilemma in *Pendennis*.

Henry Esmond sows no wild oats. His early innocent flirtation with the blacksmith's daughter is very mild, although it has important consequences as Henry and Lady Castlewood catch smallpox, and her beauty is marred. Her anger with Henry is understandable although on a second reading of the book when we realise that Lady Castlewood has been in love with Henry all the time we see jealousy in her outburst. Lady Castlewood's love for someone who is so much younger than herself is handled with delicacy, although it did meet with hostile criticism. Mature women do have sexual feelings, even though many young people like Hamlet think there is something rather shameful about giving way to these feelings. Lady Castlewood does not acknowledge that her love for Henry is sexual, although her excessive indignation at moments of crisis does betray the nature of her affection. For much of the novel she is of course married, and even when she is widowed she is handicapped by the fact that Henry seems much more likely to marry her daughter Beatrix. Most readers of the novel are surprised by its conclusion, and there are awkward questions about Lady Castlewood's age. Her daughter is twenty-six in 1712, and Lady Castlewood does not marry Henry until after 1714. The birth of her second daughter seems surprising.[22]

Thackeray had of course to work with historical dates like 1688 and 1714 for the framework of his story, and it is unfortunate that poor Lady Castlewood has to remain nubile and attractive during this lengthy period. It might have been easier to make Beatrix a little younger, although to have done so would have meant sacrificing the portrait of the breaker of hearts, engaged more than once but never satisfied. It is clearly Henry that she really loves, and she admits he touched her heart a little, but he is too melancholy for her and not grand enough. Lord Hamilton, though elderly, is certainly grand, but he dies in a duel with Lord Mohun. Beatrix's next escapade is with James Stuart, the Old Pretender. His intentions are not honourable, but Henry and Castlewood arrive in the nick of time to prevent him from dishonouring Beatrix, although in the process any chances of James succeeding to the throne are lost, and all Henry's gallantry is wasted on two lost causes. Beatrix pursues the Pretender to Paris before returning to England as the wife of a bishop, and, it is hinted, the mistress of George II.[23]

These revelations about Beatrix's future career are not found in the main narrative, but in Rachel Warrington's preface. Thackeray was not slow to observe that women are less likely than men to be charitable to fallen women, and Henry Esmond and Thackeray both treat Beatrix with a fair amount of sympathy, although, as is the case with Ethel Newcome later, she has to combine the roles of heartless jade and wicked flirt with her real personality of a woman of spirit trapped in the toils of Vanity Fair. Beatrix is more heartless and more flirtatious than Ethel, but would seem technically to preserve her virtue in the main body of the novel. This may be difficult for modern readers to swallow and would have been improbable in the eighteenth-century, but nineteenth-century convention demanded that Beatrix's wickedness should take place off-stage, as it were, after the main narrative of *Henry Esmond* and before the story of *The Virginians* begins.

By the time he came to write *The Newcomes* Thackeray knew the Brookfield affair was over, and during the composition of this novel, prolonged over two years and interrupted by bouts of ill health and foreign travel, he frequently expressed feelings of resigned despair and showed signs of premature age in his early forties. The character of Colonel Newcome, seen as a grizzled warrior at the beginning of the novel and a venerable old man at the time of his pathetic death when Thackeray finishes his story, would seem to reflect the author's own mood, since Thomas Newcome had both been forced to give up someone he loved and made an unsatisfactory marriage, although unlike that of his creator his marriage had followed rather than preceded his unlucky love affair.

We hear very little of Mrs Newcome, clearly an unsatisfactory character, whom Newcome marries out of quixotic chivalry and incompetence. After her early death Thackeray's hero seems to lead a life of chaste innocence, symbolised by his little iron bedstead and the way he rebukes Captain Costigan for his ribald songs in the opening chapter. This virginal prudery, though it made Newcome a favourite with Victorian readers and routed those who had condemned the author of *Vanity Fair* for his worldly cynicism, does seem a little at variance with Thackeray's own wish for frankness and equally frank acceptance of masculine incontinence. Indeed it seems odd that Colonel Newcome should deplore Tom Jones in view of his old-fashioned regard for eighteenth-century literature.[24] In his life he models himself on Sir Charles Grandison, but his prudery would seem to match that of Mrs Grundy.

Mrs Grundy is mentioned as the enemy of Ethel Newcome, whose flirtatious conduct is seen in some quarters as deplorable. Ethel, like many a Victorian heroine, is not allowed to be as spirited as her author would like her to be. She is unwilling to marry her cousin, Lord Kew; conducts herself outrageously at Baden, although it is hard to know what her bad behaviour involves; first throws herself at the Marquess of Farintosh, then rejects him; distresses the good Colonel by her apparently mercenary conduct and then redeems herself by her devotion and selflessness at the end of the novel. Teasingly, Thackeray does not allow us to know for certain whether she finally marries Clive Newcome, with whom she has always been in love, as he has with her. This love match had not been allowed to happen because of the wicked world which buys and sells brides as it buys and sells pictures. In trying to stand up to this wickedness, which she mocks by appearing with a sold sign taken from a picture pinned to her dress, Ethel is admirable, and Thomas Newcome's strictures on her seem unjustified. The Victorians admired Ethel, and Thackeray's daughter claimed that the popularity of this Christian name was due as much to Ethel Newcome as to another pillar of Victorian rectitude, Ethel Norman in Charlotte M. Yonge's *The Daisy Chain*, also published in 1856.[25]

Ethel refuses to allow herself to be bought and sold by anyone, not even by her uncle, who in order to win her for his son tries to accrue vast wealth. He eventually settles for second best with the insipid Rosey Mackenzie whom we first meet almost as a child, while her mother, the terrible scourge of Colonel Newcome's old age, appears as an alarming seductress. Like his father, Clive Newcome enters into an unsatisfactory marriage after an initial love affair which is prevented by interference from the family.

Lady Kew is the main obstacle to Clive and Ethel Newcome. Unlike Alethea Newcome, who nips Colonel Newcome's romance in the bud, she is not a pious but a worldly woman, being sister to the Marquess of Steyne and disapproving of her virtuous psalm-singing daughter-in-law, the mother of Lord Kew, who is intended for Ethel. Lord Kew is rather an attractive character in whose fate and faults Thackeray seems interested until he is wounded in a duel, repents of his sins and disappears from the story after marrying, presumably for love, not money, Lady Henrietta Pulleyn, the second daughter of Lord Dorking, whose first daughter Lady Clara disastrously is made to chase money rather than love. Lord Kew had become entangled with Madame d'Ivry at Baden and, we gather, had sinned elsewhere. His sins are condoned by Thackeray: 'It was not a worse life than that of a thousand young men of pleasure'; 'The easy young man passes many a year of his life in all sorts of wild company'; 'The Chaumière knew him and the balls of Parisian actresses, the countesses of the opera at home and abroad'. Later on his sick bed, 'this simple, kindly, modest and courageous soul'[26] prays that his future may make amends for the days gone by. Ethel is less forgiving and much to Lady Kew's disgust shows Lord Kew a catalogue of his sins, compiled by the jealous Madame d'Ivry, whose own loveless match to a man many years her senior has led her to a life of dissipation, too dark to be described in detail.

Most of this scandalous behaviour takes place abroad, as do the amours of another masculine sinner, for whom Thackeray shows a similar tolerant sympathy. M. de Florac, the son of Colonel Newcome's first love and the cousin by marriage of Madame d'Ivry. 'His courage was well known and his character for bravery and another kind of gallantry probably exaggerated by his bad reputation. Had his mother not been alive, perhaps he would have believed in the virtue of no woman.'[27] Unlike Madame d'Ivry, Madame de Florac had remained faithful to her elderly husband, but her example is no real encouragement to marital fidelity on the part of her son, whose marriage to the elderly Miss Hoggs seems a distasteful addition to Thackeray's attack on the marriage mart. Lord Kew, more English and less cynical than Paul de Florac, does believe in the essential purity of women. 'He chose to believe that good women were entirely good.'[28] The innocent Lady Henrietta is his reward. Thackeray is not alone in regarding the continent in general and France in particular as a hotbed of sexual sinfulness. Both Eliot and Brontë speak disparagingly of French novels. But increasingly we find in Thackeray a Podsnap-like pandering to English chauvinism.[29]

Lady Clara is less fortunate than her sister in having to meet the full might of English disapproval. She is forced to abandon her childhood sweetheart Jack Belsize in favour of the odious Barnes Newcome because the latter is rich and the former poor. Inconveniently, after Clara and Barnes are married Belsize becomes rich and inherits a title owing to the death of his elder brother. Though perhaps not as grand as his friend Lord Kew he is larger and, though rougher, has less of a dissipated past. As already shown, he is infinitely preferable to Barnes who in addition to his other faults has a sordid sexual reputation of which we are constantly reminded. Using the same metaphor as Frank Castlewood had used, but this time more correctly, Thackeray says that Barnes thought he could 'sow his wild oats as some of the young Londoners sow them, not broadcast after the fashion of careless scatter-brained youth, but trimly and neatly, in quiet places, where the crop can come up unobserved and be taken in without bustle or scandal'.[30] Such thoughts are unwise. Barnes's liaison with a lady in his neighbourhood, Mrs Delaney, is frequently brought to our attention, notably on the occasion of his marriage and the electoral contest with his uncle. It is at first sight not exactly clear why the conduct of Barnes is so much more reprehensible than that of Lord Kew or M. de Florac, although there are differences. Barnes's affair results in two illegitimate children; it is clearly not just a casual liaison; it is conducted in respectable England rather than abroad, where women were considered fairer game; and, most importantly, Sir Barnes, in spite of sowing his wild oats so trimly, makes the mistake of being caught.

Thackeray may have been a guilty of a little carelessness in the composition of *The Newcomes*, serialised over a long period. His suggestion in an early number that Barnes was a cautious philanderer seems to be contradicted when his sins so obviously find him out, although it should be noted that delayed retribution is an important theme in the novel. Thackeray does seem guilty of a certain amount of inconsistency in condemning Barnes for his moral misdemeanours while condoning those of Lord Kew and de Florac, although most of us are equally guilty in finding motes in the sexual lives of our enemies while warding off beams from the escapades of our friends. We have noted ways in which his manuscripts reflect uncertainty and inconsistency. Thackeray may also seem guilty of adopting the infamous double standard in damning Lady Clara and Madame d'Ivry for sexual sins for which they have some provocation, whereas male sinners are allowed sustained incontinence for which they have far less excuse.

In Thackeray's defence it must be urged that Lady Clara and Madame d'Ivry are married, unlike the male sinners we have named, and can be contrasted with de Florac's mother who remains loyal to her marriage vows in spite of being forced to wed someone for whom she has no affection. Nor is Thackeray totally loyal to the ideal of conjugal felicity and fidelity which his readers seemed to demand. Laura Pendennis seems to be the model wife, clucking coyly over her husband and son, while being careful to keep away from sinners like Lady Clara, but there is a certain amount of evidence that Thackeray did not like Laura. He perhaps exaggerates her self-righteousness and Pendennis's apparent approval of it to show this dislike. Finally there are times when the author breaks away from the smug narrator to question Victorian pharisaical standards in general and the double standard in particular.

Shame! What is shame? Virtue is very often shameful according to the English social constitution and shame honourable. Truth, if yours happens to differ from your neighbours', provokes your friend's coldness, your mother's tears, the world's persecution. Love is not to be dealt in, save under restrictions which kill its sweet healthy free commerce. Sin in man is so light that scarce the fine of a penny is imposed; while for woman it is so heavy that no repentance can wash it out. Ah! yes; all stories are old. You proud matrons in your Mayfair markets, have you never seen a virgin sold, or sold one? Have you never heard of a poor wayfarer fallen among robbers and not a Pharisee to help him? of a poor woman fallen more sadly yet, abject in repentance and tears, and a crowd to stone her? I pace this broad Baden walk as the sunset is gilding the hills round about, as the orchestra blows its merry tunes, as the happy children laugh and sport in the alleys, as the lamps of the gambling palace are lighted up, as the throngs of pleasure-hunters stroll, and smoke, and flirt, and hum; and wonder sometimes, is it the sinners who are most sinful? Is it poor Prodigal yonder amongst the bad company, calling black and red and tossing the champagne; or brother Straitlace, that grudges his repentance? Is it downcast Hagar, that slinks away with poor little Ishmael in her hand; or bitter old virtuous Sarah, who scowls at her from my demure Lord Abrabam's arm?[31]

Between 1855 and his death in 1863 Thackeray completed two long novels, *The Virginians* and *Philip*, one short novel, *Lovel the Widower*, and began the promising *Denis Duval*. This is not an impressive achievement in either quantity or quality. Ill health and lassitude, lecture tours and a parliamentary candidature, wealth and sloth can all be blamed for this falling off. Though Thackeray retained support among his contemporary readers, subsequent critics have found fault with the incoherent digressions and repetition of stock characters which mar both *The Virginians* and *Philip*, both of which are expansions of earlier stories, as if the author could not think of any new subject. Others have disliked Thackeray's pervasive cynicism combined apparently with a sensitivity to criticism inspired but not excused by the quarrel with Dickens and Yates. Others have seen all of Thackeray's later work from *Vanity Fair* onwards as a surrender to Victorian gentility.[32]

Many of these criticisms are justified, but in spite of them Thackeray still continues to say something about sexual behaviour which is neither stale nor obvious, but rather uncomfortable and provocative. Indeed it could be argued that in his later novels Thackeray, now confident of the support of his reading public and perhaps not unduly worried by how far this support remained constant, deliberately tried to tease this public by challenging some of their easy attitudes.

The title of *The Virginians* is part of this teasing process. Of course the two heroes come from America, but Thackeray cannot with all his talk of *virginibus puerisque* have been unaware of the sexual connotations of his title, especially since it is clear that the two Warrington brothers are meant to represent the innocence of the New World when faced with the corruption of the Old. Curiously what would seem to be a laudable aim in prudish eyes was not particularly popular on either side of the Atlantic. American audiences were mainly hostile to the portrait of George Washington, but Thackeray is also a little cruel and condescending to American naivety. In England *The Times* criticised the author for being too free-spoken, and there could have been objections to the sympathetic portrayal of obvious sexual sinners like Beatrix Esmond, revived as Baroness Bernstein, and Lady Maria Castlewood, one of the few Victorian heroines allowed to marry beneath her, while prudish pharisees like Lady Warrington are shown to be mean in spirit as well as parsimonious. But in general Thackeray was clever enough by hints and allusions to get away with a fairly frank statement of the fact that men and women have sexual needs and that society as constituted was not very good at satisfying them or describing them.

By this time Thackeray at the age of forty-six had acknowledged 'the bankruptcy of his heart'.[33] Mrs Brookfield, his own brief happiness in marriage and his juvenile misbehaviour were but memories, although memories he could analyse with skill as well as melancholy. George Warrington is not a very satisfactory mouthpiece for his reflections, being generally recognised to be no match for his brother, whose amorous entanglements are far more interesting. Writing presumably towards the very end of the eighteenth-century Sir George Warrington seems to lapse into premature Victorianism, thus destroying the contrast which is in general more pointed than in *Henry Esmond* between one generation's tastes and another's. The accession of George III had of course meant that life at court was more decent than in George II's reign, and the same thing happened when Queen Victoria came to the throne. Thackeray's lectures on the four Georges would have made him well aware of both changes. But *The Virginians* is spread over so many years that we tend to lose sight of exactly which generation is being discussed.

It was clearly a different generation from that of Thackeray's own readers. When Henry Warrington arrives at Castlewood his cousin tells the assembled company all the court scandal. 'The ladies, young and old, laughed quite cheerfully at the lively jokes. Do not be frightened, fair readers of the present day. We are not going to outrage your sweet modesties or call blushes on your maiden cheeks.'[34] This passage displays equal disdain for the loose talk of the Castlewoods and the restrictions of Victorian times, shown up when we see the virtuous Lamberts laughing over Fielding and crying over Richardson in a manner shocking to Mrs Grundy.[35] Richardson appears in person in Tunbridge Wells, enabling Thackeray to mourn the fact that *Clarissa* is now forbidden reading. He wonders whether our women are more virtuous than their grandmothers or only more squeamish. American ladies are said to be more modest than English ones. Thackeray even in jest speculates that, 'a century hence the novels of today will be hidden behind locks and wires and make pretty little maidens blush'.[36] His speculations would not have proved very profitable.

Harry remains unsullied by the temptations of Tunbridge Wells, largely as a result of the virtues of his American upbringing. It is odd that Harry's American modesty should be praised, while that of his female descendants should be blamed. The latter is of course excessive, and there is a distinction between words and deeds, although it is when hearing loose talk that Harry blushes like a girl,[37] and it is his very innocence that leads him into dubious company. Colonel Wolfe disapproves of his escorting the French dancer Cattarina, and the Lamberts are fed sad tales of his profligacy. These are unjustified. 'Mr Harry with his colonial modesty had no victories over the sex to boast of; and was shy and awkward when he heard such narrated by others.'[38]

But in the chapter entitled appropriately 'Rake's Progress' it is hinted that Harry's Virginian modesty takes a bit of a knock when he moves to London. It is true we only hear of racing, gambling and drinking, but the pointed contrasts between eighteenth-century conduct and that of the pure and outraged nineteenth-century, and the pretended shock at authors like Fielding, Richardson and Smollett make it clear that Thackeray is thinking of sexual scandals. Indeed he comes very close to repeating his attack on prudery in the preface to *Pendennis* in the following paragraph replete with ambiguity.

I often think, however, in respect of Mr Warrington's doings at this period of his coming to London, that I may have taken my usual degrading and uncharitable views of him – for you see, I have not uttered a single word of virtuous indignation against his conduct, and if it was *not* reprehensible, have certainly judged him most cruelly. O the Truthful, O the Beautiful, O Modesty, O Benevolence, O Pudor, O Mores, O Blushing Shame, O Namby Pamby – each with your respective capital letters to your honoured names. O Niminy, O Piminy, how shall I dare for to say that a young man ever was a young man.[39]

What Thackeray can say is something about old women. The reappearance of Beatrix as Baroness Bernstein is a success. As well as her shocking loose talk we get guarded references to the shocking loose ways of her youth and middle age, but she is sympathetically treated in spite of her sins. Her eventual death is a little sombre, but it is clear that the sin of which she repents is not sexual immorality, but her failure to respond to the love of Henry Esmond because of the pressure of Vanity Fair. Another lady who loves not wisely but well is her niece Lady Maria, who in spite of her advanced years falls in love first with Harry Warrington, then the handsome actor Hagan whom she marries. Lady Maria is again handled with some degree of sympathy, although it could be argued that Thackeray is rather cruel in finding something comic about the spectacle of a woman loving somebody much younger than herself and her social inferior. In the first instance Thackeray is returning dangerously and probably deliberately to Lady Castlewood, although unlike her grandmother Lady Maria is not married when she falls in love with Harry. The cruel comedy about Lady Maria's rouged cheeks is perhaps some kind of defence against the kind of criticisms with which *Henry Esmond* had been greeted in certain quarters. Lady Maria of course offends against Victorian decorum by being so obvious in her sexual needs at a time when women were not supposed to have such needs, but at least Thackeray gives a fairly honest and a fairly kind account of such a character, although she is not really respectable.[40]

Poor Hetty Lambert who loves Harry Warrington is not allowed to show her love except by some rather cross pertness since respectable young ladies were not allowed to show their feelings except by falling into a decline, as is the case with her sister Theo who loves the less dashing George Warrington. Cynical and boring George seems a less likely object to inspire passion than his dashing younger brother, and is probably the reason for the disappointing conclusion of the novel as he takes over the narration. Thackeray may have tried a little revolt against George and his boring married life when he appears to censor part of his narrative.[41]

In *Philip* we have already shown the absurdity of having a hero meant to be a dashing young fellow, but in fact doing nothing more than being rude to all and sundry. In this novel, as if determined once and for all to scout the possibility that he was vicious and irresponsible, Thackeray as well as heaping scorn on Dr Firmin for his past sins, paints several decorous pictures of family life in the home of the young Firmins and young Pendennises. Charlotte Baynes, the daughter of the incompetent General Baynes and the shrewish Mrs Baynes, like Theo Lambert falls into a decline when her parents forbid her marriage with Philip; like Rosey Mackenzie has difficult pregnancies and seems very close to Isabella Shawe, but in spite of this seems under the tutelage of Laura Pendennis to be represented as an ideal wife and mother.

In a novel which it is very surprising to find the usually reliable Ray describe as outspoken[42] there are at the end two squeaks of sexuality. We hear of the later fate of Agnes Twysden, Philip's first love, married to the brutal and mean Captain Woolcombe. She eventually leaves him for a life of adventure on the continent, having paid like Lady Clara Pulleyn the price for preferring money to love. Laura Pendennis is as harsh to her even before her fall as she is to Lady Clara Pulleyn, and indeed the account of her fall is inserted quite gratuitously since it occurs well after two episodes which seem like tired borrowings from *The Newcomes* – the election and the discovery of the will.

An equally gratuitous piece of sexual melodrama is the strange behaviour of Philip Ringwood, Philip Firmin's distant and aristocratic cousin, who makes improbable advances to Philip's wife. Since Charlotte, to remain virtuous, must be unaware of these advances, and since the reader, to remain virtuous, cannot have these advances spelt out in any great detail, the adulterous behaviour of Philip Ringwood cannot be made much of. It is presumably included as part of Thackeray's defence of family life. Eventually Ringwood pays for his sins by dying in some amorous duel on the continent. It hardly seems likely that Charlotte should have captivated him; the parallel love affair between Lady Castlewood and Lord Mohun seems far more probable.[43]

So in the end Thackeray does lapse into gentility, sentimentality and prudery. Perhaps *Denis Duval* would have struck a more original note, although it is odd that we never really know whether the Princess is guilty or innocent of adultery with the Chevalier de la Motte. Thackeray's ambivalence in this matter draws attention to the ambiguous stance he adopts in sexual matters throughout his adult writings. Is Becky Sharp a lively lady or wicked woman? Is Amelia clinging ivy or an ideal wife and mother?[44] Are we meant to hate or love Laura and Helen Pendennis? Are Blanche and Fanny more sinned against than sinning? How should we regard Lady Castlewood and her daughter, with their strong passions which the world thwarts? Is Lady Clara wicked to run away, or is the world wicked which makes her unfaithful and breaks her when she is unfaithful? It is because he does not give an easy answer to these questions that Thackeray is an uncomfortable writer. Clearly he does not fit the Victorian male stereotype that modern critics have erected, a man who divides the female sex into angels and whores. Clearly too he would find himself ill at ease with modern permissive thinking which allows unrestricted sexual expression for men and women alike. Thackeray saw both the dark and the bright side of sexuality and tried to show both in an age which tried to show neither.

6

Dickens

As with Thackeray, so with Dickens. There seems at first sight a wide gap between the writer and the man. We might be able to bridge the gap if we knew how far the man went in committing sexual sins which as a writer he seems to condemn, but this we shall never know. Dickens is less open than Thackeray. His interest in the stage, in disguise, in concealment; his insistence on being in the right, as shown in his dealings with his publishers, and his reaction to his public on his separation from his wife; his overbearing qualities as a husband and father; and even the great reverence which he demanded and received as England's major man of letters are all complications which do not feature in our consideration of the life of Thackeray.

As a young man Dickens was probably less sexually experienced than his great rival, although not more innocent of sexual vice. As a young boy he was left to fend for himself in a London still full of Hogarthian squalor where prostitutes openly plied their trade. These experiences must have left their mark, although we do not see much of the mark in the novels, where Oliver Twist and David Copperfield somehow preserve their innocence. *Sketches by Boz* gives a franker picture of the depraved people Dickens met. We must note that Dickens experienced sexual vice at a period when his family's fortunes were at such a low ebb that he was for ever afterwards ashamed to mention the blacking factory. He would, then, be likely to associate sex with dirt and degradation as something unmentionable, behaving in the same way as Mr Podsnap, that brilliant caricature of the Victorian middle class for whom Dickens wrote and to which he had risen. Thackeray is more carelessly if condescendingly aristocratic about sexual misdemeanours, which boys will commit if they are boys of a certain standing.[1]

Poverty is a fairly good incentive to chastity in the young male, and there is an endearingly pure quality about Dickens's courtship of Maria Beadnell and his swift engagement at the age of twenty-four to Catherine Hogarth. His remark to Carlyle about the impossibility of his son remaining continent, and Emerson's shocked response, has already been noted.[2] Dickens's eldest son was not yet twelve at the time, and though the remark can be used as an example of the Victorian double standard, it is almost certainly one of Dickens's confusing sexual jokes. In this case he aimed to show up the prudish Americans in the same way as in *Martin Chuzzlewit* scorn is poured on the American lady who is shocked by the expression 'naked eye', though crudely blind to the moral and physical corruption around her.[3] Likewise there would appear to be some element of joking in the nudging references to conveniences, meaning presumably brothels, that occur in a letter of 1841 to the painter Maclise.[4] Maclise was of course no saint, being caught in bed with Lady Henrietta Sykes, and Dickens's friendship with him is suspicious as is his later friendship with the dissolute Wilkie Collins with whom he went on continental jaunts. On the other hand we cannot help feeling that Dickens's jocularity on the subject of sex which occasionally creeps out in his earlier novels as well as his correspondence is the jocularity of a man who would sin if he could, as opposed to the man who has sinned, but wished that he hadn't. Sex is less present in the later Dickens novels written at a time when the weight of the evidence suggests that Dickens was an adulterer.

This period was when Dickens's life became more tragic. Earlier, tragedy had entered both his life and his work in the shape of prostitution. Prostitutes are frequently mentioned in *Sketches by Boz*; and in *Oliver Twist* Nancy is the principal female character, easily outshining the colourless and conventional heroine, Rose Maylie. In later editions of these works references to prostitutes were refined in such a way that *Oliver Twist* has remained a favourite for a century and a half with young readers whose cheeks Dickens, as well as Mr Podsnap, was anxious to preserve from blushes.[5] This is of course because *Oliver Twist* deals with childhood as does *David Copperfield* where Martha Endell really and little Em'ly nearly fall into prostitution. Alice Marwood is a prostitute like her mother in *Dombey and Son*, and her fate mirrors that of Edith Dombey, who is improbably her cousin. Edith Dombey is like Lady Dedlock in *Bleak House* a lady with aristocratic connections who falls from grace, though Edith like Mrs Strong in *David Copperfield* and Louisa Gradgrind in *Hard Times* does not actually fall.

This is not a very impressive list of fallen women in view of Dickens's impressive output and volcanic energy, the wealth of female characters in his novels and his wide ranging acquaintance with women. No student of Dickens, and certainly no student of Dickens and sexuality, can ignore his work in company with the rich philanthropist Angela Burdett-Coutts, in trying to reclaim prostitutes to a life of virtue by the foundation of Urania Cottage as an asylum for fallen women.[6] Although such an enterprise seems mildly ludicrous by modern standards, and although modern readers may find something faintly disreputable in the energy Dickens displayed towards this social problem, as they have found in the later interest shown by William Gladstone, it is difficult to fault the humanity of Dickens in this enterprise. Oddly, however, in his fiction Dickens seemed to be more anxious to swim with the tide of reticent pessimism than to fight against it with the outspoken optimism he showed in his charitable work. Nancy and Alice Marwood are lost beyond redemption, even though the former has a heart of gold; both ladies meet a sacrificial death. Prostitutes bring down others in their train, as Martha nearly brings down little Em'ly. *Sketches by Boz* shows again and again the downward spiral of sexual indiscretion leading to prostitution leading to death. There is a girl on the brink being tempted by a girl in mid-stream, with the girl over the water-fall as a further warning; and the imagery of drowning, to which Dickens constantly recurs, is used as a rather appropriate symbol for the fate of the fallen woman. If, whether able to swim or not, one jumps into a river, there is no way in which one can reclaim one's dry position on land. It is possible, however, to swim back to land or be rescued or to be dragged back as a lifeless corpse. *Our Mutual Friend* has graphic pictures of the latter two eventualities. Once a woman has lot her virginity she cannot reclaim it. She can be rescued, as Dickens tried to rescue prostitutes in Urania Cottage. She might swim back to something like respectability as Martha did in the distant climes of Australia. She might teeter on the bank and be infected by the mire, even though she does not touch it, as is the case with Edith Dombey and Louisa Gradgrind. But the odds are that she will be swept over the waterfall, as happens to Nancy in *Oliver Twist*, even though Nancy does not actually meet the watery death she anticipates.

Public opinion would seem to have demanded that once a body had passed over the brink she was lost for ever. This was the attitude of the churches, exemplified by Mrs Henry Wood, as quoted in the first chapter, and Dickens, though no sympathiser with organised religion, was a popular novelist. As a popular novelist he was also bound to keep in touch with public opinion about the degree of freedom allowed to the discussion of sexual issues. In novels up to and including *Barnaby Rudge* Dickens is fairly frank in sexual references, but the 1840s were something of a watershed in taste, as the Brontës found to their cost, and Dickens would seem to have adapted his style accordingly. It is convenient and perhaps not entirely coincidental to date this shift in popular taste with regard to sexual matters to the accession of Queen Victoria. Certainly the virginal queen was and was to be a model of sexual decorum in comparison to her two raffish uncles. In later editions of the novel Dickens omitted indelicate references that had appeared in the serial version of *Oliver Twist* just before Victoria had succeeded, whereas Hardy at the end of this reign has to excise or bowdlerise in the serial versions what he can later amplify after Victoria's death. Oddly it was in 1837, the year Victoria's reign began, that Dickens produced a farce *Is She His Wife?*, which with its allusions to bigamy, adultery and seduction would have made Mr Podsnap and his daughters blush. But public taste does not change as rapidly or as neatly as that. There were still survivals of Regency raffishness in the 1840s and the marriage of Victoria and Albert was celebrated with a plethora of improper ballads.[7]

But Dickens did not write his work to the tune of these ballads. Little Em'ly and Martha are treated with sympathy, but with hushed horror, and poor Edith Dombey is punished although she has committed no sin, and so gingerly is the treatment of her possible sin that we find it hard to understand what is happening. Later, in *Little Dorrit* and *Our Mutual Friend*, Dickens seems to attack the excessive prudery of which he himself might seem guilty when he drew satirical portraits of Mrs General reducing everything to prunes and prisms and Mr Podsnap anxious about the cheek of a young person. It could be argued that Mrs General and Mr Podsnap are concerned with disasters in general rather than sexual misdemeanours in particular, but it would be a mistake not to think of them as sexual prudes, because this gives an ironic bite to the fact that Mrs General is trying to entrap William Dorrit and that the Podsnaps nearly allow their daughter to be ensnared into a sexual disaster by Alfred Lammle.

Podsnap and those he stood for were as hypocritical as Pecksniff, but was Dickens guilty of the same fault? We have already seen a number of contradictions between the conduct he practised and the code he preached, but have reserved the greatest and most obvious contradiction until the end. In 1858 after twenty-two years of marriage Dickens separated from his wife. She had given birth to ten children and had more than one miscarriage. With selfish insensitivity Dickens blamed Catherine for the numerous pregnancies as a result of which she lost her looks and her figure. There is increasing evidence of incompatibility between the couple during the 1850s, but there is speculation about other factors. Shortly before he left his wife Dickens had met a young actress, Ellen Ternan. Their names were inevitably linked and Dickens at the time of the separation issued an indignant denial of any impropriety.[8]

Such a denial may have been true at the time, but it seems unlikely that Ellen did not become Dickens's mistress at some date during the next twelve years. Certainly he was frequently away from home and frequently abroad with her. The evidence of Ellen herself, who married a clergyman after Dickens's death, and of Dickens's daughter, would seem to point to an adulterous relationship, Kate Dickens even claiming that they had a child. The evidence of Ellen's children is ambiguous, but the behaviour of her son certainly points to something improper.[9] There are still those who like to think that Dickens remained chaste until his death, but it is a sign of the change in sexual attitudes that most readers of Dickens now assume that he and Ellen were lovers. Dickens's latest biographer is an exception, although he almost protests too much in insisting on Ellen's virginity and Dickens's technical innocence while going to great elaborate lengths to show how guilty Dickens felt and others felt him to be.[10] It is not easy to make much of this hypothesis in our reading of the later novels, where Estella and Lizzie Hexam remain obstinately unattainable, but we can see something of Dickens's unhappiness and guilt and obsession in such portraits as John Jasper or Bradley Headstone. There is also in the later works a strong emphasis on masculine guilt.

We can understood why Dickens felt guilty, because in the treatment of his wife he was guilty. The Victorians thought more severely than we do of the middle-aged man who abandons his wife for someone much younger. But apart from this guilt Dickens ought not to have felt unhappy, because after a decade of living with his wife, who could cater neither to his romantic nor his practical needs, he would now seem to have had Ellen for the former and his sister-in-law Georgina looking after his household with loyal devotion. His relationship with Georgina was again the subject of unkind gossip, this time virtually certainly untrue, but all the same Georgina and her elder sister, Mary, who died with tragic suddenness early in Dickens's marriage, are important for an understanding of the female characters in the novels of Dickens. The two sisters would seem to be the models for the series of heroines – blameless, sexless and colourless – of whom Rose Maylie is the first and Agnes Wickfield the worst. Mary Hogarth died when she was seventeen and many of the heroines of the novels, Florence Dombey, Little Nell and Little Dorrit, are preternaturally young or seem so. Mary's death occurred during the composition of *Oliver Twist*, and it was during the writing of *David Copperfield* that Dickens may have begun to realise the importance of an Agnes-like figure in his life.

David Copperfield is supposed to be Dickens's most autobiographical novel. It ends with David happy and prosperous with an adored and adoring and suitably small family, hearing news of the success of the Micawbers in Australia. Real life was very different and grew more so. Dickens's family was large and caused him trouble. His father and mother were partial models for the Micawbers, but could not be exiled to Australia. The marriages of two of Dickens's brothers collapsed in the 1850s. The complicated and unhappy sexual history of the Dickens family is not reduplicated in the novels, it being a sign of his genius that he could escape by his imagination from the unpleasant reality that surrounded him. As he impregnated his wife whom he did not love and later loved Ellen whom he could not marry, we cannot help feeling that Dickens began to hate the sexual instinct which caused him such trouble;[11] and that he took refuge from it either by making love comic, as it is with Miss Tox, or repulsive as it is with Uriah Heep, or cutting out the sexual element together as is the case with the sentimental but sexless marriages of Esther Summerson and Bella Wilfer, or turning his women into grotesque caricatures like Miss Mowcher, Mrs Gamp and Mrs Gummidge.

And yet with his inventiveness and energy Dickens does have something to say about fallen women. He has quite a lot to say in

Sketches by Boz. In the chapter entitled 'Hackney Coach Stands' the word prostitute is used quite openly. 'How many melancholy tales of the same people at different periods! The country girl – the showy over-dressed woman – the drunken prostitute. The raw apprentice – the dissipated spendthrift – the thief.'[12] Here in brief is that picture of stages on the road to ruin to which Dickens frequently returns in *Sketches by Boz*, but tried to fight against in the work he did for prostitutes and in some of his greatest novels. There is a similar triple portrait in 'The Pawnbroker's Shop', already noted in connection with *Jane Eyre*, although in this case the girl on the brink of ruin is not an innocent country girl, but a girl from a shabby genteel family with her elderly mother. Mothers and daughters come into the description of a visit to Newgate where Dickens shows in turn a mother visiting a daughter and a daughter visiting her mother, hardened criminals all four, their wretched plight forced upon them by their sordid life.[13] The most graphic picture of female corruption comes in 'The Prisoners' Van', where two girls have been thrown upon the steps by a rapacious mother. 'What the younger girl was then, the elder had been once; and what the elder then was, the younger must soon become . . . Step by step, how many wretched females, within the sphere of every man's observation have become involved in a career of vice, frightful to contemplate; hopeless in its commencement, loathsome and repulsive in its course; friendless, forlorn and unpitied at its miserable conclusion.'[14] This is a fairly standard Victorian attitude. The lurid language sadly lacking in sympathy; the absence of any practical suggestion for improvement; and the general assumption that one step on the downward path led to inevitable ruin are in strong contrast to the practical work Dickens did in trying to redeem fallen women.

Equally standard is the assertion in the original introduction of *Pickwick Papers* that the author would write nothing that any young person could find offensive. This claim is surprising in view of the early date of *Pickwick Papers*, composed before Queen Victoria had ascended the throne; in view of Dickens's later attack on Podsnappery; and indeed because there is actually quite a lot of sexual activity in the story. Of the four members of the Pickwick Club, Snodgrass and Winkle get married, Tupman is active in amorous pursuits and Pickwick is actively pursued. Pickwick finds himself in the same bedroom as a middle-aged lady in yellow curl-papers, and Jingle elopes with the middle-aged Rachel Wardle. It is true that nothing untoward occurs on either occasion, although there are some fairly arch remarks and the age of the lady in each case is a further blanket on licentious thoughts. In addition the world of Pickwick with its stage-coaches and Christmas cheer is an essentially comic one, and the comic treatment of sex has always been allowed more license, as is shown by the leniency always allowed even by the strait-laced to comic picture postcards. There is a joke in *Nicholas Nickleby* about a maternal aunt being really a maternal parent;[15] the real tragedy behind this comic statement of a woman, for respectability's sake, not being allowed to acknowledge her own child would have been treated in a more hushed and a more solemn manner if the novel had been written to instruct rather than to entertain. It was as the author of *Pickwick* that Dickens really became famous, though the jolly, innocent world of *Pickwick* may seem as unreal as a perpetual diet of plum puddings in stage-coaches. Dickens had found a formula for success, and sex didn't play a great part in this formula.

In *Oliver Twist* there are two tragedies involving fallen women, that involving Oliver's mother and that involving Nancy. Both meet the conventional early and unhappy death reserved for erring females, but both are treated with some sympathy. Agnes Fleming is betrayed by Edward Leeford into becoming his mistress, but this is largely his fault, and it is hinted that he would have married her eventually had it not been for his untimely death. There is a lot of talk of shame, and Agnes's father dies of a broken heart, leaving her sister to be brought up by poor cottagers who think that with her unfortunate lineage she is bound to go to the bad, but they are wrong because Mrs Maylie rescues her, brings up the child as her own niece, and she turns into the saintly Rose Maylie. So much for bad blood. It is only Monks who calls Oliver a bastard and he is reproved by Mr Brownlow.[16] Like Esther Summerson Oliver suffers no moral taint through being illegitimate, indeed in both cases Dickens would seem to have gone too far in the other direction and made them insipidly virtuous.

Nancy is less insipid. About her there has been considerable debate. Thackeray and Wilkie Collins, Philip Collins and Slater give very different verdicts.[17] Called a prostitute roundly in prefaces up until 1846 and referred to as a drab in the text, Nancy is not shown walking the streets, and even her role as Sikes's mistress is both discreet and domestic. The one time we see her in the same room as Sikes she is darning his waistcoat. Originally introduced with Bet as her pert partner in vice, brazen and rouged, she becomes pale and ennobled by suffering, tries to save Oliver and shows touching affection to Sikes even when he is about to murder her. The tart with a heart of gold is of course both a stock character and a not very likely one. Dickens did have models in his family for many of his female characters, but not of course for Nancy. This makes her less realistic but more interesting, although there are inconsistencies. Cruikshank's illustrations and Dickens's pen pictures do show a gradual improvement in Nancy's moral condition, but at times Dickens seems to feel he has gone too far and pulls us back into stock denunciations of stews and dens, jails and hulks, debased creatures and degraded beings.[18] The meeting with Rose is not a success and Nancy's statement 'if there was more like you, there would be fewer like me'[19] seems to contradict the general if rather disgraceful supposition that prostitutes thrived in Victorian times because young men were thwarted of their sexual outlets by virginal creatures like Rose Maylie. Nevertheless Nancy is one of the better pictures of fallen women in Victorian literature.[20]

Dickens's most famous female character in *Nicholas Nickleby* is not a fallen woman, but the feather-brained Mrs Nickleby, who quite steals the limelight from the chaste Kate and Madeline who have to resist assaults on their virtue from a degraded aristocrat and the prospect of marriage to an elderly usurer respectively. Mrs Nickleby unconsciously makes a good joke about fallen women when she suggests that in their abandoned plight they can go to the workhouse or the Magdalen Hospital. The joke playing on Mrs Nickleby's innocence is more obvious in the manuscript where she is made to add 'I think it's the Magdalen Hospital where they take in unfortunate females' and Dickens was evidently fond of it as later she mistakenly calls Madeline Magdalen.[21] The Magdalen Hospital was of course an institution for reclaiming prostitutes, and Magdalen another name for fallen woman. Behind this joke there is of course a serious point concerned with innocence and the upbringing of children. Attached as he is to virgin purity, Dickens somehow has to make Kate aware of the wicked intentions of Sir Mulberry Hawk. In an odd way she seems better prepared for the world than Madeline, although the latter's dissipated father would seem to have shown more vice to his daughter then Kate would have been exposed to in Devonshire. Dickens feels obliged to explain Kate's instinctive dislike of Ralph Nickleby's party when he says, 'however fresh from the country a young lady (by nature) may be and however unacquainted with conventional behaviour the chances are she will have quite as strong an innate sense of the decencies and proprieties of life as if she had run the gauntlet of a dozen London seasons'.[22] She later denounces Mrs Wititterly for standing by when more attacks are made on her virtue, and yet Dickens comments on Kate's lack of knowledge of the world.

Dickens also touches on another problem which he does not really explain. The admirable Nicholas and Kate are the children of a feeble father and a foolish mother. Their uncle is a villain, and yet Dickens is at pains to point out family resemblances and to start the novel with a family tree of the Nicklebys, going right back to Ralph Nickleby, great uncle of the villain of the same name. He also makes the tedious Charles Cheeryble give quite a sensible discourse on Nature in connection with Smike's dislike of Mr Snawley, mistakenly supposed to be his father.[23] In fact Smike is Ralph's son, born in wedlock, though the marriage was a peculiar one. Neither nature nor nurture can really explain how Smike and Kate and Nicholas turn out as they do and, though in the twentieth-century we are eager to explain bad behaviour by bad blood or bad upbringing, Dickens at any rate in his youth, seems to think the individual responsible for his or her own behaviour, though a happy family atmosphere undoubtedly helped. Mr Squeers does not provide this atmosphere and it is an added irony that among his charges number many natural (i.e. illegitimate) sons, sent away by their families to rot in Yorkshire where they could not be an embarrassment.[24]

The Old Curiosity Shop, by reducing the age of its heroine to fourteen, would seem to have taken her out of the sexual sphere in Victorian eyes.[25] Nowadays we are less innocent and find it difficult to imagine little Nell wandering the countryside without being involved in some kind of sexual entanglement from which her elderly and incompetent grandfather would have been totally unable to rescue her. She is of course in danger from Quilp who in spite of his size and temper is a figure of great sexual magnetism and force. His speech is rich in sexual innuendoes and one sometimes feels that having suppressed little Nell's sexuality Dickens unconsciously compensates with Quilp. There is some evidence that originally Dickens intended the Marchioness to be the child of Quilp and Sally Brass, but then rejected the idea that such a good character could come from such evil parents.[26] Or there may be some reaction against illegitimacy.

Illegitimacy does features in *Barnaby Rudge*. Unlike in *Oliver Twist* it is the legitimate son, Edward Chester, who is the virtuous hero, and the illegimate son Hugh who is the more villainous. Neither is exactly like their smooth and dishonest father. Apart from Sir John's misbehaviour with Hugh's mother there is little interest in sex in *Barnaby Rudge* in spite of its violent setting in the eighteenth-century. In Dolly Varden Dickens does succeed in creating a heroine who is not too virginal and virtuous to be sexually attractive and realistic, as is frankly acknowledged when she is locked up with the saintly Emma Haredale and prudish Miss Miggs.[27] It is curious that one of Dickens's least known books should have one of his best heroines.

There is not much about sexuality in *Martin Chuzzlewit*, a book whose early numbers failed to sell well. It is possible that we could connect this fact to the lack of sexual interest, although difficult to know whether the failure arose from Dickens wishing to pander to the new prudery or being unwilling to cater for his unreformed readers' wish for sex and violence. We have seen Dickens casting in *Martin Chuzzlewit* a cold eye on American prudery, but this is part of the general attack on America which raised the fortunes of the book. Later in the description of Pecksniff's odious courtship of Mary Graham and the narration of Ruth Pinch's sensual charms with her bright eyes and wicked little stomacher we can see Dickens fairly obviously torn between that attraction and repulsion to sex which is the lot of the average person. The fate of the two Miss Pecksniffs, one married to the brutal Jonas, the other abandoned at the altar by the feeble Rev. Noodle, is a cruel satire on the wish of women to be married at any cost, and *Martin Chuzzlewit* is not in general a book that is sympathetic to the female sex.

Four years elapse between the completion of *Martin Chuzzlewit* in 1844 and the completion of *Dombey and Son* in 1848. It is generally recognised that with the latter novel Dickens elevated his art to a higher plane. In the next five novels there is a far higher proportion of women characters and among their number a fairly impressive collection of women who are in some way fallen. On the other hand, as we have shown, the 1840s like the 1960s represent something of a watershed in sexual taste. *Jane Eyre* was attacked for sympathy with sexual sinners and too graphic descriptions of sexual scenes. Dickens was not so attacked, but we feel like attacking him for punishing Lady Dedlock and Little Em'ly, Louisa Gradgrind and Edith Dombey so severely and describing their fall so circumspectly that it is not at all clear when and whether some of these fallen women have actually fallen.

Edith Dombey is plainly innocent. She declares at the end of the book to Florence that she has not slept with Carker, although she is guilty of much. In the eyes of the world, like Maggie Tulliver whom she otherwise hardly resembles, she has compromised herself fatally, and there is much talk of shame and stain and the loss of fame and good name even after her innocence is clearly established in the tawdry magnificence of the adulterous hotel in Dijon. We assume that Edith is going to commit adultery when she crawls past Florence on the stairs, and her guilt seems established when she does not return that night. Cousin Feenix asks for forbearance until criminality is proved and we are surprised to learn that Carker and Edith have left by separate routes, but Cousin Feenix is an old fool, and we assume like Mrs Brown that the lovers have arranged to meet at an agreed rendezvous. As indeed they have, but at this rendezvous Edith rejects Carker, and, though she is not allowed complete forgiveness, she is allowed to see Florence once. Nor is retirement under the protection of Cousin Feenix all that bad a fate, since the latter, though shaky on his legs and long-winded in his speech, turns out like Miss Tox to be on the side of the angels.[28]

There is evidence that Dickens changed his mind about turning Edith into an adulteress. The elaborate parallels between Alice Harwood and Edith would make more sense if Edith had been ruined by Carker in the same way as Alice is prostituted by Mrs Brown. Alice turns out in an unlikely fashion to be the daughter of Edith Dombey's uncle, and we seem here to be reverting to a new form of the debate about nature and nurture. What prevented Dickens from turning Edith into an adulteress was probably her association with Florence, whom she befriends and wishes to save from marrying for money rather than love. It would be hard for the virginal Florence, who does indeed marry the poor but honest Walter, to be befriended by a wicked woman, and perhaps the woman is prevented from being too wicked by the example of Florence. There is also the wish to punish the odious Carker who is made to risk everything for an unpleasant rejection, although it could be argued that the cold-blooded cruelty to both Dombey and Carker that Edith shows is in fact more wicked than an adulterous passion. Edith is of course provoked and, unlike Maggie Tulliver who also causes unhappiness to two men, has no reason to be fond of these men, but her harshness, though magnificent, has a calculating quality about it wholly lacking in the heroine of *The Mill on the Floss.*

Dombey and Son was written well before Ellen Ternan had come upon the scene, but in the description of the relationship between Florence and Edith Dombey Dickens was drawing attention to an unfortunate feature of the life of a Victorian woman. Not only were fallen women condemned, but also those who were thought to be fallen women and even those who associated with them. This is why Laura Pendennis shuns Clara Newcome and St Oggs shuns Maggie Tulliver; why women could not call on the Lewes family and Dickens's daughters had a dubious reputation, probably for condoning, however unwillingly, their father's association with a lady not his wife.[29] Sadly Dickens does not seem to have been prepared to attack this blanket condemnation of friendship to sexual sinners and of unconventional behaviour, although he is relatively charitable in his next novel.

In *David Copperfield* fallen or nearly fallen women do not occupy quite such a central position. It is unthinkable to imagine either Dora or Agnes in a compromising position. Annie Strong is a different matter. At the beginning of her story when there is the incident of the cherry-coloured ribbons we suspect her of wishing to conduct an affair with her cousin Jack Maldon. The absentminded and elderly Dr Strong hardly seems an ideal husband any more than he seems an ideal headmaster. Mr Wickfield, suspecting trouble, sends Maldon off to India, but he returns and is there in the background when David renews his acquaintance with the Strongs in London. It is Uriah Heep who, in vulgar terms, opens the Doctor's eyes to the possibility of an affair. There then passes a period of unhappiness which is solved by Mr Dick, an improbable marriage counsellor, who encourages Annie to make a long speech, explaining that she had not married Strong for his money, and that the night of the cherry-coloured ribbons had revealed Maldon to have a false and thankless heart. She realises that her early love for him had been an immature one, and David Copperfield ponders on his love for Dora.

So Dr Strong and his wife live happily ever after, he with his dictionary which shows less signs of being finished than Casaubon's work on mythology, and Annie with her rock-like reverence for her husband which is perhaps less sorely tried than Dorothea's, as Dr Strong has a generous heart and genuine learning, with no room in his will for nasty codicils. Through this muddled account of a marriage which does come right in the end we do see Dickens toying with interesting ideas raised in earlier books, but then throwing away the opportunity to explore them. Dr Strong is a rich man and Mrs Markleham, Annie's mother, is like Mrs Skewton mercenary, but Annie is at pains to deny wealth as a motive for her marriage. Both Annie and her husband are innocent and reticent, and we need the unlikely combination of Uriah Heep and Mr Dick to bring out the truth. Dickens seems in favour of more plain speaking, but the message of the Strong marriage is not exactly plain, especially as David Copperfield uses it sadly to contrast with his own marriage to Dora, a maddening but attractive heroine.[30]

Annie fails to fall, but Dickens enters the lurid world of seduction and prostitution with little Em'ly and Martha. Annie Strong denies that she marries for money, whereas little Em'ly elopes with Steerforth in the hope of becoming a lady. This touch is probably put in to make little Em'ly more innocent, although it makes her very like Hetty Sorrel who shared her exile to Australia. Innocence in sexual matters is a subject which Dickens had treated in *Nicholas Nickleby*, but it had to be treated gingerly. Oddly, if successfully, it is David himself who takes on the role of the young innocent, and this explains, as the acute Rosa Dartle notices, his nickname of Miss Daisy. One can read homosexual implications into this name[31] and it would not be surprising if Steerforth, sensual and selfish, should turn his attention to small boys in a single-sex school, but probably Dickens is using David as an example of shattered innocence because the shattering of female innocence was too dangerous and too difficult. As with Eve in *Paradise Lost*, if little Em'ly is to be entirely innocent, she does not deserve to be punished as she is and, if she is not as innocent as young women ought to be, then she does not deserve her partial redemption as a single woman in Australia.

Linked to little Em'ly are two other very different fallen women, Rosa Dartle and Martha. The former, cultivated and clever, has been seduced by Steerforth in her youth, still loves him and is savagely hostile and contemptuous to little Em'ly when Steerforth has run off with her. In contrast, Em'ly is kind to Martha when everybody else, even the good-hearted Peggotys, shun her, and is rewarded for this kindness when Martha in turn rescues her from a life of prostitution in London. Both go with Mr Peggoty to Australia, where Martha marries and Em'ly could have married. She remains a spinster out of love for the dead Ham rather than any sense of her own unworthiness.

At first sight we may think of contrasting the humanity of Dickens in allowing both women to improve and to escape from the lowest depths with Eliot's harshness to Hetty. Unlike in *Sketches by Boz* one woman raises another up rather than dragging her down, and Martha and Em'ly join a series of women whose friendship is a source of mutual support. Esther Summerson and Ada Clare are the most obvious example.[32] In contrast to Dickens, George Eliot seems to be almost like Rosa Dartle in her harshness to Hetty Sorrel, who is not even allowed to survive Australia. On the other hand Dickens does raise more questions than he answers. We must first complain that, though there is some extraordinarily lurid language used to describe Martha's fate in London, which Em'ly nearly shares, it is not at all clear what exactly this fate is. In leaving Suffolk for London Martha is involving herself in greater danger, although she is trying to make a new start away from people who knew her. Is she right or not? Ham and Mr Peggoty disapprove of Em'ly befriending Martha, presumably as this involves guilt through association. Are they right or not? Martha in fact helps Em'ly later and could have warned her earlier. We would like to know more about the false friend who offers little Em'ly needlework and shelter, from which Martha rescues her when 'on the brink of more than I can say or think of', as Mr Peggoty puts it.[33] Presumably Dickens could not say too much for fear of offending his innocent readers, although one would have thought that the innocent readers might well ask embarrassing questions about what was the dreadful fate that threatened Em'ly. And indeed if Em'ly had been less innocent she might have avoided embarrassment with Steerforth and the needlework.

Dickens's next novel, *Bleak House*, has in Lady Dedlock a very different kind of fallen woman from little Em'ly. Her sin in loving Captain Hawdon and giving birth to Esther Summerson is cruelly punished. She dies near her lover's grave; he dies a worthless reject; and yet the offspring of their illegitimate love, in spite of being blinded and being offered a loveless marriage to Mr Jarndyce, does manage to secure a happy marriage to Alan Woodcourt. *Bleak House* is an important, perhaps the most important, statement of hostility to the legal and constitutional muddle which in the view of Dickens was ruining Britain. Sexual currents are there in *Bleak House*, but they tend to be lost in the whirlpool of Dickens's political imagination. It is interesting to note in this novel the hostility of Dickens to organised religion. Mrs Jellyby is keen on missions and Mr Chadband on useless questions, and neither of course is any use to anyone. A narrow religious attitude is also responsible for Miss Barbary's cruel statement, which Esther Summerson repeats, to the effect that she was a disgrace to her mother as much as her mother was a source of disgrace to her. Dickens clearly resented this slur against the innocent Esther. Lady Dedlock is less innocent and meets in death the conventional fate of the Victorian fallen woman, although her husband forgives her, and there is a certain amount of melodramatic exaggeration in the story of her frenzied flight. She is suspected wrongly of murder, and it is perhaps an indication of Dickens's hostility to conventional morality, faintly satirised in the account of the gossip after Lady Dedlock's death, that we, like Inspector Bucket, are led for a time to believe that Lady Dedlock would murder Mr Tulkinghorn to preserve her reputation in the eyes of this conventional morality. It comes as something of a surprise that it is actually Hortense who is the murderess, just as Sir Leicester Dedlock's forgiveness is surprising. It may seem out of character that Sir Leicester, bred in conventional stiffness, should turn out to be another Dr Strong with more to forgive; but perhaps this is part of Dickens's feeling that the inspiration of the human heart was more important than rules and regulations.

This is certainly the message of *Hard Times*, although here the enemy is not organised religion, but the fashionable Utilitarian philosophy. Utilitarianism does not in fact have a great deal to say on sexual morality. Bentham's belief in the maximising of pleasure, when carried to its extreme, might lead to the setting up of state brothels where a few women could be sacrificed to the lusts of many men, and most women could be freed from these lusts. Bentham of course never went as far as this, and the high-minded John Stuart Mill would have seen something wrong in it. Mill's own sexual history was odd; he was prevented from marrying Harriet Taylor for some time because she was married, but she influenced him with her feminist views. Dickens had no time for votes for women, a cause taken up by Mrs Jellyby, but the story of Stephen Blackpool and Rachel is a plea for easier divorce, for which Mill fought. Rachel is in no sense a fallen woman; Victorian taste would not have tolerated her being presented as a saint if Stephen Blackpool had sexual relations with her while his drunken wife was still living, any more than it would have allowed Louisa Gradgrind fulfilled happiness at the end of the novel. Dickens is of course angry with people like Mrs Sparsit who like to think of Louisa running off with the handsome Harthouse. In fact Louisa only goes back to her father, but she has to pay the penalty for deserting Bounderby by not being allowed to marry and only having the children of Sissy Jupe as a consolation prize.

> Herself again a wife – a mother – lovingly watchful of her children, ever careful that they should have a childhood of the mind no less than a childhood of the body, as knowing it to be even a more beautiful thing, and a possession, and hoarded scrap of which is a blessing and happiness to the wisest. Did Louisa see this? Such a thing was never to be.[34]

It may seem cowardly and conventional that Dickens had to punish Louisa in this way. As Orwell saw in *1984* the sexual instinct is too great to be controlled by rules and, though speaking against the strict rules of Utilitarianism in *Hard Times*, Dickens eventually takes refuge in the norm of Victorian sentiment which saw the family as an ideal to be protected at all costs. Kindness to Louisa might have seemed a threat to this ideal.

By 1854 Dickens's own family life may have been under some

strain. It is hard to establish exact dates. When the separation came in 1858 he claimed that tensions between him and his wife had existed for many years, but this may have been an exaggerated claim to conceal the role of Ellen Ternan whom he did not meet until 1856. There is an occasional note of impatience in correspondence with his wife and an increasing restlessness shown in absences from home, but most of those who assume that the Dickens marriage was unhappy throughout the 1850s are reading the novels as autobiography. This is dangerous, although Dickens's next novel, *Little Dorrit*, is his most unhappy. Autobiography is generally supposed to enter *Little Dorrit* when Arthur Clennam meets Flora Finching, allegedly modelled on Maria Beadnell, whom Dickens had met in 1855 years after their youthful love affair. He found her, as Arthur finds Flora, to be both fat and foolish. Little Dorrit, as her name indicates, is a reversion to Dickens's early youthful, almost sexless, heroines. The point is made clear in a strange passage where she meets a prostitute who is surprised to find her not a child but a woman.[35]

Thus the eventual marriage of Amy Dorrit and Arthur Clennam is hardly a tribute to the sexual instinct that leads Peg Neagles and Fanny Dorrit astray with worthless husbands; might have led Arthur to a marriage to a silly woman whose looks soon leave her; nearly entraps William Dorrit into an alliance with the hypocritical Mrs General; ruins Miss Wade whose befriending of Tattycoram seems marginally lesbian; and almost always leads to disaster. And yet Miss Wade and even more Mrs Clennam are hardly tributes to hostility to sex. The latter's disapproval of her husband's infidelity and Old Testament religiosity are treated as dour and narrowminded. *Little Dorrit* was clearly written at a time of crisis in Dickens's life. We have seen him torn between a violent repugnance to the mating instinct and a Lawrentian hostility to the forces that condemned this vital principle. *Little Dorrit* is the novel that reveals this paradox most clearly, and the famous prison imagery merely seems to reinforce the way man is trapped between desire and despair.

Dickens's final three and a half novels contain fewer women and practically no fallen women. It is possible that Ellen Ternan explains this absence, Dickens being cautious about treating a subject which might have raised awkward questions. Alternatively we can choose to see Ellen virtuously holding out in the way that

Lucy Mannette is out of reach for Sidney Carton and Estella is unavailable for Pip until the spurious ending of *Great Expectations*, and Lizzie Hexam unwilling to accept anything less than marriage from Eugene Wrayburn. Or we can say that the murderous obsession of Bradley Headstone and John Jasper, both characters embedded in the respectable Establishment, portrays Dickens's own infatuation with Ellen and his disgust at it. Various characters adopt disguises in these last novels; some of them are respectable like John Harman; some take a false identity for perfectly respectable motives like Sidney Carton and Dick Datchery; but it has been suggested that this emphasis on a double life reflects the concealment that was necessary in Dickens's own life.

Apart from this secret life there is of course still a rich range of female characters in the last novels. The pert Bella Wilfer, the noble Jenny Wren, the artless Rosa Bud, the enigmatic Helena Landless, cannot be fitted into the conventional division of women into angels or harlots; and although they may reflect various aspects of Ellen Ternan, it is surely an insult to the creative imagination of Dickens to see his characters solely in autobiographical terms. Nevertheless in a book about fallen women of the Victorian age it is odd that in a chapter about the greatest Victorian novelist who did take practical steps to try and improve the lot of prostitutes we have to end with an apology for the absence of any fallen women in the later novels. Madame Defarge's sister raped by Charles Darnay's father under some *droit de seigneur* ordination; and Estella's mother, the murderess who had somehow entered into sexual relations with Magwitch, are hardly major or exciting characters in *A Tale of Two Cities* and *Great Expectations*, and cannot compare with the famous anti-sexual symbols of Madame Defarge knitting shrouds and Miss Havisham petrified in her wedding dress, although of course the latter two characters are symbols of doom, and we are meant to sympathise with Madame Defarge's sister and Magwitch's mistress.

In *Our Mutual Friend* and *The Mystery of Edwin Drood* there is no illicit sex apart from that proposed by Eugene Wrayburn to Lizzie Hexam and thwarted. The earlier Dickens and Hardy might have been more sceptical about Lizzie holding out, but she does, in spite of her love for the worthless Eugene. Sin, when it occurs in the later novels, occurs within the bonds of marriage or proposed marriage, since Bradley Headstone and John Jasper have, as the old cliché has it, honourable intentions, even if they intend murder in order to see that these intentions are carried out. Mr and Mrs Lammle enter a loveless marriage for mercenary motives, and when it turns out that each party has been deceived there is not much to fall back upon except the possible prospect of enticing Georgiana Podsnap into a marriage with the far from fascinating Fascinating Fledgeby. The shadow of marriage as a form of legalised prostitution, hinted at delicately in the cousinship of Alice Marwood and Edith Dombey, and the relationship of both ladies to Carker, is stated a little more clearly in *Our Mutual Friend*, but in the later novel the emphasis is more on marriage than prostitution.

We have in this chapter interwoven biography and criticism more than with other nineteenth-century authors, as is the case with the major and successful study of Dickens's women by Michael Slater. Generally, however, Dickens is supposed to be too great an artist to be reduced to writing his autobiography as fiction, as is the case with Brontë where the biographers have had a field day, and with Thackeray, often supposed to have been capable of writing only one novel. Dickens, like Shakespeare, of whose sexual life we know almost nothing, could and did enrich and transform the women he met into memorable characters, and Slater is perhaps too schematic in trying to fit these characters into the mould of various ladies that Dickens knew. But anyone reading any of the biographies of Dickens apart from that of the discreetly loyal Forster must come away with the feeling that Dickens did not treat women fairly, either worshipping them or cursing them, and the same tends to be true of the women of his novels. Our next author, Hardy, also treated the women in his life badly, although as with Dickens there is much that is mysterious about his sexual life which no amount of speculation can solve. Remarkably, however, Hardy was able to create female characters with realistic sexual feelings with whom we can and do sympathise; and he did this in spite of a moral climate which enforced absurd bowdlerisations in the magazine versions of his novels and eventually, by condemning *Jude the Obscure* as 'Jude the obscene', brought his career as a novelist to a premature close.

7

Hardy

Thomas Hardy's life, of which his sexual life is a part, provides much the most complicated of the biographies we have had to offer. Sheer longevity is the first complication. Hardy was born in 1840, fifteen years before the last surviving brother of Jane Austen died. His youngest sister, Katherine, died in 1940; and a son of Tryphena Sparks, a younger first cousin with whom Hardy is supposed to have been entangled, died in 1976. Hardy looks back to the eighteenth-century and forward to the twentieth. He could with his interest in the Napoleonic wars and bygone knights and baronets have written a poem in his old age about Sir Francis Austen whom he could have met in his youth. But he didn't. We have to consider not just the gap in time between Austen and Hardy; nor the gap in place, Hardy's heroines moving slightly to the west of Austen's; nor the change in pace between the sedate travel of Austen's heroines and the more hectic but unhappy movements of Hardy's female characters; nor the change of class, with Jane Austen's ladies being distinctly a cut above the likes of Bathsheba who even if she does go to Bath moves to a resort which had gone steadily downhill in the nineteenth-century. We have to acknowledge that Hardy's standards were different from those of Jane Austen, and in spite of being somehow apart from the nineteenth-century and apart from slick urban mores the two authors have little in common. There are too differences in personality, although the times in which the two authors lived are another determining factor, as Hardy saw when he envisaged a bleak fate decreeing man's existence.

It is clear that Hardy lived through a minor sexual revolution. Austen and Brontë did not live long enough for a similar revolution, and reviews of Brontë novels indicate that in their time the pendulum was swinging in the opposite direction. Dickens, Eliot and Thackeray wrote during the height of Victorian prudery, as indeed did Hardy, whose career as a novelist only spans the years from 1868 when he first submitted the manuscript of *The Poor Man and the Lady* to 1896 when the outraged reception of *Jude the Obscure* persuaded him to give up the writing of novels for ever. Here is another source of confusion because the texts as we now have them, generally taken from the 1912 Wessex edition, are very different from either the original manuscripts or the absurdly bowdlerised version of the novels first submitted for serial publication.[1] Indeed, if we are looking for indications of the way in which Hardy handled sexual matters, we could do worse than consider the passages omitted from earlier serial publication and added at a later date. We could also do better, because it is clear that magazine editors were very sensitive about faint traces of explicit sexual activity, but fairly insensitive to obvious, even heavy-handed, implicit sexual observations.[2] Nevertheless there is a certain relevance about Byron's remarks in *Don Juan* describing how convenient it is that editors of classical texts relegate the indecent passages to an appendix, thus enabling the student in search of smut to skip the rest of the text.[3] Compared to Byron's schoolboy texts, Hardy's omissions and additions are less absurd, and are an apt reflection on changing standards and the way in which serial publication had always to be more delicately handled than novel publication, presumably since novels could more easily be kept out of the hands of the sensitive young person.

Hardy of course objected to the cuts he was forced to make and was hurt by the opposition with which *Tess of the d'Urbervilles* and *Jude the Obscure* were greeted. In 1890 he wrote one of the most famous attacks on Victorian prudery. His own bowdlerisations are so savage that we sometimes feel that he is deliberately spiting the Victorian conventions he would like to have flouted. The full texts by modern standards are not very shocking. Tess Durbeyfield and Sue Bridehead undergo terrible sufferings, but modern sensibilities are unlikely to be bruised by the description of these ordeals, which are handled with great discretion. On the contrary, we are shocked, as it is clear that Hardy was shocked, by the fact that these heroines should be driven to endure such suffering by a combination of malign fate and the disapproval of society.

It is tempting to look for the origins of Hardy's attitudes in Hardy's own life, but the writing of this life is no easy matter. There are two good modern biographies to aid us, but the wealth and uncertainty of sexual references in these biographies almost makes us pine for the reticent evasiveness to be found in the life of Thomas Hardy officially written by the second Mrs Hardy, but in fact virtually dictated by the author himself.[4] We do not know where we are with stories that Hardy fathered an illegitimate child by Tryphena Sparks, or again that he was impotent.[5] Before and after his first marriage Hardy was connected with a number of women, but we do not know and cannot know how close the connection was. His relations in general and sexual relations in particular with both his wives must be a matter of conjecture. Most biographers are agreed that Hardy did not treat his wives well – or indeed many women well. This is odd in view of the sympathy Hardy shows to the heroines of his novels. His poetry has been a source of information about the women he loved, but poetry is a dangerous source for biography, although it is clear that he did write many poems in memory of his first wife after marrying his second.

Some more tangible and perhaps more surprising indications of Hardy's sexual background can be derived from an inspection of Hardy's family tree. He himself was conceived well before his mother and father were married. Of his two grandmothers one was heavily pregnant at the time of her marriage, and the other gave birth to her first child seven months after her wedding. The latter was Mary Head, whose unhappy youth in Berkshire is supposed to have contributed to the story of *Jude the Obscure*. It is possible that she gave birth to an illegitimate child when very young.[6] These seemingly lurid sexual escapades all took place early in the nineteenth-century or even in the eighteenth-century, and we cannot really use them as evidence against Victorian morality. Even when Victorian morality was at its zenith it was not uncommon among members of the working class for marriage to follow pregnancy rather then vice versa. Indeed in *The Well-Beloved* there is more than one reference to island custom whereby engaged couples slept together to ensure their fertility before they were married; the eldest of the three Avices rejects this custom, but her daughter does not.[7] In *Two on a Tower*, while the hero and heroine get themselves into terrible difficulties, the troubles of Lady Constantine's pregnant maid are solved quite simply by her mistress persuading the maid's lover to marry her. Interestingly in this novel, Swithin St Cleeve and Lady Constantine go to elaborate lengths to avoid being caught by this other couple, the Greens, who do not seem to have to worry about their own reputation. Tess's mother does not really mind that Tess is going to have a baby, but thinks it a pity that Alec cannot marry her, though she senses dimly that Alec is out of her class. Jude is in the same class as Arabella, and the pretended pregnancy that leads to their marriage is the occasion of coarse ribaldry but no lasting shame to either party, although it does lead to lasting tragedy. It was only among the middle class of Angel Clare into which Jude and Sue were painfully trying to climb that sexual misdemeanours were so heavily condemned. This was of course the class to which Hardy's wife belonged, and it is not difficult to see something of a rebellion against the code of his wife in both *Tess of the d'Urbervilles* and *Jude the Obscure*.

Another member of the middle class with a complicated sexual history is Horace Moule, Hardy's mentor in many respects, born to inherit the Oxford education to which Jude aspired, and supposed by many to be a model of Hardy's unhappy heroes. Moule's death by suicide would seem to have been brought about by depression, probably resulting from drunkenness, but there are rumours of sexual scandals. An illegitimate child by a worthless woman, a broken engagement with a governess and even accusations of homosexuality have been adduced as reasons for Moule's despair.[8] No certain knowledge is possible. Unlike the working class the middle class knew they had to cover up their sexual scandals. Hardy's keen interest in class differences which may well seem like clumsy snobbery does run parallel to his interest in sexual matters.

No doubt we might have seen something of this double interest in *The Poor Man and the Lady* if this novel had survived. Hardy's first published novel *Desperate Remedies* is not concerned with the working class, to which he returned with great success in *Under the Greenwood Tree* and *Far from the Madding Crowd*. Instead in this contrived tale of marriages false and true we are in the middle-class world where appearances have to be kept up. Cytherea Aldclyffe cannot marry Cytherea Graye's father because she has had an affair and given birth to a child.[9] This child is Aeneas Manston, the villain of the book, who marries first Eunice, an American lady whom he murders but pretends has been burnt in a fire, and then Cytherea Graye, from whom he is separated on the night of the wedding by the rumour that his first wife is alive. He then persuades another lady, Anne Seaway, to live with him as if she were his first wife, miraculously returned. Much of the sexual interest in the book comes from Hardy playing with these three strange unions, reminiscent of the entanglements of Jude Fawley and Sue Bridehead. Aeneas is anxious to keep his first marriage a secret, and the village gossips on discovering traces of her in Aeneas's house speculate that she is a 'wicked one – some poor street-wench escaped from Sodom . . . only to find herself in Gomorrah'.[10] In fact Eunice and Aeneas are legally married, as of course are Aeneas and Cytherea. The latter marriage is never consummated because by a desperate rush across the country Cytherea's brother and other lover arrive in time to give the news that the marriage may be illegal. There is something both comic and prurient in this rush because, though we know why Owen Graye and Edward Springrove are in such a hurry, this fact can never be actually stated. Finally to avoid suspicion of murder Aeneas sets up house with Anne Seaway, thought to be his wife, but in fact clearly a fallen woman, whose morality and motives for joining Aeneas are never really discussed.

Early in the story there is a remarkable scene where Cytherea Aldclyffe gets into bed with Cytherea Graye with whom she has lived as her lady's maid. Critics have been keen to see lesbian implications in this episode, perhaps too keen, as Hardy is at pains to suggest that there is nothing wrong about it, and Miss Aldclyffe's two love affairs in her youth would suggest that she is heterosexual.[11] In addition her extraordinary Christian name is the name of the goddess of love, Aphrodite or Venus. She is anxious to secure the marriage of her namesake with her son in the same way as Venus interferes in the *Aeneid* to make Dido fall in love with her son Aeneas. The classical parallels do not really work, as there is a great difference between Cytherea Graye and the queen of Carthage and an even greater difference between Virgil's pious Aeneas and the murderous Manston.

There are much more useful lessons from Virgil in two of Hardy's more successful novels, *Under the Greenwood Tree* and *Far from the Madding Crowd* which can be compared to Virgil's *Eclogues* and *Georgics* respectively. Sex hardly enters into the pastoral world of *Under the Greenwood Tree* whereas the less artificial world of *Far from the Madding Crowd* contains, as does the *Georgics*, work and woe as an integral part of country life. Unlike Fancy Day, Bathsheba Everdene is a sexual being, as we can see in her provocative behaviour to Boldwood and Gabriel Oak as well as in her courtship by Sergeant Troy. The famous sword dance is full of sexual symbols which passed uncensored, whereas, as Leslie Stephen noted, Hardy had to be very careful in describing the story of Fanny Robin.[12]

This is a pity because Fanny Robin's fate becomes a little obscure. Though Troy is a man who lives entirely for the present, we are not told why he deserts her. She dies in childbirth in October, presumably becoming pregnant in January at about the same time as she ran away to the barracks in Casterbridge. The confusion between All Saints and All Souls is described just after the sending of the letter to Boldwood on Valentine's Day, and the failed marriage could presumably have been an attempt by Troy to do the decent thing when Fanny discovered she was pregnant. The ensuing humiliation might have led Troy to reject Fanny, and her to leave the northern town where Troy's regiment was stationed to take up lodgings in Melchester as a seamstress. Unlike Hetty Sorrel, Fanny Robin runs from her lover towards her home when she is pregnant, and unlike in George Eliot's novel, to which *Far from the Madding Crowd* was compared, there is no real reason why Troy and Fanny should not have married, as there was no class barrier between them, and Troy, as we discover at the time of her death, does seem if a little theatrically to show a genuine love for Fanny Robin. In the serial version of the story Fanny's pregnancy had to be handled with such care that we miss the poignant description of the mother and baby in their coffin, presumably omitted because it contained no hint of moral aversion. Much indeed is omitted in Fanny Robin's story, and in trying to fill in the gaps we are in danger of treating people in books as if they were characters in real life. It is part of the trouble of books like *Far from the Madding Crowd* written under the restrictions of Victorian prudery that characters in them have so much of their real life omitted. Fanny Robin's story does seem to be an expurgated version of Tess's tragedy. There are curious resemblances between Sergeant Troy and Alec d'Urberville, both caught rather uneasily between aristocratic pretensions and plebeian reality, evil motives and histrionic good intentions.

Hardy was later to have trouble with both kinds of hostility to his treatment of sexuality, the hostility that objected to any mention of fallen women, and the hostility that objected to them being mentioned without the appropriate denunciation of their fallen state. There could be little objection to the novels that preceded and followed *Far from the Madding Crowd*, namely *A Pair of Blue Eyes* and *The Hand of Ethelberta*. It is possible to see the strong influence of Emma Gifford in these novels. To the Cornish setting of the former, the Rouen scenes in the latter, the interest in the peerage and some fairly straightforward social snobbery we can add some prudish touches in both novels, though Leslie Stephen still found cause for complaint in the use of the word 'amorous' and a close embrace in *The Hand of Ethelberta*.[13] In both novels the heroine is courted by four suitors, but sexuality is strongly suppressed in all eight courtships. Lord Mountclere, Ethelberta's last and most successful suitor, provides a small element of sexual disreputability in that his proposal is felt initially to be dishonourable, and he does have a mistress, fancifully called Miss Grouchette, hired like Tess Durbeyfield nominally to look after the poultry. But rather flatly Miss Grouchette is sent packing, and Ethelberta succeeds in reforming the wicked viscount.

In *A Pair of Blue Eyes* sexual attraction on both sides is more apparent in the love affairs of Elfride Swancourt and her middle two lovers, Stephen Smith the architect and Henry Knight the man of letters, with both of whom Hardy could identify. Lord Luxellian, Elfride Swancourt's eventual husband, is a more shadowy figure, and his courtship seems prompted at least in part by a wish to find a mother for his two small daughters. In an episode which is reminiscent of the hurried train journeys of *Desperate Remedies*, Stephen Smith and Elfride Swancourt plan to get married first in Plymouth, then in London, but though they contrive to be alone in various railway carriages nothing untoward occurs, although there is much talk of the impropriety of these headlong travels. Later, Knight questions Elfride about this escapade and asks, 'Did you return home the same day on which you left it?'. She replies 'No', and all is over between them.[14]

One could hardly ask for a more ludicrous expression of strict adherence to Victorian propriety and yet Hardy supplied this in the previous scene, where Knight nearly falls down a cliff and Elfride rescues him with an improvised rope supplied from her undergarments to remove which she modestly has to retire. Neither the cliff nor the rope seem terribly realistic, and with a man's life at stake modesty might not seem to be the highest priority.

One cannot help feeling that Hardy was secretly laughing at Victorian conventions when he makes Knight nearly lose his life through Elfride having to observe these conventions, and when later he makes him lose his wife because he cannot ask directly whether Elfride has slept with Smith. There is also a rather distressing prurience about the repeated way Hardy returns, albeit with discreet circumlocutions, to the abandoned undergarments with phrases like 'her form was singularly attenuated'.[15] Symbolically of course the initial rescue and the later rejection do work, showing Elfride's willingness to abandon herself to sexuality, and Knight's cold-blooded rejection of it. He does not even kiss her when she has rescued him, owing to his peculiarity of nature. He has not even the excuse at that stage of knowing how scantily dressed she is.

In *The Return of the Native* Hardy succeeded in breaking free of the prudish shackles imposed by Leslie Stephen as editor of the *Cornhill*, publishing the story originally in the *Belgravia* – but not before Stephen had forced some changes to the story.[16] In this case Hardy did not revert to his original ideas, to be found in the manuscript, but kept the changes when he published the novel in book form. Originally it was intended that the marriage between Thomasin and Wildeve, which is thwarted at the beginning of the book because the licence is not correct, should have taken place but would have been discovered to be improper after the couple had been together a week. Such a change would have put the innocent Thomasin in an awkward position; and in fact traces of the original idea can be found in the frequent references Mrs Yeobright makes to Thomasin's disgrace as if it were a cause of moral reprobation rather than social embarrassment.[17] Thus Thomasin was originally cast in a more tragic role, and the tragedy would have been reinforced by making the reddleman disappear from the Heath and her remaining a lonely widow. Thomasin is an attractive if slight figure and does not deserve unhappiness, but in making her find happiness with Diggory Venn Hardy strains our sympathies. The reddleman has a portentous appearance but turns out to be rather an ordinary young man. In his spying on Eustacia Vye and Wildeve he seems like a voyeur, and his insistence that Wildeve marries Thomasin to make an honest woman of her seems a little perverted.[18] We cannot imagine Gabriel Oak creeping up on Sergeant Troy and Fanny

Robin covered in turves; and it is Boldwood who makes himself ridiculous by insisting that Troy marries Bathsheba whom he wants for himself.

Thus in making Venn and Thomasin the couple rewarded for virtue Hardy's text is not saying all that much for conventional virtue, and the same is true when we look at the erring couple Damon Wildeve and Eustacia Vye. Originally it would seem that Eustacia was intended to be a more witch-like and wicked figure, but in fact in all versions of the novel in print she attracts much of the sympathy originally intended for Thomasin. Her early death is that reserved for fallen women, although Hardy leaves it ambiguous whether this death is suicide or an accident, just as it is ambiguous whether Eustacia intended to run away with Wildeve or just to run away. Running away from Clym Yeobright may seem deplorable, but he is a tiresome character, insensitive to Eustacia's aspirations, and Eustacia is not at all to blame for the apparent rejection of Mrs Yeobright. The latter, like Mrs Morel, is no great advertisement for strait-laced morality, and we do not like her hostility to Eustacia and to Wildeve who is far too sensitive a man to fit the role of the conventional villainous seducer. It is not at all clear why Mrs Yeobright objected to the marriage of her niece with Wildeve or indeed how the couple after one false start overcame these objections. Presumably the bar was Wildeve's association with Eustacia, although this association before either party had married is treated in a very gingerly fashion. It is clear that it was a sexual association, but only just clear. Hardy added a few phrases like 'body and soul' in the 1895 version, although surprisingly he altered this to 'life and soul' in the 1912 edition.[19]

It was wrong for Eustacia to run away from her husband, and for Wildeve, whose adulterous intentions are clear, to try and join her. People leave their spouses all the time these days and are not usually drowned for their pains. In punishing Eustacia and Wildeve with death but not with disapproval Hardy shows himself as so often halfway between Victorian and modern times. Of course – and here Hardy is more modern – *The Return of the Native* is an attack on the institution of marriage, an attack somewhat camouflaged by the unsatisfactory marriage of Thomasin at the end. Both Wildeve and Eustacia marry for the wrong reasons, Wildeve out of pique and Eustacia to escape from the Heath. It was a good idea to give her Corfiote ancestry, thus associating her with Odysseus, a wanderer not notorious for marital fidelity. In many ways *The Return of the Native* anticipates, though in a less blatant fashion, the attack on marriage in *Jude the Obscure*, where nature intends Jude and Sue for each other, but a series of unlucky accidents and the force of social convention separate them.

Anne Garland marries the wrong man in *The Trumpet-Major*, preferring the scapegrace Bob Loveday to his worthy brother John, who returns to die in the Peninsular War. Bob is more dashing than John, it being typical of his feckless charm that he should become entangled with the actress Matilda Johnson. Matilda is clearly a woman of low morals, although the comic treatment of her is not without sympathy. She does her best to save Bob Loveday from the press-gang; and her eventual marriage to the comic villain Festus Derryman represents some kind of reclamation to respectability. Derryman's own attempts on Anne Garland are ineffective and ridiculous. Though *The Trumpet-Major* greatly pleased contemporary reviewers, Hardy never, except perhaps in *The Well-Beloved*, returned to the comic treatment of sex.

A Laodicean, written at a time when Hardy was gravely ill, is another novel in which the influence of Hardy's wife has been traced.[20] There is much snobbery and little sexuality, although some reviewers took exception to the rather ludicrous episode in Book 2, chapter 7, where Paula Power is watched secretly by Captain de Stancy performing gymnastic exercises in a pink flannel costume. Actually this chapter is rather useful in drawing attention to the sexual instincts of Captain de Stancy, long repressed after a youthful indiscretion as a result of which he has an illegitimate son. He professes penitence towards the mother of this son (William Dare), of whose presence he is ashamed, but carries on a long courtship of Paula, the rich heiress who owns his ancestral castle. Eventually Paula yields to his suit although she really loves the architect George Somerset. De Stancy's title and noble blood, false reports against Somerset of profligacy and drunkenness spread by Dare, and the evil influence of her uncle, Abner Power, all combine to bring about an engagement. Two hours before the wedding Paula is informed that the rumours about Somerset are false and that Dare is a villain. De Stancy confesses that Dare is his son, and Paula refuses to marry him. In view of her Low Church upbringing and her previous condemnation of Somerset, whom she loved, for drinking and gambling, this revulsion against sexual immorality is fully in character, but we need not think that in making Paula reject de Stancy for a youthful escapade of which he repented Hardy was really joining forces with Mrs Grundy. The title *A Laodicean* would seem to reflect Hardy's own uncertainty about right and wrong at the time the novel was written, and it is interesting that of the three villains of the novel de Stancy is easily the most likeable, his sexual lapse fading into insignificance when compared to his son's arson and fraud, and Paula's uncle's murderous conduct during his youth. De Stancy, like Sergeant Troy, is a soldier, but his long and clumsy courtship reminds us more of Gabriel Oak, and at times we feel sorry that it is not rewarded in the same way.

Two on a Tower represents the half-way point in Hardy's career as a novelist, and it is the first novel in which we find Hardy both attacking and being attacked by Mrs Grundy in a way that made Leslie Stephen's objections seem insignificant. Lady Constantine has strong sexual feelings for a man younger than herself and of an inferior social status. So has Lady Castlewood, but this is not made plain until the end of Thackeray's novel. Another titled lady to fall in love with her social inferior is Lady Chatterley, but Hardy handles his love affair in a very different fashion from Lawrence, because there is no open love-making, and Swithin St Cleeve and Viviette Constantine are a very high-minded couple who try to regularise their union by getting married in secret.

Unfortunately it transpires that Viviette's first husband, presumed dead in Africa at the time of the supposed marriage, had in fact survived until six weeks after it. Sir Blount Constantine is as frightful a husband as Sir Clifford Chatterley but in a very different way. He 'corrupts the village boys' at the time of their confirmation, a nice comic touch presumably inserted without any homosexual implications, and marries a native princess in Africa shortly before blowing his brains out, an improbable piece of melodrama. Nevertheless he insists on strict standards of chastity and decorum for his wife, who gains our sympathy as a result of this outrageous exploitation of the double standard. His survival after his wife has thought him dead is the final piece of vengeance on his part, although this is hardly his fault and in a way he gives some kind of warning in the macabre episode when Swithin puts on his clothes and is mistaken for his ghost at about the time of his real death.

The death is announced to Lady Constantine on 29 June. The previous night Swithin had slept in her house before going to Greenwich, but in a separate bedroom. Viviette's brother hopes to trap them together, but is foiled when Swithin is discovered to have left his room only to make astronomical observations. Lady Constantine hastens to write to Swithin and they plan to get married, but when Swithin returns she discovers that he will lose a legacy if he marries before he is twenty-five, and they decide heroically to separate until that period has elapsed. For a week she refuses to see him, but there is one prolonged meeting where they say goodbye, and Swithin prepares to depart for South Africa. He sets sail on 25 August, the day on which Viviette discovers she is pregnant. A frantic journey to Southampton and equally frantic telegrams are of no avail and, with her brother's connivance, Lady Constantine improbably marries the Bishop of Melchester in early September. A baby is born on 10 April.

Critics objected to the deception of the bishop, who is presented as a rather self-centred figure. Like Mr Collins he does most of his courtship by correspondence, and flirts archly with Viviette while at the same time hypocritically denouncing Swithin for his alleged sexual immorality. The child is passed off as the bishop's son, and here, as in the case of Hetty Sorrel, the novelist has to be very careful with dates in a very limited space of time. Viviette has to know that the child is Swithin's and for the sake of her honour has to pass it off as the bishop's. It is not clear that either Hardy or his heroine quite succeeds. Tongues wag in the village about the healthy appearance of what should have been a seven-month baby; and the bishop's premature death and Viviette's premature ageing could have been the result of tongues wagging about such a hasty birth following a hasty wedding or of suspicions by the bishop of his wife's fidelity. The novelist does not tell us about this, but perhaps the gossip and suspicions were all the worse for never being uttered.

There is one other cause for complaint, made more complicated by Hardy's additions to the text. In the third edition of the novel in 1883 he gave the date of the final meeting of the lovers before Swithin's departure as 7 July. In 1895, at the time of the composition of *Jude the Obscure* and perhaps as part of the boldness of the later novel, he added two short passages about this meeting, namely 'Viviette yielded to all the passion of her first union with him' and 'I ought not to have consented to that last interview; all was well until then'.[21] These additions emphasise that it was at this meeting that the baby was conceived, and of course this conception took place at a time when both partners knew that they were not legally married.

Unfortunately Hardy confused the issue by saying in the preface to the 1895 edition, 'there is hardly a single caress in the book outside matrimony, or what was intended so to be'. As one biographer has rather sourly remarked the final caress must have been a prolonged one, and the preface shows Hardy in an unattractive mixture of evasion and self-righteousness.[22] In addition, the date of 7 July appears to be wrong, as Hardy seems to have forgotten that Swithin was away in Greenwich for about five days after the night of 28 June when he slept in Welland House and was then banished from the company of Lady Constantine for a week after his return.

Three or four days may not seem much to worry about. Perhaps Hardy exaggerated in saying that Lady Constantine immured herself for a week. Swithin is only denied admittance to her three times, and he should have called every day. But the date, whether right or wrong, and the separation of the two lovers for at least ten days are designed to hammer home the message that the lovers conceive the child when they know they are not married. One wonders why Hardy went to such elaborate lengths to labour this point. We have shown that in Hardy's family weddings sometimes took place when the mother was heavily pregnant and Hardy must have acquired a countryman's knowledge of conception and birth, even if he lacked scientific exactitude. Lady Constantine should have guessed that she was pregnant some forty days after the conception of the child. The occurrence of St Swithin's Day on 15 July and the legend about the forty days of rain afterwards might have made 15 July a more suitable date for the last meeting. As it is Swithin seems to spend rather too long a time in England making his preparations, and Viviette takes rather too long a time in discovering she is pregnant.[23]

It would have been just possible for Viviette and Swithin to have met for the last time as lovers as late as 15 July, while thinking they were married, and for Hardy to have fitted in the news from Africa, the discovery of the legacy and the preparations of Swithin in the forty days. Presumably Hardy made Viviette conceive their child in sin, and what they knew to be sin, as part of his protest against the binding force of the marriage tie. This was a bold gesture, although modern readers can hardly find the two lovers very wicked because, after sinning for six months without knowing it, they sin for one last time in full knowledge of what they are doing. Lady Constantine's action in marrying the bishop may seem slightly more wicked, but again can be seen as part of a protest against the absurd conventions hedging in a lady's honour. Her action would of course be less explicable if she was not conscious of sin, as, if she had conceived when thinking she was married, she should have confessed all to the bishop, and he would surely as an influential master of the Establishment have been able to summon Swithin back from the ends of the earth, or find out the incompetent cleric who conducted the false marriage, or somehow arrange for a genuine mistake to be rectified.

Thus *Two on a Tower*, never regarded as one of Hardy's greatest achievements, must take its place as one of his more outspoken protests against Victorian sexual morality, even though he did not make the precise nature of his outburst clear until 1895 when with the writing of *Jude the Obscure* he was taking on Mrs Grundy for the last time. Deepening pessimism and a lack of sympathy with his wife make most of Hardy's remaining novels reinforce this attack on convention. In *The Mayor of Casterbridge* the powerful personality of Michael Henchard is such that all other characters, male and female, seem uninteresting. Henchard is of course a sexual sinner, both in disregarding the marriage tie by selling his wife in a drunken moment to Newson and in compromising Lucetta in Jersey. The degree of intimacy between Lucetta and Henchard had to be skirted over delicately in the magazine version of the novel, as indeed did the fact that Lucetta's death was caused by her perfectly respectable pregnancy.[24] Lucetta is, however, not respectable, although she does not deserve the premature death desired by respectable Victorian middle-class readers or the skimmity ride devised by the ribald Dorset peasantry. She tries to confess her sins to Farfrae, but it is hinted after her death that this death is somehow preferable to dishonour. 'Farfrae could not but perceive that by the death of Lucetta he exchanged a looming misery for a simple sorrow.'[25]

The predicament of a woman who has had a lover before her

marriage is one familiar to modern readers. Modern husbands are less likely to be so upset or so unforgiving as Farfrae or Angel Clare or Henry Knight, who has nothing to forgive; and Hardy's novels may have helped to bring about this change of attitude. While with one hand Hardy reaches out to the twentieth-century with the other he goes back to the eighteenth in that the incident where Henchard sells his wife for five pounds at the beginning of the novel seems to modern readers to be almost incredible. Susan Henchard turns out to be a colourless character, and we find it hard to remember that she lives in sin with Newson for a number of years. Hardy tries to make her respectable by getting both her and Newson to say that she was brought to admit the error of her ways.[26] Elizabeth Jane was originally intended to be Henchard's child; making her Newson's daughter is an important part of the plot, but it does render her illegitimate, although, oddly, she more than any other character in a novel full of good intentions is keen to do the right thing. She is rewarded with some degree of tranquillity as an adult when her youth 'had seemed to teach that happiness was but an occasional episode in a general drama of pain'.[27]

Henchard's life is a general drama of pain, and occasional episodes with Lucetta and the drunken escapade in the furmity tent do not seem to merit the harsh punishment he receives. His courage, generosity, strong will and honesty mark him out for admiration; and his fall seems not to be the result of his sexual peccadilloes but is to be blamed on blind chance and the vagaries of the corn trade. In creating such a character Hardy came dangerously close to flouting Victorian sensibilities, although lip service to decorum is paid by the fact that all the sexual sinners in *The Mayor of Casterbridge* meet an early death apart from Captain Newson. He heroically feigns an early death in order to release Susan from an illegal union, although ironically it is this pious tribute to conventional morality which causes such distress to the main characters.

In *The Woodlanders* it is not the sexual sinners who are the main sufferers. Giles Winterbourne nobly, though ill, remains outside in the rain to preserve Grace Melbury's honour as she stays in his hut in the woods, and dies as a result, whereas Fitzpiers who has had affairs with Mrs Charmond and Suke Damson is reunited to Grace, although it is hinted that they will not be happy and that he will have further affairs. Mrs Charmond dies a melodramatic death on the continent, shot by a former lover, although it is hinted in the 1895 version of the book that death was hastened by pregnancy. Suke Damson emigrates to New Zealand, a variation on Australia or death as the destination of fallen women. Her liaison with Fitzpiers is described much more openly in the 1895 edition than in either the serial or the first three-volume and one-volume editions prepared in 1887. As a result of criticisms made by *The Spectator* Hardy did in the three-volume edition do something to blacken the character of Fitzpiers, although he is never the complete villain.[28]

The most interesting character in the book is Grace Melbury. She marries Fitzpiers for the wrong reasons, snobbery and curiosity making him seem preferable to the homely and gentle Giles. On discovering Fitzpiers's behaviour with Suke and Mrs Charmond she realises she is in love with Giles Winterbourne, and, especially in the 1895 version, is fairly open in describing the physical nature of this love. 'Come to me, dearest! I don't mind what they say, or what they think of us anymore'.[29] Heroically Giles refuses; and dies as a result. Shattered by remorse Grace is reunited to Fitzpiers in an odd incident when they both nearly fall victim to a man-trap laid by Suke Damson's husband. She escapes, minus her skirt, and her father on hearing that the pair are united reflects bitterly, 'Well he is her husband, . . . and let her take him back to her bed if she will'.[30] The last half of this sentence and further bitter reflections on the future unfaithfulness of Fitzpiers were only added in 1895, but in all versions of the novel the nature of Grace's sexual drive is fairly clear, although disguised usually by the convention that heavy breathing is used to express desire. The man-trap does not actually catch Fitzpiers, for whom it is intended, but only Grace's skirt, and therefore it is difficult to see it as a symbol of female sexuality entrapping men, although it is possible to read some of Hardy's novels in this antifeminist light.

Tess is of course the trapped rather than the trapper, and Hardy's most famous heroine like the wounded birds she pities is the victim of male sexuality, as frequent images of piercing and wounding make clear. She is also the victim of Victorian convention which turns Angel and all respectable folk against her. Angel is no Giles Winterbourne. He has sinned in his youth and makes improper advances to Izzy when disappointed in Tess. Similarly Alec in his brief conversion to the role of Evangelical preacher has an outrageously moral side to him to balance his role as the selfish seducer. Caught between these two forces Tess stands no chance, but Hardy stood no chance against the forces of public opinion when he gave *Tess of the d'Urbervilles* the defiant sub-title *A Pure Woman*.

The two episodes most likely to call Tess's purity in question are her original seduction and her decision to join Alec when Angel has deserted her. In the serial version of the book Hardy got round these difficulties rather crudely by having a mock-marriage and by having Tess and Alec sleep in separate bedrooms in Sandbourne.[31] These changes of course make Tess's sense of guilt and her murder of Alec far less easy to explain. When the novel was printed as a book Hardy still in a sense slid past the difficulties by presenting the novel in phases, so we never actually know what happened in the few weeks between the time Tess was seduced and the time she discovered she was pregnant, or in the few weeks after Tess has written her last desperate letter to Angel and the time he discovers her and Alec together. Tess must have had some knowledge of what was happening both at the time of her first and second seduction, and, though her innocence in the first instance and her unhappiness in the second are obvious, to remove all the responsibility from her is to demean her status as a human being.

It seems odd that Hardy should not have been aware of the furore he was likely to arouse by insisting on Tess's purity and mocking the conventions that destroyed her. Tess's cruel death might seem part of these conventions, although it is recorded in conjunction with the association of Angel and Tess's sister Liza-Lu. Carping critics complained that Angel should have been in prison for complicity in murder and should not have been holding hands with Liza-Lu because he was prevented from marrying his deceased wife's sister.[32] Foolishly Hardy tried to take on these critics at their own game and equally foolishly he maintained that his next novel, *The Well-Beloved*, was totally innocent.[33] This novel was published as a serial in 1892, but not published in book form until 1897. Oddly and almost uniquely the serial version might seem to tread on more dangerous ground than the book, since in the former the hero Jocelyn Pierston first marries Marcia Bencomb, thus missing the chance of marrying the well-beloved, the first Avice Caro, and at the end of the novel marries the third Avice, granddaughter of the first, although the marriage is annulled when Marcia returns. In the final version there are none of these divorces, although it would seem that Jocelyn lives in sin with Marcia without being married to her. Most of Jocelyn's sexuality seems cerebral rather than physical, although we are not totally surprised that the critical Establishment, now used to finding fault with Hardy's novels in the same way that it had earlier attacked the novels of the Brontës, found something to cavil against in *The Well-Beloved*.

There was even, from a reviewer in *The World*, a not very kind pun about sex and Wessex.[34] Like Hardy's own more tragic pun from Father Time in *Jude the Obscure* 'we are too menny' this pun does raise the possibility that Hardy envisaged human sexuality as a ghastly mistake, entrapping men into marriages that lead nowhere.[35] This is what happens to Jude who on one reading of the novel falls like Tess through sex into another's clutches and is unable to escape from Arabella in much the same way as Tess is unable to escape from Alec. Although Sue like Angel provides the possibility of a better match, eventually both Tess and Jude return unhappily to their former lovers and an early death. Though there is some evidence for Hardy seeing Jude as the male innocent equivalent of Tess, this of course is a very schematic reading of both novels.[36] It ignores the decline of rural England in both novels; Jude's aspiration to Christminster and the curse of the d'Urbervilles; and more importantly it ignores the responsibility of both Sue and Angel for the downfall of Jude and Tess. Angel's prudery is less complicated than Sue's, although both have associations with the Church and show at times a superficial resentment against its teachings. Sue does show some sexual frigidity, although only in contact with the unattractive Phillotson; with Jude she seems to live perfectly happily and is frequently pregnant by him. The happy sex life of Jude and Sue is hardly stressed in the novel, more emphasis being laid on their companionship, but this may be a result of the absurd bowdlerisation forced upon Hardy for the serial version in which there were omitted many details of Arabella's courtship of Jude, including the false pregnancy, Sue's aversion to Phillotson, and even the fact that Jude and Sue lived together. Only one child is killed by Father Time in the serial version, and that one is adopted.[37] In the final version Sue Bridehead is still an enigmatic figure, a representative of the new woman that shocked so many in the nineteenth-century, more comprehensible in the twentieth-century where such women have asserted their rights, but have still not found their role.[38]

With Sue Bridehead and Tess Durbeyfield we return to the point from which we began. Both characters seem to represent an attack on institutions of Victorian society that are less hallowed today: the purity of the female sex and the sanctity of marriage. The shocked reception of both characters and the absurd lengths to which Hardy was forced to go in order to render their exploits palatable indicate a further difference between our age and that of the Victorians, well emphasised by Hardy in his essay on 'Candour in English Fiction', where he says that, 'English Society imposes a well-nigh insuperable bar' to a frank treatment of the relation between the sexes.[39] And yet Hardy and all the Victorian novelists under discussion did manage to overcome this bar and have something worthwhile to say on the subject of the relation of the sexes. The code under which they said it is a baffling one to modern readers, with – to take some rather ridiculous examples – heavy breathing indicating sexual desire, pregnancy indicating sexual relations, and a night together in a railway carriage or a wood being tantamount to the disgrace of the elopements in Jane Austen.[40] And of course the code demanded that a woman who had sexual relations with a man who was not her husband was disgraced for ever. Given the limitations of this code, Hardy contrived to make a powerful if pessimistic statement of the role of sexuality in human life. It is not all that pessimistic. Angel and Tess do have a brief idyll of happiness after the murder of Alec, and Sue and Jude live together quite contentedly for a number of years, even though not married. Such unions even though under obvious stress seem more satisfactory than the conventional and sentimental marriages of Laura and Pendennis or David Copperfield and Agnes. But even Dickens and Thackeray like their great female contemporaries are able to break through the restrictions of the code, better perhaps than writers of the twentieth-century, who, with no code to work with and no set of rules to rebel against, have in spite of endless explorations of male and female sexuality not come up with very many original contributions.[41]

8

Conclusion

Vague references to nineteenth and twentieth-century attitudes to sexuality are clearly misleading. Just as there were shifts in public opinion even during the reign of Queen Victoria, so, as has already been noted, there have been marked changes in sexual attitudes during the last thirty years. Some readers of this book can remember how in their youth both in literature and in life there was little mention of adultery, premarital sex or homosexuality, and how, if these subjects were mentioned, they were the objects of shocked disapproval. Twentieth-century classics like *Ulysses* were once classed as obscene publications, and Joyce like Lawrence was regarded as a dangerous author. This may seem surprising to students of literature brought up in our present sexually permissive era, and such students must find it even harder to understand the conventions under which nineteenth-century novelists wrote. Such students sometimes make the mistake of assuming that novelists of the nineteenth-century had nothing to say about sexual matters, or at any rate nothing that makes any sense in the modern world. Alternatively students are encouraged to think of the Victorians as inhabiting the same world as themselves, and write and read elaborate interpretations of nineteenth-century novels, designed to uncover hidden sexual meanings.

Modern critics have contributed to the latter tendency, and perhaps this is healthy, because the former tendency would seem to consign the nineteenth-century novel to oblivion. In *Desire and Domestic Fiction: A Political History of the Novel* (Oxford, 1987) Professor Nancy Armstrong might seem to be covering much the same ground as the present volume does, and certainly her book contains many references to Austen, Brontë, Dickens and sexuality. Her heavy concentration on theoretical issues fortunately prevents there being too much of an overlap, since this book has eschewed the fashionable reliance on theory, and concentrated instead on the texts of the novels. Rather unkindly we can select

Armstrong's book as an example of how an interest in theory can lead to a neglect of the text. In trying to show how the two most famous Brontë novels end with an ascendant heroine taming male desire Armstrong refers to the move from Wuthering Heights to the more effeminate surroundings of Thrushcross Grange and the move from Thornfield to Ferndean Manor.[1] It is unfortunate that she calls the latter 'a bungalow on the estate' and that she says that the younger Catherine asserts her feminine power over Hareton by ordering him to plant a flowerbed among the wild brambles. The wild brambles are in fact blackcurrants which Heathcliff, no stranger to homely domestic tastes, promptly orders Hareton to replace. Similarly, though there are no mad-women in the attics at Ferndean Manor, there is no evidence that the house has but a single storey, and it is not on the same estate as Thornfield was.

In modern times Rochester might well retreat to a bungalow,[2] and Jane would have had few qualms about sleeping on the same floor if not in the same room as her future husband. As it is, Jane with perfect propriety runs upstairs the first night she arrives at Ferndean before coming down to breakfast the next morning. Victorians noticed these little gems of decorum. We have seen how with an absurd sense of propriety Hardy had in the serial version of *Tess of the d'Urbervilles* to make his poor heroine sleep in a separate bedroom away from her former seducer, even though she had clearly compromised herself by going to live with him. Times have changed, although they have not changed so much that the greatest novelists cannot bridge the gap between the centuries.

Lesser novelists are less able to do this. We began with Mrs Henry Wood, whose morality seemed lax to some Victorians, ludicrous to most of us. Gaskell was censorious about Eliot's life and surprisingly about Brontë's books.[3] Fallen women are found in her own novels and stories, but with the notable exception of *Ruth* (1853) attention is deliberately diverted from the fallen woman, who occupies a subsidiary position. Thus in *Mary Barton* (1848) Esther Barton only appears, suitably rouged and degraded, to act as a warning to her niece who might have been seduced, but is not. In the short story 'Lizzie Leigh' (1850) the interest lies in the fallen woman's mother; in 'The Poor Clare' (1856) Mary Fitzgerald, who is seduced, hardly appears in the story and we instead are asked to concentrate on her mother and daughter.

Ruth does of course have a technically fallen woman as its central character. This novel caused a considerable stir. In later novels like *Sylvia's Lovers* (1863) and *Cousin Phillis* (1863) the subject of female love is handled with such delicacy that modern readers have tended to shy away from this aspect of Gaskell's work and look instead to her as the novelist of industrial unrest. She was of course interested in prostitution as a social evil, sharing this interest with Dickens, to whose periodicals she was a regular if dilatory contributor. But Ruth is not a prostitute. Her innocence is stressed and her fall is not her fault but that of her guardian, her employer and her seducer. Victorian taste did not like this innocence stressed,[4] and modern taste finds it hard to believe. Ruth is rescued in her pregnancy by the crippled minister and his sister Faith. They and the maid Sally pass her off as a widow, and she takes up employment in the sternly religious Bradshaw family. Some Victorians found this subterfuge dishonourable; modern readers find it unnecessary and cannot understand the disapproval with which the Bensons and Sally temper their support and forgiveness. Eventually the seducer re-emerges with a different name and proposes unsuccessfully to Ruth, Mr Bradshaw discovers Ruth's story and is furious, and Ruth dies through nursing her former lover. Victorian taste did not hold with Gaskell's obvious disapproval of Mr Bradshaw's unforgiving attitude; modern taste sees nothing to forgive. Even Charlotte Brontë felt that Ruth's death was a mistake, though of course the conventional fate of the fallen woman; at least one modern critic has found the death appropriate, reversing the stock response of the nineteenth and twentieth-centuries. Clearly for both categories of readers *Ruth* is an uncomfortable book.[5]

Like Mrs Gaskell and unlike a great many Victorian novelists Trollope would appear to have led a happy married life. His impoverished and unfortunate youth may have given him a natural sympathy with the underdog, and fallen women are some kind of underdog. Trollope's mother certainly showed sympathy to fallen women and underdogs in *Jessie Phillips*, a work clearly designed to stand up for bastards and put seducers in their place. Trollope's most famous books steer clear of sexuality. In the Barchester novels Eleanor Bold is inappropriately named; she is part of ecclesiastical politics, but not of sexual politics. Lady Glencora in the Palliser novels is a little bolder. She hankers after an unworthy man who is not, nor cannot, be her husband, but somehow Trollope stops short of making her dilemma a real one. The same is true of Lady Laura Kennedy, unhappily married to someone she cannot love and therefore loving others she cannot marry. In *He Knew He Was Right* (1869) there is a splendid portrait of marital jealousy, but Louis Trevelyan's jealousy becomes less interesting when we know it is unfounded. Modern readers would find *Can You Forgive Her?* (1865) and *He Knew He Was Right* more exciting if Lady Glencora needed forgiving and if Louis Trevelyan had not been wrong.

It is a mistake to dismiss Trollope as wholly playing into the hands of Podsnap. His *The Way We Live Now* (1875) is a bitter satire against Victorian complacency. He does not fit in easily with any preconceived notions of a prudish Establishment. It is perhaps worth mentioning that, though Trollope suffered the indignity of having a story censored by Thackeray, his brother did marry Ellen Ternan's sister. Three late novels, *The Vicar of Bullhampton* (1870), *An Eye For An Eye* (1879) and *Dr Wortle's School* (1880) do show some concern for the fallen woman, although in a rather different way in each novel and a rather subdued way in every novel.

In *The Vicar Of Bullhampton* there is quite a long discussion in the preface about the problem of 'unfortunate' women like Carry Brattle, but in fact she has a subordinate position in the plot. There is little about Carry's seduction or her descent into prostitution, although plenty about the well-meaning efforts of Frank Fenwick, the vicar of the title, to reconcile Carry to her family. The family are not very forthcoming, and the eventual forgiveness of Jacob, Carry's father and the miller of Bullhampton, is grudging in the extreme. It is difficult for modern readers to appreciate how merciful and how moving Jacob's forgiveness is meant to be. Carry's future life, though better than death or Australia, hardly seems a bed of roses, and it seems odd to modern liberated minds that Jacob should indicate his forgiveness by the abrupt order to Carry's sister, who has pleaded on her behalf, that she should give him his breakfast.

Carry Brattle is not all that important in a novel which also includes a murder, in which her brother is involved; an ecclesiastical quarrel, in which the vicar is involved; and a more decorous love story, in which the squire of Bullhampton is involved. In *An Eye For An Eye*, however, the illicit love affair between Kate O'Hara

and Frank Neville is central to the story, but the story is told from
Frank's point of view, and appropriately it is he who finally falls,
being pushed over a cliff by Kate's mother. Kate manages to
survive, although in France rather than in Australia. Like Tess,
Hetty Sorrel and Little Em'ly, Kate is clearly of a social status
inferior to that of her seducer, although as the heir to an earldom
Frank Neville is superior in rank to his fellow seducers. There
would have been nothing wrong in the upstart Alec d'Urberville,
or Steerforth, marrying Kate, although the whole issue of social
snobbery in relation to the Irish is a complicated one. There are
many portraits in Victorian fiction of Irish people like Captain
Costigan in *Pendennis* lying about their ancient lineage, but in
such a pleasant manner that we almost believe them. Thackeray
makes Costigan's daughter in fact succeed in marrying into the
peerage. In *An Eye For An Eye* the balance of sympathy between
the Nevilles with their grand position and the O'Haras with their
grand pretensions is finely drawn. It is a pity that modern critical
attention, rightly oblivious to the antiquated social nuances of this
story, should have ignored its interesting moral message. There
would of course be little or no sympathy with Frank Neville now.[6]

After tragedy comedy. All's well that ends well in *Dr Wortle's
School*, since it turns out that the accomplished Mr Peacocke, an
assistant master at Dr Wortle's select establishment, can after all
be legally married, since Mrs Peacocke's first husband has conveniently died in America. The bigamy novel had quite a long
innings from the early 1860s to the 1880s.[7] *Dr Wortle's School* was
published shortly before *Two On A Tower*, where there is similar
bigamy, innocently entered into but less fortunately resolved.
Trollope's treatment of the affair largely turns on the appearance
of the scandal rather than the reality of the sexual connection, and
it was probably for this reason that Trollope was more successful
than Hardy in avoiding hostility from reviewers. Modern critical
judgement has not been able to make much of either novel. It is
perhaps unfortunate that Trollope's novel is set in a school which
can be compared to the setting of another comic novel written
over fifty years later. Evelyn Waugh's *Decline and Fall* (1928) has in
Captain Grimes an anti-hero of smaller classical attainments than
those of Mr Peacocke, but with a similar matrimonial background.
Although Waugh wrote well before the twentieth-century sexual
revolution and even before private education at schools like

Llanaba Castle became a bad joke, it is the easy tolerance of Captain Grimes's peccadilloes rather than the desperate defence of Mr Peacocke's sins which seem to strike a chord with modern readers. They are inclined to ignore the fact that Captain Grimes knows he is married when he proposes to his headmaster's daughter, while Mr Peacocke, as his headmaster is aware, is perfectly innocent.

Unlike Gaskell and Trollope, Wilkie Collins did not have an innocent private life, conducting not one but two prolonged relationships with women to whom he was not married. It is difficult to be certain about how far this unorthodox matrimonial record contributed to the writing and reception of unorthodox novels which received hostile reviews. Modern readers are unlikely to be overconcerned by Collins's affairs with Martha Rudd and Caroline Graves, and are not unduly alarmed by either his language or his attitudes in describing difficult sexual situations. There has indeed been recent critical interest in Collins, but this interest has not been able to bridge the gap between nineteenth and twentieth-century attitudes. Faced with Collins's reputation as a sexual revolutionary and the rather tame sexual encounters in his novels critics have not unreasonably tried to decode these novels to show some more subversive meaning.[8] There is little that is shocking in the two most famous novels, *The Women In White* (1860) and *The Moonstone* (1868), although in the former work we can see that the odd and presumably innocent attraction between the villainous but seductive Count Fosco and the vivacious but plain Marian Halcombe, is much more dynamic than the dull but decorous affair between Laura Fairlie, appropriately dressed in white, and the virtuous Walter Hartright. Throughout his career as a novelist Collins plays on the opposition between virtue and vice, light and dark, angel and whore, and subtly shows that the distinction in each case is not clear cut. Even in *The Moonstone*, Collins's most popular novel, and perhaps not coincidentally a novel in which sexuality does not play a leading part, there are odd references to the extramarital liaisons of both Franklin Blake, actually the culprit, though the hero of the story, and Geoffrey Ablewhite, clearly the villain, although admired for his appearance of virtue. Nevertheless, both *The Moonstone* and *The Woman In White* escaped Victorian calumny.

It was not so with Collins's other novels. Even *Antonina* (1850), a not very successful early period piece, was attacked for its French connections, a useful reminder of the difficulties the Brontës faced in 1848, the year of revolution in France and elsewhere. *Basil: A Story Of Modern Life* (1852) was thought to be far too modern, although it is difficult to see why *The Athenæum* called this story revolting and unwholesome.[9] Basil overhears his wife Margaret, with whom he has not consummated his marriage, making love to the villain Mannion. He is naturally appalled, but there is nothing particularly appalling in the description of the love-making or in the way that vice is punished or virtue rewarded. Mannion has his face pushed into the tar-macadam and then after vindictively pursuing Basil is pushed over a Cornish cliff. His fate and Margaret's fate seem appropriately worse than death. So too is the fate of Lydia Gwilt, the villainess in *Armadale* (1866), although in this case Collins might seem to have overstepped the mark of propriety, both in giving Lydia Gwilt attractive features and in frankly admitting the strength of her love for Ozias Midwinter.

In between these two novels Collins wrote *Hide And Seek* (1854), *The Dead Secret* (1857) and *No Name* (1862). In all these novels illegitimacy plays an important part, particularly in *No Name*, where the illegitimate heroine is appropriately called Magdalen Vanstone. This seems an act of defiance on Collins's part, as is his refusal to condemn his heroine for her unconventional behaviour in trying to restore her fortunes. After enticing one man to marry her Magdalen ends up a reformed character, wedded to another, an eminently respectable sea-captain. In *Man And Wife* (1870) Collins returned to the attack on the marriage laws and conventions. Anne Silvester, a governess, is seduced and has a stillborn baby but, in spite of this combination of undesirable attributes, survives an attempt on her life by her husband, whom she has cajoled into an odd marriage, and after his death marries a rich lawyer. All our sympathy is meant to be with her, and the villain of the novel is her husband, Geoffrey Delamyn, an unpleasant athlete.

In his attack on athleticism and defence of sexual unorthodoxy Collins is curiously anticipating E. M. Forster, whose *The Longest Journey* (1907) contains an unattractive athlete who dies like Geoffrey, and an illegitimate birth. The athletic contests do not ring true in either novel, but Forster's work is more attractive to modern audiences because he is more able to integrate his moral preaching into the body of the novel. Collins's failure to do so becomes prominent in his later work.[10] Adulterous passion is a feature of *The Law and the Lady* (1875), seen as an attack on Mrs Grundy and attacked by her, and comes into *The Two Destinies* (1876), dismissed by the *Saturday Review* as amazingly silly; and *The Black Robe* (1881), dismissed as unnatural in *The Spectator*. In *The Fallen Leaves* (1878), described by Swinburne as 'too absurdly repulsive for comment or endurance' and *The New Magdalen* (1873), Collins returns to the theme of the reformed prostitute.

Both are very odd novels by Victorian standards. In both cases the prostitute ends up respectably married. In both cases the prostitute and Collins regret the cold-hearted charity of homes for fallen women, refuges only in name because of the stigma they carry with them. There is surprising emphasis on the beauty of simple Sally in *The Fallen Leaves* and the moral strength of Mercy Meyrick in *The New Magdalen*. Mercy, unable to find acceptance by society because of her past, takes on the identity of Grace Roseberry, supposed to be dead, but even this lie does not reduce her stature, and when Grace returns from the dead it is she like Regina in *The Fallen Leaves* who rouses our indignation because of her conventional pharisaical rejection of Mercy. *The Fallen Leaves* would not be a bad title for a discussion of unknown Victorian novels which are now totally neglected, in spite of, not because of, their far from Victorian unconventionality in sexual matters.[11]

Charles Reade is almost unknown today. There have been no recent biographical studies and only two critical books on him in the last thirty years.[12] *The Cloister and the Hearth* (1861) is vaguely known as a dim period piece, but even accomplished Victorian scholars would have difficulty if asked to say much about many of Reade's other works. It is therefore surprising to read contemporary reviews comparing Reade with Thackeray, Dickens and Eliot. Admittedly these comparisons were usually unfavourable, but not always so. Henry Kingsley, himself unfavourably compared to Reade, thought that *A Terrible Temptation* (1871) was the worst novel he had ever read and he thought *The Mill On The Floss* the best, but Henry James, a greater novelist than Kingsley, preferred *The Cloister and the Hearth* to *Romola*.[13]

Reade's popularity in Victorian times and neglect today can be attributed to various causes, but not to a change in sexual mores.

For both in his life and in his novels Reade hardly conforms to any real or imagined Victorian stereotype. Faced with celibacy by his fellowship at Magdalen College, Oxford; his inability to earn any other form of living; and perhaps by his eccentricity and the strong influence of his religious mother, Reade found some kind of compensation. An affair with a Scotswoman, the prototype of Christie Johnstone, a possible illegitimate child, friendships with actresses, and the long association with one of these actresses, Mrs Seymour, are well known and, had Reade been more studied in our permissive age, would surely have been explored. *The Cloister and the Hearth* is a frank investigation of the difficulties of celibacy. Bigamy, whether excusable or inexcusable, legitimacy and illegitimacy, and a wide range of fallen women of various classes and various degrees of guilt figure prominently in a number of novels, notably *White Lies* (1857), *Griffith Gaunt* (1866), *A Terrible Temptation* and *A Simpleton* (1873). There are some remarkably candid descriptions of sexual activity in Reade's published works and some even more remarkable passages in his rough drafts and voluminous notebooks, still imperfectly edited. Even more strikingly Reade, an unworldly bachelor, seems full of insights into feminine sexuality. *Hard Cash* (1863) is, as its title implies, more about money than love, and Reade's obsession with the laws governing lunacy in this novel as in others turns the work into a piece of dated propaganda, a fact which must contribute to the ephemerality of its appeal. Nevertheless the references to David Dodd's enforced celibacy at sea are interesting; this character appears in other Reade novels, and probably autobiography plays some part here. In addition, both the heroine of *Hard Cash*, Julia Hardie, who dies a virgin, and Mrs Archibald, the appropriately named villainous keeper of the lunatic asylum in which both Dodd and Julia's brother Alfred are incarcerated, have sexual longings which are described in an unusually explicit fashion.[14]

Reade did not of course escape censure. *A Terrible Temptation* was blasted in America as 'this mass of brothel garbage'.[15] Reade reacted to similar criticisms by publishing an article entitled 'The Prurient Prude'. The article is an unwise one, although it is possible to see in it Reade's curious innocence. In addition, though he does not establish the truth of the maxim that to the pure all things are pure, he is able to show that there is a good deal of impurity in the minds of those dedicated to stifling impurity in literature. Dickens, less innocent than Reade, objected to his contemporary's sexual frankness, although he also found much to praise, and his criticisms seem very odd to us today. Thus in writing to the far from innocent Wilkie Collins he found it indecent that Griffith Gaunt's two wives should examine his sons' 'little points' together. When Reade adapted Trollope's *Ralph the Heir* for the stage there were objections to the phrase, 'he must marry her in her smock'.[16]

In spite of these occasional excrescences of prudery Reade seemed to pass muster in Victorian circles. *Griffith Gaunt* first appeared in a magazine edited by Mrs Henry Wood. Reade is less anxious than Wood to preserve the technical innocence of his heroines, but as a general rule the truly virtuous are rewarded even if they are led by some mistake into sexual sin. So in *White Lies* Josephine Dujardin, who never intended to commit bigamy, is rewarded by the discovery that her first marriage could be dissolved because it had never been hallowed in church. So in *Griffith Gaunt* Mercy Vint, who has married Griffith in genuine error, is rewarded by marriage to Sir George Neville although she is only a publican's daughter. Kate Gaunt and Bella Bassett in *A Terrible Temptation* are suspected of adultery with clergymen, but the suspicions, though not unfounded, are false. In this novel the conduct of Rhoda Somerset, a courtesan, and her half-sister Peg is not exactly condoned. The former ends up as a nun, while the latter, whose gypsy ancestry is seen as an excuse for immoral actions, has her son, whom she has tried to pass off as heir to the Bassett estates, sent off to Australia, the traditional home of fallen women. It seems rather sad that what seemed so unconventional to the Victorians should seem so trite to us, but perhaps this is an explanation of the collapse of Reade's reputation.

In contrast Meredith's reputation has worn a little better, although he too was subject to hostility for certain of his publications. His own marital difficulties did not help his early career, although it seems extremely odd to us that *The Ordeal of Richard Feverel* (1859) should have been thought shocking.[17] Feverel's sexual misconduct with Mrs Mount is hardly described in graphic fashion or in any way condoned. *Rhoda Fleming* (1865) with its seductions and bogus marriages seems more shocking. As reader for Chapman & Hall Meredith had contact with major literary figures like Dickens, Eliot and Hardy, and there are odd references to his own literary prudery. *Modern Love*, published in 1862, is clearly not designed to appeal to Mr Podsnap, but poetry was not much read by the likes of Mr Podsnap, although *Modern Love*, like *The Ordeal of Richard Feverel* helped to preserve the reputation of Meredith as a dangerous author. In later works Meredith occasionally touches on sexual themes, but it seems to be a sign of the naughty nineties that *Diana of the Crossways* (1885), *One Of Our Conquerors* (1891) and *The Amazing Marriage* (1895) did not meet with all that many attacks, and that Meredith, awarded the Order of Merit in 1905, should have ended his life in a blaze of glory, respected as the chief writer of England.[18]

Hardy ended his life in a similar fashion, but *Tess of the d'Urbervilles* and *Jude the Obscure* met with all the hostility that Meredith's early works suffered and his later works escaped. It is hard to explain this phenomenon. Meredith does not make his sexual propaganda as blatant as that of Hardy, and seems to have carried into his own work prescriptions to Hardy about the need for caution. It is possible that the fact that Meredith wrote about aristocrats and Hardy about peasants in his two most outrageous novels may explain the different treatment the two novels received. Meredith's high-flown obscurity may be another factor. The aristocracy and the peasantry both in fiction and in fact were less subject than the middle-class to attacks from middle-class Podsnappery. Rather pathetically both Meredith and Hardy tried to rise above their humble origins. Meredith made the transition more successfully than Hardy, and was thus more popular with his contemporaries and less popular today.

Gissing's life and novels also show, almost too painfully, the difficulties of a sensitive late-Victorian man in disentangling the complex web of contemporary sexual and social politics. Heroically cutting the Gordian knot by marrying first a drunken prostitute and then an unintellectual member of the working class was clearly no answer, and few modern readers of Gissing can blame him for seeking refuge from this second marriage in an irregular liaison with a sympathetic Frenchwoman. Nor can they blame him for moving from portraits of prostitution and destitution in his earlier novels to more familiar middle-class territory in his later novels, or for often making his heroes have to choose between an available woman from the working classes and an unattainable middle-class lady. Indeed modern readers have done much to rescue Gissing from oblivion. There have been many modern studies of his life and his work.[19] These studies have shown, surprisingly, that Gissing was not all that unpopular in the nineteenth-century. There were general complaints about the grimness of his portraits, but reviews were satisfied with the propriety of his language, and could hardly complain that his general gloom supported the rewarding of vice. It is true that Bentley first censured and then suppressed a volume entitled *Mrs Grundy's Enemies*, and that *Punch* brutally excoriated *The Unclassed* in an article entitled rather salaciously, 'Gissing the Rod', but in general those who noticed Gissing showed remarkable restraint in their praise of the novelist for so bravely and so discreetly mentioning the unmentionable.[20]

Gissing's favourite novelist was Charlotte Brontë. He admired and was admired by Hardy, and he wrote a serious critical work on Dickens. His experiences as a novelist were very different from those of Gaskell. In part this can be attributed to the age in which he lived, in part to his gender. Eliot and Brontë suffered when it was known that they were women. One of the aims of this chapter and this book is to show how difficult it is to master the complexities of the Victorian age which spread over eight decades. Another is to show the different standards of sexual behaviour which were expected from men and from women. A third is to show the great gap in sexual morality and its depiction in fiction which seems to have opened up between ourselves and our forebears, and the ways in which the greatest novelists miraculously close this gap.

Eliza Lynn Linton, who lived from 1822 to 1898, is a minor novelist whom nobody now reads if indeed they have heard of her.[21] Conveniently the dates of her adult life almost coincide with the reign of Queen Victoria, and thus she could be seen as a barometer of taste during this reign. Equally conveniently she mixed with the great Victorian authors. Dickens bought Gads Hill from her. Brontë discussed Linton's novels with Lewes before the latter had met Eliot whom Linton knew before Eliot had met Lewes. Towards the end of her life Linton wrote disparagingly of the relationships of Lewes and Eliot. This disapproval seems oddly inconsistent with her own books being sternly regarded by Brontë and Eliot on account of their sexual immodesty. Brontë indeed in a surprising contrast preferred the prim and proper novels of

Austen to the windy wordiness of *Azeth the Egyptian* (1846).[22] Linton disapproved of, as well as inventing the name of 'The Girl of the Period' in 1868. This girl we feel is the mother of the New Woman of the 1890s, and yet Linton joined Hardy in 1890, albeit in a less violent form, in the debate on 'Candour in Fiction', saying sensibly that restraints imposed by circulating librarians 'cut off from fiction one of the largest and most important areas of that human life we preferred to portray'.[23] Not surprisingly Mrs Linton did not approve of Mrs Henry Wood.[24]

Linton, whose views on women are contradictory but hardly fashionable,[25] has for obvious reasons not been taken up by the twentieth-century any more than has Rhoda Broughton, the vicissitudes of whose reputation we have already charted in Chapter 1. In spite of the change of heart among her readers Broughton was always popular in her lifetime, but her reputation has never revived since her death. Her own life remains a mystery: an unhappy love affair is possible, but less easy to prove than Linton's unhappy marriage. Unlike Linton Broughton did not seem to dislike her own sex. Her heroines, longing to fall, but prevented almost by accident from falling, are attractive if artificial creations, just about passing muster in late Victorian times, but almost incomprehensible today. *Belinda* (1883) is an interesting novel in that Professor Forth, like Casaubon in *Middlemarch*, is supposed to be modelled on Mark Pattison. In Broughton's novel the equivalent of Dorothea is about to elope with the equivalent of Ladislaw, but is forced by their mutual guilt to return before anything untoward has occurred, only to discover that Forth/Casaubon has died, and that in this case his death has released her from a fate worse than death. We cannot see Eliot writing this novel, and this is not just because times had changed. In *Cometh Up as a Flower* (1867), written well before *Middlemarch*, Nell le Strange falls in love with a penniless soldier, but marries a boring if virtuous plutocrat. She dies technically innocent, but for loving someone other than her husband meets in her early death the conventional fate of a fallen woman. We cannot imagine such a novel meeting with any revival of interest among modern readers.[26]

In 1969 John Fowles published *The French Lieutenant's Woman*, a story about Victorian sexuality, involving appropriately a governess, written from a twentieth-century point of view. The one description in this book of sexual activity, lasting ninety seconds precisely, was considered fairly exciting in the swinging sixties, although now it seems fairly tame. In the novel Fowles makes several pointed references to the difference between present and past standards of sexual morality, to Hardy, and to Dickens. He also has a long chapter (35) describing how times have changed, beginning appropriately with the words 'What are we to make of the nineteenth-century?'. This chapter reinforces the rather obvious thrust of *The French Lieutenant's Woman*, that hidden behind the surface of nineteenth-century respectability twentieth-century sexual licence was rampant, and that a twentieth-century novelist was needed to give the key to this secret. Such a message is repeated in the film version of the novel, where unable to repeat the double if not triple ending of the book, the producers of the film have the characters in it behaving almost with nineteenth-century propriety and the people acting these characters rushing off in sin. Much the same message is found in Antonia Byatt's *Possession* (1990), where a Victorian love affair is a heavily shrouded scandal, revealed by two happy twentieth-century lovers who fall into bed when they have finally solved the nineteenth-century mystery.

Victorian novelists were interested in all aspects of human life, of which human sexuality is clearly an important part, if not the most important. Byatt's brilliant pastiche of her two Victorian lovers, poets rather than novelists, with its heavily concealed heady sexual symbolism, reinforces this point. Even if nineteenth-century novelists were prohibited by Mrs Grundy, Mr Podsnap, Mudies Circulating Library and various other pillars of the Victorian establishment from describing the sexual act in the graphic detail which was permitted to Victorian pornographers and modern novelists, they could still give interesting insights into sexual activity before and after, within and without, the institution of marriage, another topic of perennial interest. The lesser novelists, of whom this chapter has given an inadequate summary, failed to achieve true or perennial greatness, possibly because they were too anxious to impress or depress Mrs Grundy and her fellows, either taming their sexual scenes to suit the censor, or introducing these scenes and judgements on them as pieces of propaganda that fit in uneasily with the novels as a whole. Some novelists like Wood, with whom we began, both confront and collaborate with

Mrs Grundy in such a ridiculous fashion that they have vanished almost without trace. Not so Austen, Brontë, Eliot, Thackeray, Dickens and Hardy. They have transcended the barriers of sex, of class, of nation and of generation. *Jane Eyre* and *Oliver Twist* were read, enjoyed and approved of by Queen Victoria, and one hopes by the present Queen. One doubts if the novels of Jilly Cooper or Frederick Forsyth, allegedly the favourite reading of our modern rulers, would have been approved of by Queen Victoria.[27]

Notes

1 INTRODUCTION

1. H. Wood, *East Lynne*, with introduction by S. Davies (London, 1984). *East Lynne* was originally published in 1861. Davies supplies an excellent introduction and a short bibliography.
2. W. Hughes, *The Maniac in the Cellar* (Princeton, 1980), p. 111 makes the point. She is one of the few critics to consider Wood in a general discussion of Victorian fiction.
3. Spectacles of various shades occur in *East Lynne*; the pink eyeshade in *Lady Adelaide's Oath* (1867). There is a clumsy disguise involving a kind of return from the dead in *Verner's Pride* (1863) and in *Within the Maze* (1872) a genuine return from the dead and a character in green spectacles who turns out not to be the revived Sir Adam Andinnian, although we know he is going to be revived.
4. This happens in *Within the Maze*. Like the green spectacles the baronetcy is a clumsy device to enable the supposed Lady Andinnian to meet the recently revived baronet's wife and spread alarm and confusion. It may seem, and probably is, snobbish and pedantic to worry about these small details, but as Jane Austen might have cruelly pointed out, this carelessness in small details does suggest a certain crudity in major moral issues.
5. In *Mrs Halliburton's Troubles* (1862) the Halliburtons are helped on their way to respectable professions by the kindly Ashley family and hindered by their relatives, the wicked Dares. Very rarely does the help take the form of financial assistance; and the Dares who come to financial and sexual ruin do not receive much charity on their downward path.
6. This is the phrase of J. Sutherland, *The Longman Companion to Victorian Fiction* (London, 1988), p. 264, a book whose short plot-summaries make it clear that Victorian novels were full of references to sexual misdemeanours. The summaries of Wood's novels are perhaps inevitably hardly fair to the fallen heroines. In half a page a Victorian three-decker about an erring wife tends to reduce itself into the easy formula of 'Going, Going, Gone'.
7. Anti-Semitism is of course not confined to *East Lynne*. See A. Nanon, *The Jew in the Victorian Novel* (New York, 1980). Jews are commonly associated in Victorian fiction with financial difficulties, into which many of Wood's characters fall. One suspects her husband fell in the same way. Again, one cannot help condemning Wood for her crudity in dismissing Jews as mercenary agents of ruin, in the same way as she seems to be dismissing fallen women as inevitably ruined.

8. *East Lynne*, pp. 288–9.
9. Oliphant is quoted by Hughes, p. 107, at the beginning of an excellent chapter on Braddon and Wood.
10. *The Newcomes*, p. 616.
11. Ibid., p. xxxvi.
12. As Philip Larkin with a brilliant mixture of precision and vagueness put it, 'Sexual intercourse began/In nineteenth sixty-three/(Which was rather late for me)/Between the end of the Chatterley ban/And the Beatles' first LP.' P. Larkin, *Collected Poems* (London, 1988), p. 167. The poem was first published in 1967.
13. Sutherland, p. 63, gives an excellent account of bigamy novels in the 1860s, though he does not mention *Philip, Griffith Gaunt* or *East Lynne*.
14. H. Mathew, *Gladstone, 1809–74* (Oxford, 1986).
15. For Rhoda Broughton see Chapter 8. I have been unable to trace the source of the remark about Zola and Yonge, though it appears in almost every article on Broughton from the *Dictionary of National Biography* onwards.
16. In *Pillars of the House* (1873) there are of course pillars of Victorian rectitude like Felix Underwood who has to sublimate his sexuality to look after his large family of brothers and sisters. One of these brothers, an archetypal Victorian black sheep, fights a duel over a married woman, marries a fallen woman and is eventually scalped by Indians. Another pillar, Wilmet, marries her fiancé, who appears to be mortally wounded, in order that she may nurse him back to life with propriety. So Yonge does give us some insights into sexuality, although her world is a far cry from the world of S. Marcus, *The Other Victorians* (London, 1964), and a brave attempt by S. Foster, *Victorian Women's Fiction: Marriage, Freedom and the Individual* (London, 1985) to bring Yonge into the frame of Victorian feminist fiction is probably as mistaken as any attempt to pretend that Marcus's Victorians were anything other than other Victorians.
17. T. Winnifrith, *The Brontës and Their Background* (London, 1973), pp. 76–83.
18. K. Tillotson, *Novels of the Eighteen Forties* (Oxford, 1954), pp. 54–73. Sutherland's summaries of mid-Victorian novels tend to argue against Tillotson's case.
19. There is an almost inexhaustible supply of books about women in the nineteenth-century, literary treatments of women in this century, the history of sexuality, the constraints of prudery, the existence of pornography, homosexuality and prudery, and modern attitudes to all these problems. In the slightly narrower focus of this study the following books, over and above those cited in the notes, are useful: R. Barrikman, S. Macdonald and M. Stark, *Corrupt Relations: Dickens, Thackeray, Trollope and the Victorian Sexual System* (Columbia, 1982); G. Cunningham, *The New Woman and the Victorian Novel* (London, 1978); C. Fernando, *'New Women' in the Late Victorian Novel* (Pennsylvania, 1972); J. Gribble, *The Lady of Shalott*

in the Victorian Novel (London, 1983); S. Mitchell, *The Fallen Angel: Chastity, Class and Women's Reading* (Bowling Green, 1981); E. Showalter, *A Literature of Their Own: British Novelists from Brontë to Lessing* (Princeton, 1977); P. Stubbs, *Women and Fiction: Feminism and the Novel 1880–1920* (London, 1979); P. Thompson, *The Victorian Novel: A Changing World* (Oxford, 1956).

20. Neither J. Halperin, *Jane Austen* (London, 1984) nor P. Honan, *Jane Austen* (London, 1987) are wholly satisfactory. R. Fraser, *Charlotte Brontë* (London, 1988) and T. Winnifrith, *A New Life of Charlotte Brontë* (London, 1988) supply some new information about the Brontës, also supplied by E. Chitham, *Emily Brontë* (London, 1987) and *Anne Brontë* (London, 1991). Haight's works on Eliot and Ray's works on Thackeray are so monumental that other works on these authors, e.g. R. Redinger and A. Monsarrat, seem a little trivial, but neither Haight nor Ray are totally frank on sexual matters. R. Ashton, *G. H. Lewes* (London, 1991) is a new source of information. F. Kaplan, *Dickens, A Biography* (London, 1988) and P. Ackroyd, *Dickens* (London, 1990) provide different interpretations of Dickens's life. C. Tomalin, *A Hidden Life* (London, 1990) is another essential source. Biographies of Hardy by Gittings and Millgate, though written in an era of sexual frankness, probably need supplementing in view of the fact that there are still people living who can supply first-hand information about the author.

2 AUSTEN

1. J. Halperin, *Jane Austen's Lovers and Other Studies: Fiction and History from Austen to le Carré* (London, 1988) pp. 7–26.
2. See the preface and introduction in R. Chapman, *Jane Austen's Letters* (Oxford, 1952) and *Jane Austen: Facts and Problems* (Oxford, 1948).
3. The old-fashioned view that Austen was unconcerned with the world around her is now exploded. For some examples of this view see W. Roberts, *Jane Austen and the French Revolution* (London, 1979). Roberts joins M. Butler, *Jane Austen and the War of Ideas* (Oxford, 1975; second edition, 1987); more recently M. Evans, *Jane Austen and the State* (London, 1987) and O. Macdonagh, *Jane Austen: Real and Imagined Worlds* (Yale, 1991) have thoroughly refuted this approach. Austen's class is well explored by D. Spring, 'Interpreters of Jane Austen's Social World' in J. Todd, ed., *Jane Austen: New Perspectives* (London, 1983), pp. 53–72, although to call this class 'pseudo-gentry' is a little unkind.
4. *Northanger Abbey*, p. 43 (silence and politics); p. 197 (newspapers and voluntary spies).
5. Butler's view of Austen as an essentially conservative figure, slightly modified in the introduction to her second edition, has been challenged most notably by M. Kirkham, *Jane Austen: Feminism and*

Fiction (Brighton, 1984), some of the essays in Todd, and fairly cogently by C. Johnson, *Jane Austen: Women, Politics and the Novel* (Chicago, 1988). The chapter on Austen in S. Gilbert and S. Gubar, *The Madwoman in the Attic* (Yale, 1976) is disappointing; it is hard to feel that all much sympathy for Mrs Norris in spite of Sir Thomas Bertram's patriarchal blundering.

6. Chapman, *Letters*, pp. 256, 259, 287.
7. Ibid., pp. 256, 410. Note also p. 420, 'We only affix a different meaning to the word *Evangelical*'.
8. Honan, pp. 330–1; Macdonagh, pp. 123–4.
9. *The Dictionary of National Biography*, vol. XV (Oxford, 1896–1901), pp. 1321–6. For more information about James Plumptre see M. Quinlan, *Victorian Prelude* (New York, 1941).
10. Chapman, *Letters*, p. 106.
11. Ibid., p. 127. I discuss this episode more fully in 'Jane Austen's Adulteress', *Notes and Queries*, 135 (March, 1990), pp. 19–20.
12. Chapman, *Letters*, p. 197; 'staid' presumably means 'stayed for' rather than 'refused'; a sign of good faith rather than guilt.
13. Ibid., pp. 251, 258.
14. *Alumni Oxonienses, 1715–1886* (London, 1887), ed. J. Foster, p. 910.
15. Roberts, p. 113.
16. Chapman, *Letters*, p. 504; Honan, pp. 334–335.
17. Chapman, *Letters*, p. 120.
18. Ibid., p. 485.
19. Ibid., p. 480.
20. Most interestingly her son Herbert, probably without her mother's knowledge, maintained an entire illegitimate family. One of Fanny's brothers and one of her stepsons had to be rescued from entanglements with governesses in a way that reflects upon the reputation of Becky Sharp and Jane Eyre. There was great disapproval in 1826 when one of Fanny's brothers, Edward, married one of her stepdaughters, Mary, although oddly less disapproval when her uncle Charles legally in 1820 married his deceased wife's sister and her sister Louisa illegally in 1847 married her deceased sister's husband, Lord George Hill. These and other sexual misdemeanours, most notably the behaviour of Fanny's husband's half-brother, a bigamist eventually hanged for murder in Australia, are recorded by M. Wilson, *Almost Another Sister* (Canterbury, 1990). They seem an odd contrast to Fanny's primness and the idea that the destiny of fallen women was death or Australia. On the other hand the idea that Fanny Price's marriage to Edmund Bertram is virtually incestuous (Johnson, 116–19) seems rather far-fetched in the light of these real life marriages.
21. Honan, pp. 43–5 for Philadelphia Hancock. For Frances Austen see Chapman, *Letters*, p. 206.
22. Honan, pp. 101–2 and 339–40 makes this assumption a little too easily.
23. *Life of Mary Russell Mitford, Related in a Selection from her Letters to her Friends*, ed. A. L'Estrange (London, 1870), I, pp. 305–6.

24. 'His affection for her soon sunk into indifference; hers lasted a little longer', *Pride and Prejudice*, p. 387.
25. *Pride and Prejudice*, p. 289.
26. *Mansfield Park*, p. 420.
27. Chapman, *Letters*, p. 298 and Honan, pp. 335–6 for the correct punctuation.
28. *Sense and Sensibility*, p. 209.
29. Ibid., p. 379.
30. Alfred Tennyson, *Poems and Plays* (Oxford, 1967), p. 92.
31. It is true, of course, that Jane and Churchill are on thin ice with the aunt in Yorkshire and dare not jeopardise their marriage by a premature publication of their engagement. Any disapproval that attaches to this enforced secrecy is complicated by our knowledge that they are not guilty of criminal conduct or even criminal designs, though their behaviour, being the same as those who were licentious, will inevitably be associated with license.
32. Macdonagh, pp. 153–7.
33. Butler, p. 280, calls William Elliot's behaviour with Mrs Clay undermotivated and inconsistent with the worldly wisdom he has hitherto displayed. But, like his uncle and unlike Professor Butler, William Elliot is interested in the baronetcy.
34. *Sanditon, A Novel by Jane Austen and Another Lady* (London, 1975).
35. C. Rawson, 'The Seductive Hero in Fiction and Life: A Note on Jane Austen and Fanny Burney', *Notes and Queries*, 203 (1958), pp. 253–4.
36. Butler, pp. 92–3, 232–6 and Kirkham give different accounts of this play, printed in *Pride and Prejudice*, pp. 414–539.
37. *Mansfield Park*, p. 468.
38. This is well brought out by Macdonagh, pp. 110–28.
39. Part of this chapter was first delivered to the Midlands Branch of the Jane Austen Society, in April 1992.

3 BRONTË

1. T. Winnifrith, *The Brontës and Their Background* (London, 1973), pp. 23–4, 96–7.
2. Ibid., pp. 116–38. See also J. Maynard, *Charlotte Brontë and Sexuality* (Cambridge, 1984).
3. T. Winnifrith, op. cit., pp. 84–109.
4. 'I love the Church of England with all its faults.' T. Wise and J. Symington eds, *The Brontës: Their Lives, Friendships and Correspondence* (London, 1932), II, p. 166.
5. C. Alexander, *The Early Writings of Charlotte Brontë* (London, 1987) gives an excellent account of these fantasies.
6. *The Spell: An Extravaganza*, written between 21 June and 21 July 1834.
7. Alexander, pp. 139, 169, 227–30 and 246.

8.   After comparing Jane Austen's juvenilia with Charlotte Brontë's it
      is easy to see that what Austen satirises, Brontë takes seriously.
      Even in the mature novels there is a certain amount of madness
      and fainting.
9.   *The Professor*, pp. 163, 192.
10.   Ibid., p. 233.
11.   Gilbert and Gubar's now famous interpretation of *Jane Eyre* relies
      heavily on such symbols.
12.   *Jane Eyre*, pp. xii–xv. *The History of David Grieve* has a chapter set in
      Haworth; the fairly respectable hero is allowed a few indiscretions
      in France.
13.   G. Haight, ed., *The George Eliot Letters* (Oxford, 1954), 1, pp. 268.
14.   The idea that men's sexual urge was inescapable and fairly con-
      stant was standard medical opinion. The comparison was with
      women who had no sexual urges until they were deflowered. See
      M. Poovey, *Uneven Developments: The Ideological Work of Gender*
      (London, 1989), pp. 24–50.
15.   T. Winnifrith and E. Chitham, *Brontë Facts and Problems* (London,
      1989), pp. 11–12.
16.   This book, first published in 1966, has undoubtedly led recent
      critics to look at Bertha Mason in a more favourable light as a
      member not only of an oppressed sex but of an oppressed race.
      Neither reading is wholly compatible with Rochester's account of
      his first marriage.
17.   The film version was made in 1970, starring Susannah York as Jane.
18.   *Jane Eyre*, p. 384.
19.   Ibid., p. 547.
20.   Ibid., p. 380.
21.   Poovey, pp. 126–63.
22.   Chapter 2, note 20.
23.   M. Allott, *The Brontës: The Critical Heritage* (London, 1974), pp.
      105–12.
24.   I am grateful to Dr Germaine Greer for first drawing this fact to my
      observation.
25.   Gilbert and Gubar, *The Madwoman in the Attic* (Yale, 1976), pp.
      372–98, seize on Eva's dream and the myth of Mother Nature, but
      are rightly conscious of the pessimism in *Shirley* about this myth
      being able to survive in the real world.
26.   *Shirley*, pp. 360; 249–50.
27.   *Vanity Fair*, pp. 624–5.
28.   *Villette*, p. 306.
29.   The change in both men really occurs in chapter 27. Paul Emanuel
      is there, jealous as usual of John Graham, but he also speaks kindly
      to Lucy and is described as fierce and frank, dark and candid, testy
      and fearless. He gives a good lecture. In contrast John Graham
      seems detached and unintellectual and we do not mind that Paul
      Emanuel calls him 'ce grand fat d'Anglais' (p. 382). The two char-
      acters appear in a very different light in chapter 21, when Paul

Emanuel is described as a dreadful little man (p. 287), but this is before John Graham has met Paulina.

4 ELIOT

1. G. Haight, *George Eliot: A Biography* (Oxford, 1968), p. 160. R. Ashton, *G. H. Lewes: A Life* (Oxford, 1991) gives a very fair account of the Lewes ménage, including the quite extraordinary statement (pp. 180–1) made by one of the daughters of Agnes Lewes and Thornton Hunt that her mother could never have committed adultery. This statement is a good insight into the gap between Victorian practice and post-Victorian theory. Ashton also suggests (pp. 211–12) that Lewes did try to get a divorce in order to marry Eliot.

2. Haight, *George Eliot*, pp. 49–95. There are also good and frank discussions of Bray, Brabant and Spencer in K. Adams, *Those That Loved Her* (Warwick, 1980). G. Haight, 'George Eliot's Bastards' in *George Eliot: A Centenary Tribute*, ed. G. Haight and R. van Arsdell (Toronto, 1982), pp. 1–10, gives details of Bray's illegitimate children and suggests that the prevalence of illegitimate children in Eliot's novels is due to this fact.

3. It is a sign of the times that in his first Eliot book, *George Eliot and John Chapman* (London, 1940), Haight is remarkably circumspect. In his justly famous life, published in the swinging sixties, he still is unwilling to make a definite statement that Eliot slept with Chapman, although admitting that Chapman recorded his amours with Elizabeth Tilney in the same way as he marked Marian Evans's initial. More recently, Adams assumes a physical affair and Haight is very frank in the *Centenary Tribute* about Bray. A similar frankness can be noticed among the biographers of Dickens, with the notable exception of the latest Ackroyd book.

4. D. Holbrook, 'Holy Vows', *London Magazine*, 30, nos 7, 8 (October/ November 1990), pp. 20–28.

5. See Ashton, p. 117, for the episode with Eliza Lynn, including the fact that Lynn was urged to submit her work to the censorship of Thornton Hunt.

6. S. Dentith, *New Readings in George Eliot* (London, 1986), p. 16, says that Isaac Evans was especially harsh, refusing to write to his sister for twenty-four years, and then having the effrontery to appear as the chief mourner at her funeral.

7. Haight, *George Eliot*, pp. 159–68; and Ashton, pp. 153–8, give a good picture of the reaction to Eliot's affair with Lewes. Ashton speculates, p. 134–9, that Lewes and Eliot became lovers in the winter of 1852–3, a year and a half before the irretrievable step of fleeing to Germany and more than four years before Isaac Evans was informed.

8. Haight, *George Eliot*, pp. 396–7.

9.   *Daniel Deronda*, I, p. 368. The Clarendon edition of *Middlemarch*, ed.
      G. Handley (Oxford, 1989), p. 227, prints 'properties'. There is no
      textual explanation for this reading, but it does seem to make sense
      in the context of Klesmer's proposal to Miss Arrowpoint. Yet Eliot
      wrote 'proprieties' in the manuscript and passed 'proprieties' for
      the Cabinet edition; and P. Gay, *The Bourgeois Experience: Victoria to
      Freud* (Oxford, 1986), II. p. 169 certainly takes the remark to indicate
      that Eliot could not be as frank as she would like to have been.
      Recently, in K. Newton, ed. *George Eliot* (London, 1991), two arti-
      cles by C. Chase, 'The Decomposition of the Elephants: Double
      Reading of *Daniel Deronda*', pp. 215–17, and K. Newton, '*Daniel
      Deronda* and Circumcision', pp. 218–31, have raised not very deli-
      cately the delicate issue of whether Daniel should have known he
      was Jewish.

10.   A Mr Gwyther was the original of Amos Barton. He was annoyed
      by his portrait. Eliot said to him that a great deal of her story was
      imaginary, but to Bray she said that Mr Gwyther had been let off
      lightly, as Amos is made a much better man than he really was and
      far more unimpeachable in conduct. This suggests that there may
      have been something between him and the Countess, but Eliot is
      not very helpful about this, saying the affair of the Countess was
      never fully known to her. Mr Gwyther is more informative, saying
      that he had never seen the Countess and her alleged father, the
      Rev Sir John Waldron, since they left for Holyrood. Clergymen and
      knights and baronets are easy to trace, but there is no trace of the
      Rev Sir John Waldron in any reference book. He seems very dif-
      ferent from the vulgar Mr Bridmain who is really the Countess's
      half-brother, and it may well be that Waldron was the Countess's
      lover and that Mr Gwyther's behaviour in associating with such a
      disreputable woman was in some sense disgraceful. If so Eliot
      seems unusually censorious. There is a John Waldron, said to be a
      clergyman but not apparently preaching, of about the right date in
      Alumni Oxonienses, p. 1482. Some detective work could be done
      here.

11.   Eliot discourages us from equating facts with fiction when she says
      most of the scenes are derived from a 'combination of subtle shad-
      owy suggestions with actual objects and events' (*Letters*, II, 459).
      The character of Sir Christopher Cheverel would seem to be based
      on Sir Roger Newdigate and the description of his house is in-
      stantly recognisable by any visitor to Arbury Hall. But although
      there was a vicar of Chilvers Cotton, the Rev Bernard Ebdell, who
      married a collier's daughter, there seems no parallel to the story of
      Captain Wybrow; and the collier's daughter Sally Shilton enjoyed
      twenty years of married life as Mrs Ebdell. In the case of *Janet's
      Repentance*, Eliot does say that the story was based on real people
      with the difference that 'the real Dempster was more disgusting
      and the real Janet, alas, had a far sadder end than mine' (*Letters*, II,
      347). The real Janet was born Nancy Wallington and married Robert

Buchanan. He had a fall as Dempster did, but this coincided with his wife's death seven years before his own. Nancy Buchanan was the daughter of the headmistress of Eliot's school at Nuneaton and we learn of her in Eliot's letters to Maria Lewis, her Evangelical teacher. This links Nancy with Janet's Evangelicalism, but there is nothing in Eliot's rather tiresome juvenile correspondence with Miss Lewis to suggest drunkenness or anything worse in Mrs Buchanan's conduct. Blackwood did not like *Janet's Repentance*, as giving too bleak a picture; and there may be some special pleading in Eliot's letter. One would like to think that drunkenness was a euphemism for sexual immorality, but as with Amos Barton this is hard to prove.

12. *George Eliot: The Critical Heritage*, ed. D. Carroll (London, 1971), gives a fair selection of reviews.
13. *Adam Bede*, II, p. 379.
14. Ibid., p. 183.
15. Ibid., p. 37.
16. *The Mill on the Floss*, II, p. 350.
17. Ibid., pp. 362–3.
18. Almost all the reviewers of *The Mill on the Floss* cited in *The Critical Heritage* compare this novel, usually unfavourably, with *Adam Bede*, and make many references to the sex of the author.
19. Gilbert and Gubar, pp. 463–5.
20. *Felix Holt*, I, p. 102.
21. T. Wise and J. Symington, eds, *The Brontës: Their Lives, Friendships and Correspondence* (London, 1932) I, p. 122.
22. A number of critics have pointed out the way in which Esther is saved from becoming the second Mrs Transome by the discovery that Harold's first wife was a real-life Giaour.
23. *Felix Holt*, I, p. 40.
24. Ibid., II, p. 348.
25. *Middlemarch*, III, p. 253.
26. Ibid., I, p. 401.
27. Ibid., II, p. 247. Eliot does not exactly stand up for bastards. Rigg, Hetty's baby, Lydia Glasher's children and Lawyer Wakem's illegitimate brood make an unimpressive team. Eliot's own decision not to have children suggests she was aware of the stigma attached to illegitimacy. Lewes was himself illegitimate.
28. B. Hardy, 'Implication and Incompleteness: George Eliot's *Middlemarch*' in *The Appropriate Form: An Essay on the Novel* (London, 1964), pp. 105–31, gives the best account of Casaubon's impotence. See also R. Ellmann 'Dorothea's Husbands', in *Along the Riverrun* (Harmondsworth, 1989) pp. 115–31.
29. *Middlemarch*, I, p. 84. The vulgar meaning of 'wick' is not attested by Partridge until the 1880s, but the name does suggest that the flame of Casaubon's passion did not burn very brightly.
30. *Daniel Deronda*, II, p. 66.
31. Ibid., p. 120.

32. B. Zimmerman, 'Gwendolen Harleth and 'The Girl of the Period', in A. Smith, ed., *George Eliot: Centenary Essays* (London, 1980), pp. 196–217.

33. Here of course Eliot goes against the most powerful statement of conventional Victorian ideology about sexual and other kinds of sin, Tennyson's *Idylls of the King*. Instalments of this work were being published throughout the span of Eliot's career as a novelist. In the Poet Laureate's story, 'one sin', Guinevere's adultery, is supposed to bring about the moral corruption of Camelot and the society Arthur reigns over, and eventually the downfall of the Arthurian regime itself.

34. *Daniel Deronda*, I, p. 206.

35. Ibid., II, p. 325.

36. She studied Dante most thoroughly after Lewes's death and after the completion of her last novel; but earlier references to *The Divine Comedy* can be found in her correspondence.

5 THACKERAY

1. M. Stealts, ed., *The Journals of Ralph Waldo Emerson* (Cambridge, Mass., 1973), X, pp. 530–1.

2. The Austen Leighs were fairly scholarly defenders of Austen's reputation, but cannot compete with Anne Thackeray and the wife of Leslie Stephen. Ray's edition of Thackeray's letters and his two volumes of biography, *Thackeray: The Uses of Adversity* (Oxford, 1955) and *Thackeray: The Age of Wisdom* (Oxford, 1958) give an admirable and candid account of the control exercised by Thackeray's family.

3. Haight's biography of Eliot and his edition of her letters can be compared to Ray's treatment of Thackeray. Both are monuments to American scholarship. Haight was more fortunate in dealing with a rising rather than a falling star, and perhaps more fortunate in being able to complete his work in a more permissive age, although even Haight is not quite so frank on sexual matters as a more modern biographer would have been.

4. Ray, *Thackeray: The Uses of Adversity*, p. 301.

5. Ray, *Thackeray: The Age of Wisdom*, p. 348.

6. Ray, *Thackeray: The Uses of Adversity*, pp. 49–55.

7. *Pendennis*, p. xlviii.

8. *A Shabby Genteel Story*, p. 20.

9. G. Ray, ed., *The Letters and Private Papers of William Makepeace Thackeray* (Oxford, 1945), I, pp. 230, 235.

10. Ray, *Thackeray: The Uses of Adversity*, p. 283.

11. J. Carey, *Thackeray: Prodigal Genius* (London, 1977) and C. Peters, *Thackeray's Universe: Shifting Views of Imagination and Reality* (London, 1987).

12. The 'Silver Fork' genre, most notoriously the province of E. B. Lytton, is said to have dealt rather luridly with aristocratic society, as of course do some of the early sections of Disraeli's *Sybil*. See Roger Henkle, *Comedy and Culture: England, 1820–1900* (Princeton, 1980).

13. *Barry Lyndon*, pp. 140–56.

14. Thackeray's preface can be found in G. Tillotson and D. Hawes, eds, *Thackeray: The Critical Heritage* (London, 1968), pp. 88–9. The same volume has some mildly critical reviews of *Vanity Fair* on pp. 53–8, and of *Pendennis* on pp. 93–8. There is a very long and favourable review of *The Newcomes* on pp. 230–49.

15. Ray, *Thackeray: The Uses of Adversity*, p. 283. For governesses see M. Poovey, *Uneven Developments*, pp. 126–63.

16. J. Sutherland, *Thackeray at Work* (London, 1974) and E. Harden, *The Emergence of Thackeray's Serial Fiction* (Georgia, 1979) disagree about the extent to which Thackeray's serial fiction is carefully thought out, or brilliantly improvised. Both critics, however, supply valuable evidence about how Thackeray changed his mind about Becky Sharp and Lord Kew and Barnes Newcombe in *The Newcomes*. Thackeray's instinctive liking for Becky Sharp, like his dislike of Laura Pendennis, should not be ignored.

17. *Vanity Fair*, p. 521.

18. Regarding this sequence, Barbara Hardy has argued in a conference on 'Adultery and the Novel', December 1990, that Thackeray, in common with the other major Victorian novelists, probes men's vulnerability to their partners' lack of devotion. For her, the novel is admirable for portraying violated intimacy and in this becomes a novel for all time. Rawdon is not only incensed by the episode of the thousand-pound note, but bewildered and wounded by it. It doesn't remind him of what Becky might have done with Lord Steyne, but of her secretiveness and indifference to his fate in contrast with his candour and generosity towards her – 'I never kept anything back from you'.

19. *Vanity Fair*, p. 624.

20. *Pendennis*, p. 64.

21. *Henry Esmond*, p. 297.

22. As Sutherland, *Thackeray at Work*, shows, Thackeray had difficulties with dates even in *Vanity Fair*, where Rawdon Crawley has to become middle-aged very rapidly. This does not really matter any more than it matters that we do not know how old Lady Castlewood was when she first married, but if she was sixteen at the time of her first marriage, she cannot have been less than forty-five at the time of her second.

23. *Henry Esmond*, p. 20.

24. *The Newcomes*, p. 40.

25. Ibid., p. xxix. Ethel Newcome and Ethel Norman are good representatives of Victorian womanhood. Neither represent the extremes of angel and whore, nor do they exactly converge into the para-

digm sketched out by an article in *Blackwood's Edinburgh Magazine* in 1859. See Note 29.

26. *The Newcomes*, pp. 351, 347, 395. For Thackeray's uncertainty about Lord Kew and Barnes, see Harden, pp. 91–2.

27. *The Newcomes*, p. 281.

28. *Ibid.*, p. 347.

29. 'The purity of our English women', as the phrase went, was integral to British racism in the period. This characterisation didn't mean that Englishwomen were praised for being prudish, hyper-refined or infantile. On the contrary, it was thought that English-women were models of feminine perfection because they combined intelligence with diligence, independence with the desire to be valued by husbands and good humour with moral perceptiveness. The Englishwoman conducted herself in an attractive way, not because she was manipulative, made up or mincing but because her competence and vivacity made her naturally desirable. She was neither slavish nor threatening; and was sexually attractive without being sexually in charge. Within this paradigm, sexiness which didn't spill into sinfulness, selfishness or moral subservience was the aim. It was a contradictory one of course, since it still applied the model of a male fantasy to real women. The relation of this paradigm of English womanhood and girlhood to the notion of the fallen woman is an obvious one. (See 'Sentimental Physiology', *Blackwood's Edinburgh Magazine*, 86 [July 1859], 87–98.)

30. *The Newcomes*, pp. 80–1.

31. *Ibid.*, p. 585.

32. Carey, pp. 150–76.

33. Ray, *Thackeray: The Age of Wisdom*, p. 370.

34. *The Virginians*, p. 125.

35. *Ibid.*, p. 195.

36. *Ibid.*, p. 221.

37. *Ibid.*, p. 233.

38. *Ibid.*, p. 255.

39. *Ibid.*, p. 347.

40. In this regard, it is worth comparing Elizabeth Barrett Browning's portrayal of this theme in the verse novel, *Aurora Leigh*. Lady Waldemar, in that work, suffering from the pangs of love, tries to open her heart to the rather disgusted Aurora, likening the reaction of society to women who make no secret of their love to the repulsion created by garlicky breath. While the author makes no comment on the exchange, Aurora herself is suitably offended, even though she too has asserted her independence as a woman by rejecting an offer of marriage to the philanthropist, Romney Leigh, the man whom Lady Waldemar wants. Lady Waldemar goes on to 'lose caste' by joining Romney Leigh, who at no point returns her feelings, on his phalanstery. Like Lady Maria, she is hardly a respectable woman, in spite of her bluntness and high position.

41. See Harden, pp. 207–8, and Sutherland, pp. 107–8, for the irony involved in this censorship.

42. Ray, *Thackeray: The Age of Wisdom*, pp. 38–9.
43. It is possible, though difficult to prove, that there may have been some autobiographical basis for Ringwood and Charlotte; some aristocratic admirer of the innocent Isabella may yet be found, or would Thackeray be thinking of his young unmarried daughters? In *Dennis Duval* we have an adulterous wife who goes mad, another half link with Isabella.
44. Interestingly, an author whom this study does not treat in detail, Antony Trollope, uses precisely this image to describe that quintessentially ideal wife and mother, Eleanor Bold, in *Barchester Towers/ The Warden*. There the weight of the image is that the ivy adorns and decorates the husband. Even more pertinent is Tennyson's use of the image in 'Isabel', which shows quite exquisitely the ambiguity of men like Thackeray toward the perfect woman. 'A leaning and upbearing parasite,/Clothing the stem, which else had fallen quite/With clustered flower-bells and ambrosial orbs/Of rich fruit-bunches leaning on each other – /Shadow[s] thee forth' (ll. 33–8).

6 DICKENS

1. P. Ackroyd, *Dickens* (London, 1990), pp. 89–90 makes much of the fact that sex is linked with the idea of confusing class boundaries, thus bringing down victims like Lady Dedlock.
2. See Chapter 5, note 1. E. Johnson, *Charles Dickens* (London, 1953), p. 645 takes this view.
3. *Martin Chuzzlewit*, I, p. 447.
4. Unpublished letter sold at Sotheby's as reported in *The Times Literary Supplement* of 14 August 1987.
5. The changes are noted in the Clarendon edition of *Oliver Twist*, ed. K. Tillotson (Oxford, 1966).
6. P. Collins, *Dickens and Crime* (London, 1965), pp. 94–116.
7. R. Pearsall, *The Worm in the Bud* (London, 1969) – an arch but useful guide to Victorian sexuality.
8. The article by P. Collins on Dickens in G. Ford, ed., *Victorian Fiction: A Guide to Research* (New York, 1978), gives the state of play in the 70s when defenders of Dickens's innocence were in a minority. F. Kaplan, *Dickens: A Biography* (London, 1988), assumes that Dickens and Ellen were guilty though he cannot prove it, whereas Johnson, writing thirty-five years previously, was prepared to leave the matter in doubt. Ackroyd exceptionally is prepared to give Dickens the benefit of the doubt, although laying heavy emphasis on his feelings of guilt.
9. There is a revised edition of Tomalin in 1991 with an appendix suggesting that Dickens actually died in Ellen Ternan's house. Tomalin is an excellent literary detective, giving surprising details of the Ternan family before the meeting with Dickens's and after

Dickens's death, when the behaviour of Ellen's son seems to suggest that he found conclusive evidence of his mother's misconduct.

10. Ackroyd, pp. 791–99, 914–20.
11. There is a certain amount of evidence that Gladstone did not, for religious reasons, make love to his wife when she was pregnant. See Matthew, pp. 88–90. Dickens is unlikely to have had similar religious convictions, but must have gone through periods of abstinence as Catherine Dickens gave birth to so many children.
12. *Sketches by Boz*, p. 97.
13. Ibid., pp. 235–6.
14. Ibid., p. 318.
15. *Nicholas Nickleby*, I, p. 115.
16. *Oliver Twist*, pp. 480–1.
17. M. Slater, *Dickens and Women* (London, 1938), p. 221, gives the favourable verdict of Wilkie Collins on Nancy as 'the finest thing he ever did', and is in general agreement with this verdict and opposed to Thackeray's condemnation, quoted on the same page, to the effect that Nancy is no more like a thief's mistress than one of Gesner's shepherdesses resembles a real country wench. P. Collins, *Dickens on Crime*, p. 261, says 'few would now wish to attack Nancy on moral grounds, her unreality as a literary creation removing her from the area of discussion'. My debt to both Slater and P. Collins in this chapter is considerable.
18. *Oliver Twist*, p. 367.
19. Ibid., p. 368.
20. This is a good discussion of her in G. Watt, *The Fallen Woman in the Nineteenth Century English Novel* (London, 1984), pp. 11–18. Clearly this book covers much the same ground as the present work, although the singular noun does indicate some kind of difference.
21. Quoted in the Penguin edition of *Nicholas Nickleby* (Harmondsworth, 1978), p. 963.
22. *Nicholas Nickleby*, I, p. 268.
23. Ibid., II, pp. 217–18.
24. Ibid., I, p. 43.
25. Although the problem of child prostitution was well known, as shown by Marcus, *The Other Victorians* (London, 1964), and Mayhew, *London Labour and the London Poor* (London, 1862), IV, pp. 210–72.
26. Slater, p. 227. Quilp is able to rout dominating females and is perhaps an embodiment of Dickens's suppressed masculine destructiveness.
27. *Barnaby Rudge*, II, p. 9. 'What mortal eyes could have avoided wandering to the delicate bodice, the streaming hair, the neglected dress, the perfect abandonment and unconsciousness of the blooming little beauty.'
28. Miss Tox has of course been mocked previously for her feelings towards Mr Dombey.
29. Ackroyd, pp. 974–5.
30. *David Copperfield*, II, p. 271. 'The first mistaken impulse of an undisciplined heart' clearly refers to Annie and Jack Maldon as well as

David and Dora, but the sexes are confusingly reversed, and it seems odd to equate by implication Dr Strong and Agnes, although both are a bit of a bore.

31. Daisy has never had the same implications as Pansy, and only the Miss suggests homosexuality.

32. There was a certain amount of interest in the 1850s/60s in the notion of sisterhood as a paradigm for female strength and mutual support. It led to the setting up of Anglican nunneries and was also prominent in the poetry of Christina Rossetti, for instance *Goblin Market*.

33. *David Copperfield*, II, p. 348.

34. *Hard Times*, p. 572.

35. *Little Dorrit*, I, pp. 212–13.

7 HARDY

1. S. Gatrell, *Hardy the Creator: A Textual Biography* (Oxford, 1988), gives a general account of these changes. The Clarendon editions of *The Woodlanders* (Oxford, 1981), ed. D. Kramer, and *Tess of the d'Urbervilles* (Oxford, 1983), ed. J. Grindle and S. Gatrell, show changes in particular texts.

2. P. Boumelha, *Thomas Hardy and Women* (Brighton, 1982) gives some excellent examples of how Hardy contrived to keep Mrs Grundy at bay by avoiding explicit sexual statements and insinuating sexual implications. R. Morgan, *Women and Sexuality in the Novels of Thomas Hardy* (London, 1988) sees Hardy openly attacking Mrs Grundy right from the start of his career, with obvious emphasis on the sexuality of Bathsheba and obvious attacks on the sterility of Knight.

3. *The Poetical Works of Byron* (Oxford, 1964), p. 642.

4. F. Hardy, *The Early Life of Thomas Hardy, 1840–1891* (London, 1928).

5. M. Millgate, *Thomas Hardy: A Biography* (Oxford, 1982), pp. 105–7, is contemptuous of the illegitimate son, but thinks that Hardy may have slept with Tryphena. R. Gittings, *Young Thomas Hardy* (London, 1975), pp. 29–31, speculates on Hardy's virility.

6. Millgate, p. 18.

7. *The Well-Beloved*, p. 36, 39, 58, 130–1.

8. Millgate, pp. 153–6.

9. Graye is an architect, Cytherea Aldclyffe is the daughter of a naval officer married to someone from an ancient family. This was a class to which Hardy did not belong, and which did not forgive marital misdemeanours.

10. *Desperate Remedies*, p. 173.

11. Gittings, *Young Thomas Hardy*, p. 143.

12. Ibid., pp. 195–6, shows that Stephen's perhaps obsessive anxiety was exaggerated.

13. Gatrell, pp. 19–20. P. Widdowson, *Hardy in History: A Study in Literary Sociology* (London, 1989), makes a brave attempt to turn *The*

Hand of Ethelberta into a major Hardy novel, but in sexual matters at any rate it seems to strike a minor key.

14. *A Pair of Blue Eyes*, p. 271.
15. Ibid., p. 175.
16. J. Paterson, *The Making of 'The Return of the Native'* (Berkeley, 1960).
17. Gatrell, pp. 34–7.
18. Boumelha, pp. 48–62, has a good discussion of Thomasin.
19. Only in 1895 was Hardy able to suggest that Wildeve and Eustacia were lovers before Wildeve married Thomasin. See Gatrell, p. 132.
20. R. Taylor, *The Neglected Hardy* (London, 1982), p. 99.
21. R. Purdy, *Thomas Hardy: A Bibliographical Study* (London, 1954), p. 46. Gatrell, pp. 191–3.
22. *Two on a Tower*, p. 29. Millgate, p. 230, argues quite well that Hardy's preface is hypocritical.
23. Although not as long as Hetty Sorrel. See the discussion of this delicate subject in Chapter 4.
24. Gatrell, p. 132.
25. *The Mayor of Casterbridge*, p. 304.
26. Ibid., p. 99, p. 206.
27. Ibid., p. 333.
28. See the introduction to the Clarendon edition of *The Woodlanders*, ed. D. Kramer, pp. 43–9.
29. *The Woodlanders*, p. 321; 'dearest' was not added until 1912.
30. Ibid., p. 372.
31. These changes can be found in the Clarendon edition of *Tess of the d'Urbervilles*, ed. J. Grindle and S. Gatrell (London, 1983). Hardy had differences with *The Graphic* when publishing his collection of short stories, *A Group of Noble Dames*.
32. *The Collected Letters of Thomas Hardy*, R. Purdy and M. Millgate, ed., (Oxford, 1978), 1, p. 290, for Angel's possible imprisonment. Angel could not have married his sister-in-law until 1907.
33. Taylor, pp. 152–3. There is a good discussion of *The Well-Beloved* and its two versions in P. Ingham, *Thomas Hardy: Feminist Readings* (London, 1989).
34. Gittings, *The Older Hardy* (London, 1978), p. 90.
35. We could compare Hardy in this regard with the rather odd ideas of George Bernard Shaw, writing a few years later in *Man and Superman* (1907). In this play, it is the object of the man to escape marriage as long as possible, in the full knowledge that in the end the biological drive of women to find the best mate and prospective father will entrap them. The Don Juan hero of *Man and Superman* flees the Dona Anna heroine all over Europe, but is eventually tracked down and forced to abandon his social revolutionary ideals to produce children. To make matters worse, he actually loves the woman he marries.
36. Some contemporary reviewers took this line, as can be seen by the comparison of Tess and Jude to be found in R. Cox, ed., *Thomas*

Hardy: The Critical Heritage, (London, 1970). J. Bayley very neatly shows the difference between Hardy's heroine and hero in *An Essay on Hardy* (Cambridge, 1978).

37. M. Chase, *Thomas Hardy from Serial to Novel* (Minneapolis, 1927).
38. This aspect of *Jude the Obscure* has received extensive attention.
39. *Thomas Hardy: Personal Writings*, ed. H. Orel (London, 1966), pp. 125–33.
40. We should note, however, that these symbols were not as ridiculous as those imposed by Hollywood cinema in its early years.
41. This is a deliberately provocative remark, but it must be admitted that neither Forster nor Conrad is a name to conjure with in discussing insights into sexuality and that Lawrence's pioneer approach largely discusses sexuality from the masculine point of view. This point is well made by Gilbert and Gubar, 'The Female Imagination and the Modernist Aesthetic', in *Women's Studies*, 13 (1986), pp. 1–11.

8 CONCLUSION

1. N. Armstrong, *Desire and Domestic Fiction* (Oxford, 1987), p. 54.
2. It is possible that 'bungalow' has a slightly different meaning in America from that it has in Britain. Stairs are interesting for Brontë, as can be seen from the sad scene in *Jane Eyre*, p. 364, where in a mournful parody of his wedding night, Rochester carries Jane downstairs.
3. J. Chapple and A. Pollard, eds, *The Letters of Mrs Gaskell* (Manchester, 1966). Mrs Gaskell, p. 594, refers to 'the awkward blot in [Eliot's] life'; p. 860, bans her daughter from reading *Jane Eyre*, and, p. 228, says that Brontë 'puts all her naughtiness into her books'.
4. A. Easson, ed., *Elizabeth Gaskell: The Critical Heritage* (London, 1991), pp. 200–329.
5. Watt, p. 39. P. Stoneman, *Elizabeth Gaskell* (London, 1987), pp. 114–17, points out that Ruth dies mad, and has some shrewd observations about the incoherence of the novel's conclusion.
6. There is little mention of these novels in the standard Trollope critical works, e.g., J. R. Kincaid, *The Novels of Anthony Trollope* (Oxford, 1977), A. Pollard, *Anthony Trollope* (London, 1978). *The Vicar of Bullhampton* and *An Eye for an Eye* are discussed extensively by Watt, *The Fallen Woman in the Nineteenth-Century Novel* (London, 1984), pp. 41–96.
7. Bigamy is also found in *Is He Popinjoy?* (1878) and *John Caldigate* (1879).
8. S. Lonoff, *Wilkie Collins and His Victorian Readers* (New York, 1982).
9. N. Page, ed., *Wilkie Collins: The Critical Heritage* (London, 1974), pp. 47–8. *The Athenæum* did not not like Collins, warning him

against 'vices of the French School' and 'catering for a prurient taste' in *Antonina*, p. 41, and seeing *Armadale* as part of a period of 'distorted invention', p. 147.

10.		Few now read *Poor Miss Finch* (1872), *The Law and the Lady* (1875), *Jezebel's Daughters* (1880), *Heart and Science* (1883), *I Say No* (1884), *The Evil Genius* (1886) or *The Legacy of Cain* (1889). Page does show that the later novels did merit some contemporary attention.

11.		Most modern studies of Collins concentrate on the earlier novels. The revival of interest in his work started with biographies by K. Robinson, *Wilkie Collins: A Biography* (London, 1951), R. Ashley, *Wilkie Collins* (New York, 1952) and N. Davies, *The Life Of Wilkie Collins* (Illinois, 1956).

12.		W. Burns, *Charles Reade: A Study in Victorian Authorship* (New York, 1961) and E. Smith, *Charles Reade* (London, 1976). M. Elwin, *Charles Reade: A Biography* (London, 1931) is the latest major biographical study.

13.		Burns, p. 11; Smith, p. 87. James compared Kingsley unfairly with Reade, citing the realism of Reade's Australian scenes, although Reade had never been to Australia.

14.		Burns, pp. 200–30, includes several passages in Reade's notebooks which were not incorporated into the final version.

15.		Smith, pp. 87–8.

16.		Smith, pp. 47, 79–80.

17.		As well as being banned by Mudies, *The Ordeal of Richard Feverel* was attacked for impurity in *The Critic* and impropriety in *The Spectator*. See I. Williams, ed, *Meredith: The Critical Heritage* (London, 1971), pp. 61–85.

18.		Williams charts the rise in Meredith's fortunes. See also J. Lucas, 'Meredith's Reputation', in I. Fletcher, ed., *Meredith Now* (London, 1971), pp. 1–14.

19.		J. Halperin, *Gissing: A Life in Books* (Oxford, 1982) gives (pp. 363–7) some notes on the Gissing revival, pioneered by J. Korg, *George Gissing: A Critical Biography* (University of Washington, 1963).

20.		P. Coustillas and C. Partridge, eds, *Gissing: The Critical Heritage* (London, 1972), give the *Punch* review, pp. 72–3, but it is hard to find many parallels. We can note, p. 142, the way F. Farrar, author of *Eric, or Little by Little* (1858), that masterpiece of Victorian piety, called *The Nether World* 'an English book' with 'none of that leprous naturalism which disgusts any honourable reader in the works of Zola and his school'.

21.		There is a good, if slight, study of her by H. Van Thal, *Eliza Lynn Linton: The Girl of the Period* (London, 1979).

22.		T. Winnifrith, *The Brontës and Their Background*, p. 23.

23.		'Candour in English Fiction', *The New Review* (January, 1890), pp. 8–15.

24.		Van Thal, pp. 67, 182.

25.		She wrote an early article praising Mary Wollstonecraft for *The English Republic*, but bitterly attacked the move for female emancipation in articles for the *Saturday Review*.

26.   *Belinda* has been reissued by Virago Press (London, 1984). For information about Broughton's life see M. Sadleir, *Things Past* (London, 1944), pp. 84–116.
27.   For the reading by Queen Victoria of *Oliver Twist* and *Jane Eyre* see Viscount Esher, ed., *The Girlhood of Queen Victoria* (London, 1912), II, pp. 86, 89, 91, 144 and *Transactions of the Brontë Society*, 59 (1949), p. 247. For knowledge of the reading of Frederick Forsyth and Jilly Cooper by British Royalty and a former British Prime Minister I am indebted to the popular press.

Bibliography

Ackroyd, P., *Dickens* (London, 1990)

Adams, K., *Those That Loved Her* (Warwick, 1980)

Alexander, C., *The Early Writings of Charlotte Brontë* (London, 1987)

Allott, M., *The Brontës: The Critical Heritage* (London, 1974)

Armstrong, N., *Desire and Domestic Fiction: A Political History of the Novel* (Oxford, 1987)

Ashley, R., *Wilkie Collins* (New York, 1952)

Ashton, R., *G. H. Lewes* (London, 1991)

Austen J., *Emma*, ed. R. W. Chapman (Oxford, 1933)

Austen, J., *Mansfield Park*, ed. R. W. Chapman (Oxford, 1933)

Austen, J., *Northanger Abbey and Persuasion*, ed. R. W. Chapman (Oxford, 1933)

Austen, J., *Pride and Prejudice*, ed. R. W. Chapman (Oxford, 1933)

Austen, J., *Sense and Sensibility*, ed. R. W. Chapman (Oxford, 1933)

Barrett-Browning, E., *Aurora Leigh* (London, 1857)

Barrikman, R., Macdonald, S., and Stark, M., *Corrupt Relations: Dickens, Thackeray, Trollope and the Victorian Sexual System* (Columbia, 1982)

Bayley, J., *An Essay on Hardy* (Cambridge, 1978)

Boumelha, P., *Thomas Hardy and Women* (Brighton, 1982)

Braddon, M., *Lady Audley's Secret* (London, 1862)

Brontë, C., *Jane Eyre*, Haworth edition (London, 1899–1900)

Brontë, C., *Shirley*, Haworth edition (London, 1899–1900)

Brontë, C., *The Professor*, Haworth edition (London, 1899–1900)

Brontë, C., *Villette*, Haworth edition (London, 1899–1900)

Broughton, R., *Belinda* (London, 1984)

Broughton, R., *Cometh Up as a Flower* (London, 1867)

Burns, W., *Charles Reade: A Study in Victorian Authorship* (New York, 1961)

Butler, M., *Jane Austen and the War of Ideas*, 2nd edition (Oxford, 1987)

Byatt, A., *Possession* (London, 1990)

Byron, Lord, *The Poetical Works* (Oxford, 1964)

Carey, J., *Thackeray: Prodigal Genius* (London, 1977)

Carroll, D., ed., *George Eliot: The Critical Heritage* (London, 1971)

Chapman, R., *Jane Austen: Facts and Problems* (Oxford, 1948)

Chapman, R., *Jane Austen's Letters* (Oxford, 1952)

Chapple, J., and Pollard, A., eds, *The Letters of Mrs Gaskell* (Manchester, 1966)

Chase, M., *Thomas Hardy from Serial to Novel* (Minneapolis, 1927)

Chitham, E., and Winnifrith, T., *Brontë Facts and Problems* (London, 1983)

Chitham, E., *Anne Brontë* (London, 1991)

Chitham, E., *Emily Brontë* (London, 1987)

Collins, P., *Dickens and Crime* (London, 1965)

Collins, W., *Antonina* (London, 1850)

Collins, W., *Armadale* (London, 1866)

Collins, W., *Basil: A Story of Modern Life* (London, 1852)
Collins, W., *Hide and Seek* (London, 1854)
Collins, W., *Law and the Lady* (London, 1875)
Collins, W., *Man and Wife* (London, 1870)
Collins, W., *No Name* (London, 1862)
Collins, W., *The Black Robe* (London, 1881)
Collins, W., *The Dead Secret* (London, 1857)
Collins, W., *The Fallen Leaves* (London, 1878)
Collins, W., *The Moonstone* (London, 1868)
Collins, W., *The New Magdalen* (London, 1873)
Collins, W., *The Two Destinies* (London, 1876)
Collins, W., *The Woman in White* (London, 1860)
Coustillas, P., and Partridge, C., eds, *Gissing: The Critical Heritage* (London, 1972)
Cox, R., ed., *Thomas Hardy: The Critical Heritage* (London, 1970)
Cunningham, G., *The New Woman and the Victorian Novel* (London, 1978)
Davies, N., *The Life of Wilkie Collins* (Illinois, 1956)
Dentith, S., *New Readings in George Eliot* (London, 1986)
Dickens, C., *A Tale of Two Cities*, Illustrated Library edition (London, 1874)
Dickens, C., *Barnaby Rudge*, Illustrated Library edition (London, 1874)
Dickens, C., *Bleak House*, Illustrated Library edition (London, 1874)
Dickens, C., *David Copperfield*, Illustrated Library edition (London, 1874)
Dickens, C., *Dombey and Son*, Illustrated Library edition (London, 1874)
Dickens, C., *Great Expectations*, Illustrated Library edition (London, 1874)
Dickens, C., *Hard Times*, Illustrated Library edition (London, 1874)
Dickens, C., *Little Dorrit*, Illustrated Library edition (London, 1874)
Dickens, C., *Martin Chuzzlewit*, Illustrated Library edition (London, 1874)
Dickens, C., *Nicholas Nickleby*, Illustrated Library edition (London, 1874)
Dickens, C., *Oliver Twist*, Illustrated Library edition (London, 1874)
Dickens, C., *Our Mutual Friend*, Illustrated Library edition (London, 1874)
Dickens, C., *Pickwick Papers*, Illustrated Library edition (London, 1874)
Dickens, C., *Sketches by Boz*, Illustrated Library edition (London, 1874)
Dickens, C., *The Mystery of Edwin Drood*, Illustrated Library edition (London, 1874)
Dickens, C., *The Old Curiosity Shop*, Illustrated Library edition (London, 1874)
Dictionary of National Biography (Oxford, 1885–1901)
Easson, A., ed., *Elizabeth Gaskell: The Critical Heritage* (London, 1991)
Eliot, G., *Adam Bede*, Cabinet edition (London, 1878–80)
Eliot, G., *Daniel Deronda*, Cabinet edition (London, 1878–80)
Eliot, G., *Felix Holt*, Cabinet edition (London, 1878–80)
Eliot, G., *Middlemarch*, Cabinet edition (London, 1878–80)
Eliot, G., *Middlemarch*, Clarendon edition (London, 1989)
Eliot, G., *Romola*, Cabinet edition (London, 1878–80)
Eliot, G., *Scenes of Clerical Life*, Cabinet edition (London, 1878–80)
Eliot, G., *Silas Marner*, Cabinet edition (London, 1878–80)
Eliot, G., *The Mill on the Floss*, Cabinet edition (London, 1878–80)
Ellmann, R., *Along the Riverrun* (Harmondsworth, 1989)

Elwin, M., *Charles Reade: A Biography* (London, 1931)

Esher, Viscount, ed., *The Girlhood of Queen Victoria* (London, 1912)

Evans, M., *Jane Austen and the State* (London, 1987)

Farrar, F., *Eric, or Little by Little* (London, 1858)

Fernando, C., *'New Women' in the Late Victorian Novel* (Pennsylvania, 1972)

Fletcher, I., ed., *Meredith Now* (London, 1971)

Ford, G., ed., *Victorian Fiction: A Guide to Research* (New York, 1978)

Forster, E., *The Longest Journey* (London, 1907)

Foster, J., ed., *Alumni Oxonienses, 1715–1886* (London, 1887)

Foster, S., *Victorian Women's Fiction: Marriage, Freedom and the Individual* (London, 1985)

Fowles, J., *The French Lieutenant's Woman* (London, 1969)

Fraser, R., *Charlotte Brontë* (London, 1988)

Gaskell, E., *'Lizzie Leigh'* (London, 1850)

Gaskell, E., *'The Poor Clare'* (London, 1855)

Gaskell, E., *Cousin Phillis* (London, 1863)

Gaskell, E., *Mary Barton* (London, 1848)

Gaskell, E., *Ruth* (London, 1853)

Gaskell, E., *Sylvia's Lovers* (London, 1863)

Gatrell, S., *Hardy the Creator: A Textual Biography* (Oxford, 1988)

Gay, P., *The Bourgeois Experience: Victoria to Freud* (Oxford, 1986)

Gilbert, S. and Gubar, S., 'The Female Imagination and the Modernist Aesthetic', *Women's Studies*, 13 (1986), pp. 1–11.

Gilbert, S. and Gubar, S., *The Madwoman in the Attic* (Yale, 1976)

Gissing, G., *The Nether World* (London, 1889)

Gissing, G., *The Unclassed* (London, 1884)

Gittings, R., *The Older Hardy* (London, 1978)

Gittings, R., *Young Thomas Hardy* (London, 1975)

Gribble, J., *The Lady of Shalott in the Victorian Novel* (London, 1983)

Haight, G., *George Eliot and John Chapman* (London, 1940)

Haight, G., ed., *The George Eliot Letters* (Oxford, 1954)

Haight, G., *George Eliot: A Biography* (Oxford, 1968)

Haight, G. and van Arsdell, R., *George Eliot: A Centenary Tribute* (Toronto, 1982)

Halperin, J., *Jane Austen's Lovers and Other Studies: Fiction and History from Austen to le Carré* (London, 1988)

Halperin, J., *Gissing: A Life in Books* (Oxford, 1982)

Halperin, J., *Jane Austen* (London, 1984)

Harden, E., *The Emergence of Thackeray's Serial Fiction* (Georgia, 1979)

Hardy, B., *The Appropriate Form: An Essay on the Novel* (London, 1964)

Hardy, F., *The Early Life of Thomas Hardy, 1840–1891* (London, 1928)

Hardy, T., *A Laodicean*, New Wessex edition (London, 1975)

Hardy, T., *A Pair of Blue Eyes*, New Wessex edition (London, 1975)

Hardy, T., *Desperate Remedies*, New Wessex edition (London, 1975)

Hardy, T., *Far from the Madding Crowd*, New Wessex edition (London, 1975)

Hardy, T., *Jude the Obscure*, New Wessex edition (London, 1975)

Hardy, T., *Tess of the d'Urbervilles*, New Wessex edition (London, 1975)

Hardy, T., *Tess of the d'Urbervilles,* Clarendon edition (Oxford, 1983)
Hardy, T., *The Hand of Ethelberta,* New Wessex edition (London, 1975)
Hardy, T., *The Major of Casterbridge,* New Wessex edition (London, 1975)
Hardy, T., *The Return of the Native,* New Wessex edition (London, 1975)
Hardy, T., *The Trumpet-Major,* New Wessex edition (London, 1975)
Hardy, T., *The Well-Beloved,* New Wessex edition (London, 1975)
Hardy, T., *The Woodlanders,* New Wessex edition (London, 1975)
Hardy, T., *The Woodlanders,* Clarendon edition (Oxford, 1981)
Hardy, T., *Two on a Tower,* New Wessex edition (London, 1975)
Hardy, T., *Under the Greenwood Tree,* New Wessex edition (London, 1975)
Henkle, R., *Comedy and Culture: England, 1820–1900* (Princeton, 1980)
Holbrook, D., 'Holy Vows' *London Magazine* 30 (October, 1990), pp. 20–8
Honan, P., *Jane Austen* (London, 1987)
Hughes, W., *The Maniac in the Cellar* (Princeton, 1980)
Ingham, P., *Thomas Hardy: Feminist Readings* (London, 1989)
Johnson, C., *Jane Austen: Women, Politics and the Novel* (Chicago, 1988)
Johnson, E., *Charles Dickens* (London, 1953)
Joyce, J., *Ulysses* (London, 1960)
Kaplan, F., *Dickens, A Biography* (London, 1988)
Kincaid, J., *The Novels of Antony Trollope* (Oxford, 1977)
Kirkham, M., *Jane Austen: Feminism and Fiction* (Brighton, 1984)
Korg, J., *George Gissing: A Critical Biography* (Seattle, 1963)
L'Estrange, A., ed., *Life of Mary Russell Mitford, Related in a Selection from her Letters to her Friends* (London, 1870)
Larkin, P., *Collected Poems* (London, 1988)
Linton, E., 'Candour in English Fiction', *The New Review* (January, 1890), pp. 8–15
Linton, E., *Azeth the Egyptian* (London, 1846)
Lonoff, S., *Wilkie Collins and his Victorian Readers* (New York, 1982)
Macdonagh, O., *Jane Austen: Real and Imagined Worlds* (Princeton, 1991)
Marcus, S., *The Other Victorians* (London, 1964)
Mathew, H., *Gladstone, 1809–74* (Oxford, 1986)
Mayhew, H., *London Labour and the London Poor* (London, 1862)
Maynard, J., *Charlotte Brontë and Sexuality* (Cambridge, 1984)
Meredith, G., *Diana of the Crossways* (London, 1885)
Meredith, G., *One of Our Conquerors* (London, 1891)
Meredith, G., *Modern Love* (London, 1862)
Meredith, G., *The Amazing Marriage* (London, 1895)
Meredith, G., *The Ordeal of Richard Feverel* (London, 1859)
Millgate, M., *Thomas Hardy: A Biography* (London, 1982)
Mitchell, S., *The Fallen Angel: Chastity, Class and Women's Reading* (Bowling Green, Ohio, 1981)
Monsarrat, A., *An Uneasy Victorian: Thackeray the Man, 1811–1863* (London, 1980)
Morgan, R., *Women and Sexuality in the Novels of Thomas Hardy* (London, 1988)
Nanon, A., *The Jew in the Victorian Novel* (New York, 1980)
Newton, K., ed., *George Eliot* (London, 1991)
Orel, H., ed., *Thomas Hardy: Personal Writings* (London, 1966)

Page, N., ed., *Wilkie Collins: The Critical Heritage* (London, 1974)

Paterson, J., *The Making of 'The Return of the Native'* (Berkeley, 1960)

Pearsall, R., *The Worm in the Bud* (London, 1969)

Peters, C., *Thackeray's Universe: Shifting Views of Imagination and Reality* (London, 1987)

Pollard, A., *Anthony Trollope* (London, 1978)

Poovey, M., *Uneven Developments: The Ideological Work of Gender* (London, 1989)

Purdy, R. and Millgate, M., eds, *The Collected Letters of Thomas Hardy* (Oxford, 1978)

Purdy, R., *Thomas Hardy: A Bibliographical Study* (London, 1954)

Quinlan, M., *Victorian Prelude* (New York, 1941)

Rawson, C., 'The Seductive Hero in Fiction and Life: A Note on Jane Austen and Fanny Burney', *Notes and Queries*, 203 (1958), pp. 253–4

Ray, G., *Thackeray: The Age of Wisdom* (Oxford, 1958)

Ray, G., *Thackeray: The Uses of Adversity* (Oxford, 1955)

Ray, G., *The Letters and Private Papers of William Makepeace Thackeray* (Oxford, 1945)

Reade, C., *A Simpleton* (London, 1873)

Reade, C., *A Terrible Temptation* (London, 1871)

Reade, C., *Griffith Gaunt* (London, 1866)

Reade, C., *Hard Cash* (London, 1863)

Reade, C., *The Cloister and the Hearth* (London, 1861)

Reade, C., *White Lies* (London, 1857)

Redinger, R., *George Eliot: The Emergent Self* (New York, 1975)

Rhys, J., *Wide Sargasso Sea* (London, 1966)

Roberts, W., *Jane Austen and the French Revolution* (London, 1979)

Robinson, K., *Wilkie Collins: A Biography* (London, 1951)

Rossetti, C., *Poetical Works* (London, 1904)

Sadleir, M., *Things Past* (London, 1944)

Sanditon, *A Novel by Jane Austen and Another Lady* (London, 1975)

Shaw, G. B., *Man and Superman*, (London, 1907)

Showalter, E., *A Literature of Their Own: British Novelists from Brontë to Lessing* (Princeton, 1977)

Slater, M., *Dickens and Women* (London, 1938)

Smith, A., ed., *George Eliot: Centenary Essays* (London, 1980)

Smith, E., *Charles Reade* (London, 1976)

Stealts, M., ed., *The Journals of Ralph Waldo Emerson* (Cambridge, Mass., 1973)

Stoneman, P., *Elizabeth Gaskell* (London, 1987)

Stubbs, P., *Women and Fiction: Feminism and the Novel 1880–1920* (London, 1979)

Sutherland, J., *Thackeray at Work* (London, 1974)

Sutherland, J., *The Longman Companion to Victorian Fiction* (London, 1988)

Taylor, R., *The Neglected Hardy* (London, 1982)

Tennyson, A., *Poems and Plays* (Oxford, 1967)

Thackeray, W. M., *A Shabby Genteel Story*, Biographical edition (London, 1898)

Thackeray, W. M., *Barry Lyndon*, Biographical edition (London, 1898)

Thackeray, W. M., *Denis Duval*, Biographical edition (London, 1898)

Thackeray, W. M., *Henry Esmond*, Biographical edition (London, 1898)

Thackeray, W. M., *Lovel the Widower*, Biographical edition (London, 1898)

Thackeray, W. M., *Pendennis*, Biographical edition (London, 1898)

Thackeray, W. M., *Philip*, Biographical edition (London, 1898)

Thackeray, W. M., *The Newcomes*, Biographical edition (London, 1898)

Thackeray, W. M., *The Virginians*, Biographical edition (London, 1898)

Thackeray, W. M., *Vanity Fair*, Biographical edition (London, 1898)

Thackeray, W. M., *Catherine*, Biographical edition (London, 1898)

Thompson, P., *The Victorian Novel: A Changing World* (Oxford, 1956)

Tillotson, G. and Hawe, D., eds, *Thackeray: The Critical Heritage* (London, 1968)

Tillotson, K., *Novels of the Eighteen Forties* (Oxford, 1954)

Todd, J., ed., *Jane Austen: New Perspectives* (London, 1983)

Tomalin, C., *A Hidden Life* (London, 1990)

Trollope, A., *An Eye for an Eye* (London, 1879)

Trollope, A., *Barchester Towers* (London, 1857)

Trollope, A., *Can You Forgive Her?* (London, 1865)

Trollope, A., *Ralph the Heir* (London, 1871)

Trollope, A., *Dr Wortle's School* (London, 1880)

Trollope, A., *He Knew He Was Right* (London, 1869)

Trollope, A., *Is He Popinjoy?* (London, 1878)

Trollope, A., *John Caldigate* (London, 1879)

Trollope, A., *The Vicar of Bullhampton* (London, 1870)

Trollope, A., *The Warden* (London, 1856)

Trollope, A., *The Way We Live Now* (London, 1875)

Trollope, F., *Jessie Phillips* (London, 1843)

Van Thal, H., *Eliza Lynn Linton: The Girl of the Period* (London, 1979)

Ward, Mrs H. *The History of David Grieve* (London, 1892)

Watt, G., *The Fallen Woman in the Nineteenth Century English Novel* (London, 1984)

Waugh, E., *Decline and Fall* (London, 1928)

Widdowson, P., *Hardy in History: A Study in Literary Sociology* (London, 1989)

Williams, I., ed., *Meredith: The Critical Heritage* (London, 1971)

Wilson, M., *Almost Another Sister* (Canterbury, 1990)

Winnifrith, T., *The Brontës and Their Background* (London, 1973)

Winnifrith, T. and Chitham, E., *Brontë Facts and Problems* (London, 1983)

Winnifrith, T., 'Jane Austen's Adulteress', *Notes and Queries*, 145 (March 1990), pp. 19–20

Winnifrith, T., *A New Life of Charlotte Brontë* (London, 1988)

Wise, T. and Symington, J., eds, *The Brontës: Their Lives, Friendships and Correspondence* (London, 1932)

Wood, Mrs H., *East Lynne*, with introduction by S. Davies (London, 1984)

Wood, Mrs H., *Lady Adelaide's Oath* (London, 1867)

Wood, Mrs H., *Mrs Halliburton's Troubles* (London, 1862)

Wood, Mrs H., *Verner's Pride* (London, 1863)

Wood, Mrs H., *Within the Maze* (London, 1872)

Yonge, C., *Pillars of the House* (London, 1873)

Yonge, C., *The Daisy Chain* (London, 1856)

Index